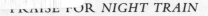

PRAISE FOR *NIGHT TRAIN*

"I hadn't planned to read all of *Night Train* in one sitting, but I found myself doing just that. David Quantick's novel sets up a vast mystery and barrels deliriously toward a conclusion you'll never see coming like, I don't know, some kind of railed vehicle that operates in the dark."

DAVID WONG

"If you're looking for an escapist, absorbing, full-throttle read, then you need to hop aboard *Night Train* immediately. *Snowpiercer* on acid, it's weird, intriguing, wickedly funny, and wholly entertaining. I loved it and didn't want the journey to end."

SARAH LOTZ

"A dark, nightmarish journey into a brand new sort of *Twilight Zone*, David Quantick's *Night Train* is breathless, frantic, and creepy as hell. You'll never see the twists coming."

CHRISTOPHER GOLDEN

"Starting a trip on the *Night Train* is like waking up in a scary game with no rules. I enjoyed trying to work out the parameters of this strange new world with Garland and exploring its ever-more-surreal carriages. When we finally start to discover where we are, we realise there's no going back. *Night Train* is pacy, amusing, and gory, and an entertaining companion on a dark journey."

LOUIS GREENBERG

NIGHT
TRAIN

Also by David Quantick
and available from Titan Books

All My Colors

NIGHT TRAIN

—

DAVID QUANTICK

TITAN BOOKS

Night Train
Print edition ISBN: 9781785658594
E-book edition ISBN: 9781785658600

Published by Titan Books
A division of Titan Publishing Group Ltd
144 Southwark Street, London SE1 0UP
www.titanbooks.com

First edition: August 2020
10 9 8 7 6 5 4 3 2 1

This is a work of fiction. Names, places and incidents are either products
of the author's imagination or used fictitiously. Any resemblance to
actual persons, living or dead (except for satirical purposes), is entirely
coincidental.

A CIP catalogue record for this title is available from the British Library.

Printed and bound in Great Britain by CPI Group Ltd.

To Simon

"All aboard the night train!"

ONE

Night. Blackness, anyway. Darkness. No light. Nothing. Just night.

Then a thundering crash. A deafening noise, too much to bear. A huge, smashing shock to the ears.

Everything shaking. Walls, roof, floor.

Still no light.

She managed to move, somehow, and tried to stand. At once she was slammed back into the ground. She tried again, but it was as if the floor had its own gravity. This time at least she was thrown across the room. She hit the wall, which means she found the wall. Now she could figure out the borders of her confinement.

Feeling her way along the wall, as she stumbled to her feet and was thrown down again, she marked the perimeter of the room she found herself in. It was big, at least twice as wide as her length, taller than her – the shaking of the room so violent that she didn't even think about reaching for the ceiling, let alone trying to touch it – and, as she was beginning to find out, much, much longer.

She made her way along the wall in pitch blackness. Her eyes adjusted to the dark, but as there was nothing but dark, she still could not see anything. For a moment she touched her eyes to make sure she still had eyes: it was a horrible, lurching moment, but right then anything was possible.

She found a fingerhold in the wall. The darkness was total, and the noise around her still a random crunching, roaring thunder, as if an ocean were pouring into every room of a house, so she used her remaining senses instead.

The wall she was touching was not cold. She felt along it with a finger. A snag, like a splinter. It might have been wood.

She inhaled. The air was metallic, oily, but there were other smells, more animal.

She decided to take stock of her situation. There were too many thoughts to process, so she started with the basics.

Where is this?

What is it?

How did I get here?

How do I get out?

Another question came into her mind. Even though it was her question, it both surprised and frightened her.

Who am I?

Remembering things is easy, she thought, *you either remember them or you don't.* Nevertheless, she tried to remember, strained as though her memory was a physical thing like a muscle that she could make work. Nothing came. She could only remember the last few minutes. If she tried to rewind her memory back any further than that, she hit a wall.

Nothing doing, she thought, and decided to concentrate on some other basic questions. *Where is this?* seemed like a good place to start. She began to concentrate on her surroundings, which was far from easy, as her surroundings did not make it easy to concentrate, might even actually have been designed to make concentration impossible. *All this needs is a death metal band playing in the background and it would be perfect*, she thought, and then wondered how it was she knew what a death metal band was yet could not remember her own name.

Maybe whoever I am just really likes death metal, she thought and, to her surprise, actually laughed. The laugh was immediately swallowed up in the hammering noise of the pitch-black room, which was now shaking like a skyscraper at the peak of an earthquake. She lost her grip and slid across the floor, slamming into the wall on the other side.

She decided to give up on standing up, and instead began to crawl across the floor, sticking close to what felt like planks beneath her body. This was a slow but effective means of movement, and she was able to crawl forwards further than she was thrown backwards.

The noise, and the blackness, continued. Whatever was causing them did not care, or probably even know, that she was there.

She made her way towards she didn't know what, almost flush with the floor now, using the weight of her limbs and the roughness of her hands to try and grip the floor. Once she was thrown backwards half the length of the room, and once she even slammed sideways into the wall again, but she was making some kind of progress.

And then, after what seemed like hours, her finger touched the wall at the front of the room. She slipped her fingernails into the cracks between the planks, the nearest she had to a handhold, and raised herself onto her knees. She waited for a moment in case the room threw her back across its floor, and then slowly got to her feet. She began to move sideways crab-fashion across the width of the wall.

If this is a room, she told herself, *it's got a door. Every room has a door.*

She didn't actually know if she believed this, but it was a good premise to act on. After a minute or two, she found something on the wall. A raised piece of wood. She felt up and down and confirmed that the wood was vertical. Hardly daring to hope, she reached out to grip the almost-flush post. She had just managed to get a weak grip on what she presumed was a door frame when, with a gigantic crashing sound like a truck being dropped from the top of a building, the room shook and convulsed and she was thrown several metres back again.

I'm getting angry now, she thought, and was pleased to discover that whoever she may be, she clearly wasn't the kind of person who gave up easily. Slowly she crept her way back to the front of the room. With great care she got to her feet, and once more felt for the door frame. This time she managed to stand and was even able to reach up on tiptoe and find the top of the frame. Her hands moved hopefully across the wood in the middle of the frame and then – *yes!* she thought – there was, incredibly, what felt like a handle in the middle of the door.

She held onto the handle for a minute or two, more for reassurance than anything else. And then, when she felt that the room wasn't going to once more throw her back, she closed her eyes (*why? I can't see anything*) and turned the handle.

At once she was blinded. A yellow light filled her eyes and rendered them useless. When the blindness faded, she saw that she was in a doorway. She stepped forward, and her foot met cold air. The room was not connected to anything, but led out to –

Another door. A door shaking like this one in its frame and suspended over something moving.

She looked down. In the glow of the yellow light, which she now saw was a lamp hanging from the wall in front of her, all she could see below her were metal rails. The rails seemed to be moving at an incredible speed, but of course she knew it wasn't the rails that were moving but her.

A train, she thought. *I'm on a train.*

She stood there for a few moments, her body crucified in the door frame, swaying in the gap between what she now saw were two carriages. Behind her, blackness. Ahead of her, she had no idea. She was about to reach out for what she hoped was another door into the next carriage when the train lurched, bucked and nearly threw her down (*onto the rails*, she thought).

She steadied herself, then something slid abruptly towards her and jarred her heel. Still holding the frame with one hand, she lowered herself, reached down to pick up the object and lifted it up. In the yellow lamplight it was clear what the object was: a set of manacles, its chain broken in half. Unconsciously she felt her wrist, and for the first time noticed that the skin was broken.

Suddenly horrified, she dropped the manacles. They fell onto the tracks and were gone in seconds. She was filled with a powerful desire to get away from there and nearly stumbled as she stepped over the gap between the two carriages.

There was a metal handle on the second door and she was forced to hold onto it to avoid falling. She pulled it back, and the door swung open, almost pushing her over. She slammed it shut, thought for a moment and then, holding her breath, opened the door again. As it swung out, she reached round with her free hand and found a handle on the other side. In one sudden move she slid herself around the door and, as it slammed shut again, rolled onto the floor.

She lay there for a moment, her heart thundering as though it too were part of the train. This carriage was warmer than the first, and quieter too. Compared to what must have been her prison, it was like a womb. Reluctantly, she opened her eyes and got to her feet.

She was in an ordinary train carriage. There were windows, but they only reflected the lights of the carriage. A thin strip of carpet ran the length of the carriage, and on each side of it seats, with tables. Every seat was occupied.

Men and women, on their own, or in pairs, and sometimes even three or four. And every single one of them was dead.

She walked up and down the carriage, not touching anyone, looking carefully for signs of life. There weren't any. None of the fifteen dead people – she did a head count – was moving, breathing or showing any indication that they were anything but dead. Without disturbing the corpses, she could not see if they died violent deaths or even (it occurred to her) if they were dead when they were put in the carriage. There were no wounds, no cuts, no signs of disease or even distress. Just fifteen dead people, slumped in their seats like commuters asleep on an early morning train to work.

The fifteen dead were an unremarkable lot. They wore unremarkable clothes in an unremarkable variety of styles. A young man in a cheap work suit, his tie loosened at the neck. A middle-aged woman in a thick woollen coat, scarf laid neatly in her lap. An old couple, his head on her shoulder, her face turned to the window. A big fat man with a shaven head in a sleeveless T-shirt, prostrate over a table, his huge hands like fleshy books spread flat on either side of his facedown pink skull as though he were praying to some pagan idol. A soldier in combat uniform, kitbag occupying the seat next to his. Two teenage girls in floral tops, mouths open, eyes shut, their mobile phones still close to them.

She moved the soldier's kitbag to the floor and sat down next to his body. She remained there for a while, not quite listening, not quite seeing, just letting the situation flow into her. The train continued to bluster its way through the dark. This made her think. She leant over the soldier's body and, making a tunnel with her cupped hand, peered out of the window.

It was hard to see anything with the reflection in the glass from the brightly lit carriage, but after a while she was able to distinguish the inside from the outside. Not that there was much to see. Most of the external world was in darkness. She thought she could see smoke, far off, and perhaps light, but with no idea of where she was – high up, in the country, or even a tunnel – it was impossible to gauge. And then she saw, with a start, something explode into brightness. She stared through the glass as a faraway object – or a small one close by – erupted into flame and sparks and smoke, like a volcano going off, or (this thought is less agreeable) a bomb. The explosion, if that was what it had been, was entirely silent.

From further away to her right there was a second explosion, and then a third. Suddenly the whole landscape was lit up by explosions. *It must be a bombing attack*, she thought. But now she considered it, the explosions did not look like bombs going off. They seemed to be coming up from the ground, not down from the sky. Like furnaces all triggered to go off at once.

Then, as quickly as they had burst into existence, the explosions stopped, and she was left in a silent carriage with fifteen dead people.

She felt the soldier's kitbag at her feet. Suddenly inspired, she hoisted it up and spilt its contents over the table. A half-drunk bottle of water, a pair of underpants, a T-shirt and a balled-up pair of socks. Trousers, a jersey, two pairs of training shoes. A washbag, containing a toothbrush, a razor (she nearly sliced her fingertip before she saw it) and a tube of facewash.

And crumpled up in balls inside the training shoes, a newspaper. She pushed it all off the table except for the newspaper, unfolded it and flattened it down on the table. She tried to read it, but none of the words made any sense. Not because they were written in a different alphabet, or even a different language, but because she could not make the component parts of the words link up. The letters just floated there, refusing to join up. It was like being a victim of a mental disorder that refused to let the brain assemble eyes and ears and a mouth to form a recognisable face.

After a few seconds looking at the letters on the printed page actually began to hurt, and she had to close her eyes.

She opened them again and looked at the dead soldier beside her.

"This isn't normal," she told him, and her voice almost squawked from lack of use. "Someone's done this to me."

She picked up the newspaper again and – not looking at the letters – started to tear through the words and around the images, the photographs and maps and even cartoons in the paper.

I'm not done yet, she thought, as she discarded the printed words and smoothed out her cache of torn-out images. She had no idea what to do with these pictures and photographs, but there is, she believed, no such thing as useless information. She folded the small squares of paper and was about to put them in her pocket when she stopped, and for the first time looked at what she was actually wearing.

It was a green jumpsuit, the same colour as the dead soldier's uniform, except that where the soldier's clothing was rough and cheaply made, the jumpsuit was woven from a more expensive cloth and was well tailored. Clearly whoever made these clothes was working to a sliding scale of equality.

The jumpsuit had breast pockets and blank epaulettes, and a blouse underneath of a similar, but softer fabric. There were long zip pockets – empty, she checked quickly – and on her feet she was wearing functional but comfortable boots (*monkey boots*, she knew they were called).

Above one of the pockets was a thin green script with lettering on it. Looking down on it gave her a headache, so she had to stop, but naturally she could not help wondering what it said. *It might be my name*, she thought. *Someone's name, anyway*.

She put the tiny pile of photos in one of her pockets and, after a moment's thought, decided she was thirsty.

"Excuse me," she said to the dead soldier and unscrewed the top of his water bottle. She sniffed it, decided that whatever killed him probably wasn't in the water, and took a swig. It tasted fine, if a little bit stale.

"Thanks," she said and just managed to stop herself offering him a swig. She put the lid back on, stood up and looked around the carriage at her fifteen dead companions.

"Sorry to do this," she said, and began to loot their corpses.

The fifteen dead gave up few surprises. None of them had any wallets or purses, and there were no identifying labels in their coats or shirts (she considered looking in their underwear but decided against it). There were no photographs in their belongings: in fact, very few of them had any belongings. She found no small items, either: no keys, no coins, no sweet wrappers, nothing that could be called a clue. For train travellers, they were surprisingly lacking in train tickets.

The only personal possessions she found, oddly, were phones, and even then the only people who had them were the two teenage girls, their mobiles placed carefully in their laps like precious dolls. The phones themselves, despite being fully charged, were no use to her. There was nothing in or on them, no call records or applications. They were not receiving a signal of any kind and even the photo folders contained nothing but generic background swashes. As an experiment, she pressed "call" on each phone and tried a couple of random numbers, and got nothing but silence. Still, she pocketed the phones (and a charger she found in the soldier's kitbag, which she checked and found compatible) because, while they might have been nothing, they were all she had.

Not really knowing why, she rearranged the fifteen dead as she found them, finally putting the kitbag next to the body of the young soldier. She was about to decide on her next move when she heard a *click*.

She turned, a second late, to see the compartment door ahead of her open and something hurtle at her, a massive forward-moving blur. Before she could see what it might be, it was on her. A blow to the head and she was on the ground. Something was keeping her down. Sprawled on her back, eyes closed from the pain, she held her arms in front of her face to prevent more blows.

None came. She opened her eyes, and saw that her attacker was – she could not say. It looked, and felt, like a giant torso was on top of her. Then she became aware that the torso had a head, quite a few metres up from where she was lying. Two arms and two legs framed the torso, each arm with a clenched fist at the end.

The head was shouting at her now from its massive mouth, and at first the shouting was so loud she could not make out what the head was saying.

"I can't hear you!" she shouted back, which struck her as an absurd thing to say to a head shouting at you from a few metres away.

"Who are you?" shouted the head.

She was about to reply when a fit of laughter struck her. The head stopped shouting and the fists dropped as she laughed uncontrollably. Finally she managed to stop and, wiping her eyes, said to the enormous figure sitting on top of her:

"I don't know! I don't know!"

And this set her off again.

• • •

The torso got to its feet and, without asking, pulled her up. Now she saw that the man who'd attacked her was not quite as big as she'd thought, just very tall and very thin.

He pushed her, not roughly, into a seat and looked down at her. His face was creased by a bony ridge where his eyebrows should be, and his nose was squat between two large brown eyes. His head was bald and his big pink ears looked like someone had stuck two gigantic slices of bacon to the sides of his head.

This thought set her off giggling again. The giant leaned in and studied her.

"Who are you?" he said.

"Please don't start that again," she replied, and managed to control herself. She looked him in the eye. If she didn't think of the bacon ears, she was all right.

She said to the giant, "I don't know who I am. Who are you?"

The giant frowned at this. He pointed at his chest, and she saw that he was wearing the same green uniform as her, just more generously made. He pointed at the strip of writing over his pocket.

She shook her head.

"I can't read that," she said.

"BANKS," said the giant, making the words big in his mouth. "I am BANKS."

Banks pointed to the strip on her jacket.

"And you are GARLAND."

She looked down at the writing. Now, bizarrely, she could read the letters without pain. Looking at them now even upside-down, she saw that the giant was right. Her name, if the words were to be believed, was Garland.

She shrugged.

"I'm Garland, then," she said. "Hello."

"Banks," said the giant, and extended his enormous hand. She looked at it for a second, then took it.

"Pleased to meet you, Banks," she said.

Then Banks winced and suddenly grabbed his arm.

She looked at his sleeve; it was bloody. Without asking, she grabbed the fabric and began to roll the sleeve up. Banks said nothing as she peeled the stiff fabric back. Underneath the cloth, the massive arm was reddish brown with dried blood.

"Wait here," she said. She had seen a door with an image of two stick figures on it. She went to it, and it was unlocked. Inside there was a toilet, a washbasin and some thick tissues. She turned on the tap and hot water flowed out: soaking as many tissues as she could find, she took them back to Banks.

"This may hurt," Garland told Banks.

"Everything hurts," said Banks as she began to wipe the blood from his arm. He looked to one side throughout the cleaning process.

Garland got through six or seven tissues before the arm – hairless, like a wax dummy's – was free of blood. There was a deep cut, healing but still raw.

"How did this happen?" she asked Banks.

Banks looked at her and smiled.

"I don't know," he said.

He looked round, and took in the fifteen dead.

"This is a bad room," he said. "I know a good room."

She was about to ask him what he meant when he smiled. It was a smile full of teeth, and they were extraordinary teeth. For a moment she thought that no two of them were alike: there were gold teeth, silver teeth, big teeth, broken teeth and even, she was sure, a glass tooth. She wanted to ask Banks about the glass tooth but decided that it could wait.

"Are you hungry?" asked Banks.

Garland nodded. She was very, very hungry.

"Come on, then," said Banks, and almost dragged her out of the seat.

He strode up to the connecting door. Garland hesitated.

"Come on," he repeated.

"I don't know what's through there," she said.

"I do," he said. "I live there. Been living there since – since I got there. It's a good room. Got food."

"Food is always good," Garland admitted. Later she would regret this remark.

Banks pushed open the door between the two carriages and held it for her, a gigantic gentleman.

"Wait," she said. She went back down the carriage and, stopping in front of each of the fifteen dead, closed their eyes for them.

She walked back to Banks.

"I don't know what else I can do."

"Nothing anyone can do," he shrugged, and stood back to let her pass into the next carriage.

The next carriage was the buffet car.

"Of course," said Garland. "Where else would food be on a train?"

It was quite a nice buffet car. There was even a table with four fixed chairs beneath it. There was a counter, and a coffee maker, and a refrigerated display cabinet, which was empty. Garland felt her stomach tremble, as if with disappointment.

"I thought you said there was food here," she said, slightly sullenly.

"There's food," said Banks. He reached up and opened a door in an overhead compartment above the counter, and then pulled down a plastic crate, which he set down with a thud on the table. Inside the crate were about twenty small tin cans, each fitted with a large ring pull.

Garland picked one up. The label had no writing on it, just a drawing of a large green circle.

"Apple," said Banks. He picked up another can, this one with a purple circle on it.

"Plum," he said. The next can had a yellow circle on the label.

"Banana?" asked Garland.

Banks shook his head.

"Cheese," he said. He pulled the ring and showed the inside of the can to Garland. It appeared to be a solid, rubbery piece of cheese that had somehow been got into the can.

"Is all the food in cans?" she asked.

Banks looked away. "No," he said.

"What is it? What's wrong?"

Banks opened a door below the refrigerated cabinet. Cold steam billowed out from a small freezer compartment. Garland went over and stuck her hand in. She pulled out a cold package, vacuum-sealed and opaque.

"Have you got a knife?" she asked Banks.

"Don't!" he said. There was fear in his voice.

Garland rubbed the outside of the packet with her finger. Then she dropped the packet and stepped back in alarm.

Inside the packet, set into a flat piece of flesh, was an eye.

"I told you," said Banks, as he picked up the packet and dropped it back into the freezer compartment.

"What the hell is that?" she said.

"Same as it says on the packet," Banks said. "Eye."

"Is it a medical specimen?" she said, disbelieving. "Is it – food?"

Banks shrugged. "Buffet car," he said. "Must be food for someone, if not some*thing*."

"Jesus," said Garland, and sat down. "Is there anything to drink here?"

Banks shook his head. "Don't know," he said.

"Shame, I could do with a drink," said Garland (*do I drink?* she thought) and got up on a chair. She reached into the compartment and pulled out another crate. It slammed onto the table.

"Same as the first," Banks said. "They're all the same. Apple, plum, cheese, other food. You want drink –" and he indicated the counter, "– look under there."

Under the counter was a metal box. Someone, she presumed Banks, had prised it open. Inside were a few small cardboard cartons with tiny straws taped to them. These also were decorated with green circles and purple circles (but not, Garland was relieved to notice, yellow circles). There were one or two small cans of what Garland guessed was soda. And there were several tiny bottles, each labelled with

27

a word. Garland couldn't read the words without her head hurting, but she recognised the colours of the liquids inside the bottles.

"Thank goodness," she said, and unscrewed the top of the first bottle. She drank the contents down in one sudden gulp.

"Good?" asked Banks.

A puzzled look appeared on Garland's face, which was then replaced by anger.

"The fuckers," she said, slowly.

"What's wrong?" Banks said as Garland snapped open a second bottle and downed it.

"I can just about cope with not being able to read," she said slowly and with fury in her voice. "But this is an outrage."

She opened a third miniature. This time she spat out the contents.

"Is it unpleasant?" Banks asked.

"Unpleasant?" she said. "If it was that, at least I'd be getting *something* from it. This – this is nothing."

"I don't know what you mean."

"That's because you don't drink. This stuff – there's nothing to it. There's nothing in it. Nothing I can taste, anyway. The one thing in this stupid place that I could really do with right now and it doesn't work."

She grabbed a handful of bottles and threw them at the wall.

"It doesn't *work*!" she shouted.

Banks looked at Garland as she hunched her shoulders and began to cry.

"I think you have a drinking problem," he said.

Garland tidied up the mess as Banks put together a colourful meal from the tins. There was a microwave oven behind the counter and he made them bowls of cold plum with hot apple sauce, followed by slices of tinned cheese. It was a surprisingly pleasant and warming meal, and Garland felt better immediately she had eaten it.

"Thank you," she said to Banks. "I'm sorry about earlier."

"This is a strange life," said Banks. "It's OK to react to things."

"Let me wash up," she said, and took the bowls from him.

There was a bathroom, and when she had washed the dishes in the sink, she used the toilet, which seemed to be amply stocked with toilet paper, at least for a train bathroom.

"Time to get cleaned up a little," she said, and ran some hot water to wash her face. It was only then that she noticed the difference between the bathrooms. This one had a mirror over the sink.

Garland looked in the mirror. She saw a young woman with light-coloured hair and greenish-brown eyes. The eyes looked tired and frightened.

"So you're Garland," she said to her reflection. "Nice to meet you."

Let's hope so, her reflection beamed right back at her.

"Yeah," Garland said, "I know exactly what you mean, Garland. Now let's go."

• • •

When she got back, Banks was sitting at the table.

"You look a lot better," he told her.

"Thanks," she said.

"Before," he went on, "you looked horrible. Dirty and awful. But now you look OK."

"Great," she said. "You look amazing, too. Now shall we get on?"

Banks looked surprised. "Get on what?"

"What, you just want to sit in here eating canned cheese all the time?"

"I have been doing that so far," said Banks. "Hasn't done me any harm."

"Well, something has done me harm," Garland said, "and I would like to find out what it is, and why it is doing it."

"OK," said Banks. "I'll give you some cans."

She looked at him.

"You're not coming with me?"

Banks shook his head.

"I like it here," he said. "I've got light, heat… I've got cans."

"All the basics," she said. She looked at Banks. He was sitting in a semi-foetal position, his arms clutching his knees. For a giant, he looked very frail.

"You're frightened," she said, and regretted it instantly. Banks looked angry.

"I know I am," he said. "Because this is a frightening place."

"But you can't stay here," she said.

"Of course I can," he said.

"What about when the cans run out?"

"There's always…" Banks nodded at the refrigerated drawer.

"You can't –"

"How do you know?" Banks was getting agitated. "How do you know what I can't do? Or what I can? Because I don't know, so how can you?"

He put his face between his knees and, to her surprise, began to heave his huge shoulders back and forth.

She was about to ask Banks if he was being sick when a thought came into her mind:

He's crying. That's what he's doing. He's crying because he's very upset.

Garland went over to Banks and sat next to him. She wasn't sure if she should touch him or not, so she slid her arm through the crook of his enormous long leg and held his calf. It felt, even to her, like an odd thing to do, but she couldn't think of anything else and, besides, it seemed to calm Banks, whose heaving subsided like the receding aftershocks of a small earthquake.

"Where are we?" he said. "What's happening? Why don't I know anything?"

Garland let out a sigh.

"I've said it before and I'm sure I'll say it again," Garland replied. "I don't know."

Banks wiped his face and she realised she had been right, and he had been crying.

"When I was... somewhere else, I don't know," he said, "I read, or I was told, that not knowing anything was a good thing. Like children don't know anything, and that makes them better than us, because we know things, bad things."

He gazed at her. His eyes were deep and wet from the crying.

"'*Suffer the little children to come to me*'," he said. "Only suffer doesn't mean suffer."

Garland looked around. She thought of the eye in the freezer drawer.

"What does it mean, then?" she said, and got up.

• • •

Banks watched as Garland collected a few supplies.

"Where are you going?" he said.

"That way," she said.

"You don't know what's up there," he said.

"No, but I know what's back there," she replied. "Dead people and darkness."

"Could be the same the other way too."

"I know that. But I'm not sitting here for the rest of my life."

Banks looked at her.

"I'm not a coward, you know," he said.

"I didn't say that."

"It's just – I know where I am here. I know what's going on. If I go with you –"

"Sure. I get it."

Suddenly the lights went out. Banks shouted in alarm. Garland dropped down beside him.

"Don't move!" she hissed and grabbed his arm.

She had no idea why she had told him not to move, but she remained there in the dark and stayed silent.

After a while, Banks whispered, "Are we waiting for something to happen?"

"I don't know," she admitted.

"Then can we —" Banks began, when a screeching noise filled the air, like an entire wall of metal being torn in half. Garland felt Banks curl up beside her, and she wanted to do the same but something inside her would not let her move. Instead she remained half crouched as the screeching got louder and louder.

The darkness inside the compartment was total, but outside she could see tiny lights, miniature stars exploding in the gloom of the night. The stars burst and vanished like bubbles made of light, illuminating for a second or two and then disappearing back into the darkness.

As the noise got louder, Garland saw that the lights seemed to be getting bigger, or nearer, she wasn't sure which. Now the noise was so loud that Banks was also screaming, whether in distress or physical pain she couldn't say. The lights were flashing pools of colour: whatever they were made by was all around now, wave after wave of exploding splashes of illumination that reminded Garland, crazily, more of jellyfish than stars.

She barely had time to marvel that she could remember what a jellyfish was when, with a firework's fizz, one of the lights exploded right outside the window. Banks screamed and clenched himself into a tight mass as ball of light after ball of light slammed against the windows. The screeching now was a high-pitched intolerable whine as the balls of light increased in size and frequency, until soon the carriage was drenched in a constant unceasing barrage of light and sound. Garland closed her eyes and tried to block her ears, but still the noise and light got in. She could feel Banks shaking next to her, and she was about to risk her own sight and hearing and put her arms round him when, as abruptly as it had started, everything stopped.

. . .

They sat for a while, not moving, not sure if it was going to start again. The carriage lights came back on, accompanied by the faint hum of the refrigerated cabinet. *Whatever it was*, thought Garland, *must have generated a field that stopped the power to the carriage.*

Slowly, Banks stopped shaking.

"Are you OK?" she asked him.

"I'm coming with you," he said.

. . .

Banks insisted on returning to the dead compartment. He returned with the soldier's kitbag, which he filled with cans.

"You need to kick that habit," Garland said.

Banks shook his head

"Cans are everything," he replied, and hoisted the kitbag over his shoulder.

Garland looked around to see if there was anything else worth taking. She found a drawer in the counter which contained some paper clips, a few pens and a small pad of paper covered in figures.

"Looks like this was a real train at some point," she said. "These must be price calculations."

"Interesting," said Banks. "What's that?"

Garland looked down. Something had rolled out from the back of the drawer. It was a keyring. On it were a couple of small keys and a miniature torch. She flicked the switch.

"It works," she said, and put it in her pocket.

• • •

Banks led the way to the end of the carriage. Garland looked at the door. "Onwards, I guess," she said.

Banks gripped the door handle.

"Ready to leave home?" she said.

"No," said Banks, and opened the door.

• • •

As they stepped into the next carriage, they were met by a gust of cold air. Banks and Garland moved forward with difficulty, because the windows of the carriage had been either removed or stove in, and a freezing wind buffeted them from either side.

But this was not what made them hurry. The carriage was empty, and there were no signs of life present. There was nothing at all there, in fact, save for a large cage in the middle of the carriage. It was made of steel, with thin, strong bars and a door from which hung a broken padlock. Inside the cage (not that they went in) there was a heap of discoloured straw.

Garland and Banks only had time for a brief look at the cage before passing it as quickly as possible and finding the door to the next carriage.

• • •

This door opened easily, and the reason for this was not hard to see, as the handle had been wrenched off. There was a deep jagged track where the handle once was, and the door itself was barely on its hinges.

Banks and Garland stopped for a moment.

"Whatever did that to the door might be through there," said Banks.

"Whatever did that is gone," Garland replied. She pointed down at the gap between the two coaches. The same track was gouged into the metal footplate with a dark stain beside it.

"I'd say it got out and in its hurry to escape it fell between the carriages," said Garland. It was more what she wanted to believe than what she actually believed, but still.

"If you say so," said Banks, clearly just as keen to be convinced as she was. "This door looks OK."

The next door did look OK. There were no scratches on it and no blood. Banks turned the handle and they went in.

• • •

The next carriage, to their relief, was completely ordinary. It was just a carriage. There were seats, tables, luggage racks and windows with glass in them.

"Wait here," said Banks, who seemed to have appointed himself as a kind of forward scout. He searched the carriage with such a serious expression that Garland found herself suppressing laughter again.

After Banks had stood on his tiptoes and run his fingers across the luggage racks, and come up with nothing but dust, he nodded at Garland.

"Clear," he said.

"Thank you," she replied, forcing back a smile.

Banks sat down at a table and opened the kitbag.

"You want a juice?" he asked.

Garland joined him.

"What kind you got?" she said.

Banks gave her a look.

"Apple and plum, what else?"

"Just testing," she said. "I thought you might have changed the choices."

Banks gave her an apple juice and took a plum juice for himself. She stabbed the straw into the carton, drank some and looked at her reflection in the window.

"What did you think you'd look like?" said Banks.

"Excuse me?"

"Before you knew what you did look like," Banks said. "After you… woke up, but before you saw your face in a mirror. What did you think you'd look like?"

Garland considered this for a moment.

"You first," she said.

"All right," said Banks. He turned his face to the window and raised his hands to his reflection.

"Before – I don't know really," he said. "I'm just me, you know. That's how I saw myself, if I saw myself at all. When I woke up – after, you know, after the panic… when I'd calmed down I had a lot to think about, like where was I and –"

"We've been through this," said Garland, and was surprised at how hard she sounded.

"Another word I remember from before," Banks said sharply, "is *empathy*. You know that one?"

"I'm sorry," said Garland, and she was. "Go on."

"All right," Banks said. "After I'd gone through the first

confusion, and I'd worked out I wasn't, you know, dead, I found the cans."

"I bet that was a big deal for you," said Garland.

"I like the cans," Banks said defensively. "The cans kept me going. This is, what, your first day?"

"Maybe," she said. Now it was her turn to sound defensive. "Hard to know what a day is, here."

"You'll know," he said. "A day is when you're awake. Night is when you sleep. Doesn't matter if it's an hour or six hours, night is when you sleep and day is when you don't."

"I'll remember that," she said. "So – how many days have you been here?"

"It's hard to be precise," said Banks.

"Don't be precise, then," she said. "Sorry, forgot. Empathy."

"Right," he said. "I would say – given I wasn't counting at first, then I thought it might be good to count, so –"

He looked down at his enormous hands, and for a moment Garland wondered if he was counting on his fingers.

"How many then?" she said. "Six? Seven?"

"More than that," said Banks. "About fifty."

There was silence in the carriage for a moment or two, and then Garland said, "Fuck. Off."

• • •

She leaned over towards him, not conscious she was doing it.

"You've been here for *fifty* days?"

Banks shrugged.

"Like I say, it's hard to count. And the days aren't exactly –"

"I thought you were going to say a week or something."

"No." He shook his head. "More than a week."

"Wow," said Garland. "No wonder there's hardly any cans left."

She drank some juice.

"The first time I saw my face," Banks said, "was in one of those –" and he pointed to a glass divider by the luggage shelf of the compartment. "I remember because it was also the first time the lights went out."

"The lights have gone out before?" said Garland.

"This really is your first day," Banks said. "Yeah. The lights go out for a few seconds most days, sometimes a few minutes. Never more than that. You learn how to sleep with them on."

"I used to sleep with the light on as a kid," said Garland, and wondered again how she knew that.

"This really isn't the same thing. Strip lights are different to a night light by your bed. You have to find stuff to cover your eyes with. Here…"

Banks reached into his pocket and pulled out a creased strip of cardboard.

"Made a sleep mask," he explained. "From a box."

She looked at it. It was just a piece of card, with dents torn out presumably to fit Banks's ears.

"Pretty good," she said.

"Not really," Banks replied, and put it away. "I'm thinking of using something more flexible. Like socks."

"I feel we've strayed," said Garland. "Tell me about seeing your face some more."

In the empty carriage, under the strip lights, on a train hurling itself through endless night, talking to this bony, bald giant, Garland found she was almost at ease. It was a strange feeling, but these days, what wasn't?

"The lights went off," Banks continued, "and I felt scared. I was alone, I was lost, and I hadn't found the cans yet."

"Pretty bad," Garland agreed.

"I remember I just stood there. I didn't even get the chance to adjust my eyes to the darkness before there was this flash from outside —"

"Yeah, what *are* those things?" said Garland.

"I have theories," said Banks. "Anyway, there I was, in the glass. I saw my face, for the first time."

"What did you do?"

"What did I *do*? You've seen my face. What do you think I did?"

Banks looked at her.

"I screamed."

He put his juice down.

"For about a minute. I stood there looking at my reflection and I just screamed."

"It's not such a bad face. First time I saw it, it was shouting at me and its owner was trying to hurt me and I didn't think, yeesh, look at that face."

"Yeah, well, you're different," Banks said.

"How so?"

"When I... met you, you were just leaving a carriage full of dead people. Whose clothes and bags you had just gone through. And when I attacked you, you just lay there and laughed."

Garland felt uneasy.

"Shock. That's all it was," she said, knotting her plastic drink straw.

"You're not in shock," Banks said. "I know what shock is. I saw it in my own face. I didn't see it in yours."

"I think you're overreacting. About your face, I mean. It's unusual, I give you that. But it's your face. It suits you, your body. If you had, I don't know, a cute heart-shaped boy face, you'd look wrong." Garland was aware she was overdoing it a bit, but she meant what she was saying.

"No."

"Yes. I'm just saying, it suits you because it's your face."

"That's it, though," Banks said. "It's not my face."

Garland turned to an imaginary waiter.

"Can we get the check, please? I suddenly have to go."

Banks looked puzzled.

"Who are you talking to?" he asked.

"I was just making a joke," she said.

"To the person who isn't there?"

"To myself," she said.

"Why would you do that?"

Banks seemed genuinely concerned.

"OK," she said. "I have empathy issues, you have humour issues. Looks like we're a great team."

Garland finished her drink with a definitive slurp.

"I really, really don't want to ask this," she said. "But when you said –"

"– about my face not being my face?" Banks finished for her. "It's true. This –" he indicated his face with a long bony finger. "It's not my face."

She sat back, and laughed.

"Is this another joke to yourself?" said Banks.

"No," she said. "I've just realised you set me up. This whole conversation was just you softening me up for the whole 'this isn't my face' business."

"It's a difficult thing," said Banks.

"Yeah," agreed Garland. "I certainly wouldn't open with it. How do you *know* it isn't your face?"

"I just do," Banks said.

"Good reasoning," Garland said. "Convincing."

"I know it's not logical," said Banks, "but I know this isn't my face."

"Wait, this isn't like body dysmorphia?"

"What's that?"

"When you think your leg or something isn't yours so you try and get it amputated."

"No," Banks said. "I don't want to lose my face. I don't have another one to replace it."

"So if this isn't your face, what happened to your old one?"

"I can't remember," Banks said. "All I know is this isn't it."

There was a period of silence then. Garland found it hard to think of more things to ask Banks about his face.

She said, "When I saw my face – earlier, in the bathroom back there – I was surprised."

"How?" Banks said. "Was it not your face?"

She smiled. "No, it's my face all right."

"How do you know?" Banks asked, tight-lipped.

"I don't," she said. "I just looked at my reflection and I thought, *oh, OK, there you are.* Like I wasn't expecting to see someone I know, but when I did, it wasn't a surprise. You know?"

"Not really," said Banks. "Like I said, not my face."

Garland ignored this. "I think I remember my face being less tired, but that makes sense, because I am tired. And I was wearing make-up, and I was clean, but, you know, circumstances. The only thing..." and now she frowned.

"Yes?" said Banks. "What's wrong? You look upset," he explained.

Garland was upset. When she finally spoke, she said, "When I looked at my face – the thing I remembered about it that was different, really different, was..."

"Was what?"

"It was younger," Garland said. "I was younger."

• • •

Now Banks was silent.

"How much younger?" he asked.

She shrugged. "Not a lot. I mean, not like twenty years, or like I was a kid. But there were, last time I remember seeing it, fewer lines, and things like that."

"OK," said Banks. "So you're old and I have someone else's face. Great."

Garland looked at him.

"I didn't say I was *old*," she said.

Banks wasn't listening.

"Hey," she said, "I said –"

"Be quiet," Banks said.

"What?"

"Be *quiet*."

Banks was listening to something.

"I can't hear anything."

"That's because you're talking."

"What is it?"

"Listen."

She listened, and then she heard it. Faint, fuzzy, rhythmic.

"It's music," she said. For some reason, this was the strangest thing yet.

"It's coming from up there," said Banks. He stood up, head cocked to one side.

"Here," he said, indicating a small round grille in the ceiling.

"It's a speaker," said Garland. She stood on the seat and put her ear to the grille. Barely audible drums fizzed out and she could hear a voice.

"Miami, Florida… Atlanta, Georgia…"

"What is it?" asked Banks.

"It's a song," she said. "Or a list. Or both."

"Baltimore… Philadelphia…"

"Do you know these places?"

"New York City…"

"I think so," said Garland. "I'm not sure."

They listened to the voice for a few more minutes, then –

"And don't –"

The music stopped, mid-phrase.

"What was that?" Garland said.

"Like you said." Banks shrugged. "Music. Not what I'd call music."

"What do you call music?"

"No idea," admitted Banks. "But not like that."

"I liked it," said Garland.

If Banks had something more to add, she never found out. At that moment the train seemed to fly into the air.

With a grinding lurch, the carriage rose up and leapt. They couldn't see outside for the dark, but they could tell by the shift in gravity and the position of the flaring lights outside that something had dramatically changed.

"Hold onto something!" Banks shouted.

Garland gripped the back of a seat as the train rattled and then, gut-sickeningly, started to race downwards.

"What's happening?" she shouted. "Are we falling?"

Banks, his fingers curled round the rim of the luggage rack, shook his head.

"I don't think so," he shouted. "It's some kind of run."

"What? What do you mean, run?"

Then she understood what he meant. The train was somehow trying to gather momentum, first climbing – could it be? – some sort of steep ramp, and then throwing itself down a different, even steeper ramp.

"Here it comes," shouted Banks. "Are you scared of heights?"

She shrugged. "I have no idea!"

At that moment, the train shot down its presumed ramp

and they were surrounded by fire.

No, not surrounded, she thought. The fire wasn't around them, but below. It was bright enough to illuminate the night outside them for a few metres in all directions. She ran to the window.

"I really wouldn't look down," said Banks.

Garland looked down. Then she closed them again.

"Fuck," she said.

She opened her eyes. The train was racing along a narrow track on a bridge supported on long crisscrossed struts, over small flat pools of molten orange. One of the pools suddenly spurted out a gout of fire which nearly touched the bottom of the train. She could actually feel the heat from the gout.

"What does this train run on?" she asked.

Banks smiled. "I have no idea what it runs on, but it surely runs on *something*. Which means –"

"Which means it has engines," she said. "Which means it has machine parts that can get hot."

"Tell me," Banks said. "Do you hear engines right now?"

It was hard to tune in to anything over the rattling and the roaring of the carriages, but after a while Garland noticed that something was missing from the overall din of the train.

"No engine," she said.

"You got it," Banks said. "That's why we have the run-up. I think the engine shuts down automatically when it comes to one of these bridges."

"The whole time? You said this bridge could be days long."

"Not the whole time, no, just long enough."

"Long enough for what?" she asked.

"I don't know," explained Banks.

Garland looked out again.

"So right now we're freewheeling down a narrow track with no power over a lake of heat and fire?"

"That's about the size of it," said Banks.

"Fuck," Garland said.

"I knew you were going to say that," said Banks.

. . .

"Now what?" said Garland, after they had tired of looking at the lake of fire.

"You tell me," said Banks. "You're the one with the plan."

"Me? I don't have a plan."

"You got me out of my carriage," Banks said. "You're moving forwards. Moving forwards is a plan."

"OK, but that's all," said Garland. "I have no idea where I'm going, or what I'm going to do when I get there. If I get there, you know, wherever there is. So yeah, moving forwards is the entirety of my plan."

"It's enough," said Banks, and took a can from the kitbag.

"Have you thought about what you're going to do when you run out of cans?" Garland asked as Banks opened it.

"No," said Banks. "Have you thought what you're going to do when you run out of train?"

. . .

The next few hours passed quietly. The train shook and rattled, the fire below erupted and belched and occasionally the engine came on with a low whine, ran for a while, and then went off again. Banks and Garland got up from time to time to use the compartment's bathroom which – like the other bathrooms on the train – was clean, supplied with rough tissues and toilet paper, and had hot and cold running water. Sometimes Garland napped for a while, sometimes Banks did, but mostly they just sat there and looked at their faces reflected in the fire-dappled glass of the window.

Garland remembered something. She felt in her pocket for the newspaper she had taken in the carriage full of dead. She unfolded it and looked at it quickly, long enough to establish that trying to make out words still hurt her.

"You can read, right?" she said to Banks.

He looked offended. "Of course I can read," he said. Then he saw what she was getting at. "Can't you?"

"It hurts my head," she said. "Might be something I was born with, but I doubt it. Anyway, I found these –"

She gave him the bits of paper. He flicked through them.

"Photographs," he said. "You should have brought the whole paper."

"I would have, if I'd known I was going to meet you."

Banks didn't reply. He was sifting the pieces of paper, placing them side by side on the table between them.

"Who *are* these people?" he asked.

"No ideas?"

"I can make guesses," he said. "These people," and he pointed at a picture of a young couple, looking gloomy in very few clothes at night, "are *famous*."

"You know that, or you're guessing?"

"Both. I mean, they look rich but not really rich, and they're glamorous, so they must be famous. But also they look familiar in a way. Like if I could remember things, I would know who they are."

Garland nodded. "Anyone else?"

"Not really." Banks flicked through the pages. "And this – what is this meant to be?"

He was looking at a drawing. It showed a giant with protuberant teeth and squinting eyes kicking a house. The giant had a military helmet on like he was an evil giant soldier. Inside the house, tiny women and children were apparently screaming. Beside the building a figure in black robes holding a farm implement stood, arms folded.

"I have no idea," said Garland.

"I recognise that one," said Banks, indicating the black-robed figure. "That's Death."

Garland frowned. "Two famous people and Death. This is a great newspaper."

Banks flicked through the remaining pieces of paper.

"Wait," he said, and stopped at a photograph of a small crowd gathered round a man in glasses. The man was saying something and it was making the crowd excited and angry. Some of them were clapping and others had their fists in the air. Whatever he was saying was obviously both important and emotional.

"What is it?" said Garland.

Banks pointed at a figure at the side of the picture.

Whoever it was had turned their back to the camera, and the photo was cropped so that they were partly out of shot. Only their back and shoulder were visible.

"I don't get it," Garland said.

"That person there," Banks said.

"What about him?"

"What about *her*," corrected Banks.

"How do you know it's a woman?"

"Because," said Banks, "it's you."

. . .

Garland snatched the photograph from him. She studied it closely, as though hoping the figure in the photograph would suddenly turn to the camera and reveal themselves.

"How do you know it's me?" she said. "It could be anyone."

"Look at the hand," Banks said.

Garland looked. "It's just a hand," she said.

"The way she's holding it," Banks said. "Placing it at the base of her throat. You're doing it now."

"No I'm not," said Garland, moving her hand away from the base of her throat.

"It's you."

"Nonsense," said Garland. She scrunched up the paper and threw it across the carriage.

"What did you do that for?" cried Banks, and scrambled up to get it.

Just then the train hit a sharp curve on the track, lurched, and threw Garland to one side. Banks, who was still moving across the train aisle, caught the full shift of the train's mass, and was slammed into the wall opposite. Garland leapt to her feet and ran over to where Banks lay.

He wasn't moving. A drop of blood had appeared in the corner of one eye, while the other was half covered by its lid.

"Banks!" she shouted. "Banks, wake up!"

Banks moved, slumped back, and this time a yellow sliver of drool ran down his chin. He closed his eyes and began to moan. Garland looked around for some water. The kitbag was still on the other side of the aisle. She stood up and got it. The water bottle wasn't in the kitbag.

"Fuck," she muttered, and realised Banks had been holding the bottle in his other hand when he had been looking at the newspaper photos. She stuck her head under the table and saw the bottle, bumping feebly under Banks's seat. Reaching for it, she banged her forehead, said "Fuck!" again and rolled the bottle out with her fingertips.

When she finally stood up again, Banks wasn't there.

• • •

"Banks?"

She looked around. How could a man as tall as Banks just vanish?

"Banks, where the fuck are you?" He was right, she really did say that word a lot. She turned round to look back down the compartment. Nothing. She crouched down – perhaps he had got under something. It seemed unlikely: he would have just as easily got into an eggcup as under one of the train tables.

51

"Banks!"

She threw open the door of the bathroom, but he wasn't there. And then she saw the compartment door, the one they'd just come through. It was banging softly against something, and the thing it was banging against was Banks. Arms wrapped around folded legs, he was mumbling to himself rhythmically, almost chanting. She lowered herself beside him.

"What are you saying, Banks?" she asked gently. Banks didn't reply. He carried on muttering his chant.

"*Seven... four... nine... six... seven... fourteen... five... one...*" he said.

"What are you doing, Banks?"

"*Six... eight... twenty... zero... eighteen... nine...*"

"Banks? What are these numbers?"

Banks lifted his head and looked at her. She recoiled. His eyes were completely white.

"*Four... eight... four... three... four... thirty...*"

There was nothing she could do, so she waited. She waited as Banks counted out his seemingly random numbers. She waited as his eyes stayed white in their sockets. After a while, she did what anyone else would have done (or so she told herself). She went and got a pen from the kitbag and wrote down the numbers.

• • •

"*Twenty-nine... three... two... six... three... two... four... ninety...*"

The numbers made no sense to Garland but then, she reflected, they wouldn't. She had no way of cross-referencing them or looking them up to see if they had some external significance. After a while, she did notice one odd thing about them. The bigger numbers, the ones she thought of as *the two-digit numbers*.

Most number chains, so far as she was aware, didn't have two-digit numbers in them. There was no need. You didn't need to say "twenty-one", you just said "two" and "one". The same for "nineteen", or "seventy-four", or any other two-digit number. There was just no place for them. But every so often, Banks would say "thirty-seven" or "forty-six" or even, on one occasion, "ninety-nine". He never, Garland noticed, went any higher than that, so presumably he hadn't been – she didn't want to, but she decided it was the right word – *programmed* to go any higher than that. So no three-digit numbers. None of it made any sense to her. There were no recurring groups of numbers. No mathematical formulas that she was aware of. Nothing. She was just writing down random numbers that a man with white eyes was chanting.

After a while Garland gave up writing. She put down the pen and placed her hand on Banks's arm. If he noticed this, he gave no sign. Soon, despite the cramped nature of their location, she grew sleepy, lulled by the repetition of the numbers.

Beats counting sheep, she thought, and just had time to remember what sheep were before she fell fast asleep.

• • •

When she awoke, she could hear banging. She sat up and opened her eyes. Banks was thumping his head against the wall.

"*One*," he said, every time his head hit the wall. "*One. One. One.*"

Garland tried to restrain him, but Banks was too strong.

"*One*," he said, again and again. "*One.*"

Garland emptied the rucksack and placed it between Banks's head and the wall. It softened the thumping at least and would ensure that Banks didn't injure himself.

The problem with repetition is that it is very repetitive. After fifteen minutes of unvaried "*ones*", Garland longed for the sparkling variety of the previous number lists. She was about to look for something to block her ears with when Banks stopped chanting.

The silence was unnerving, but no more than the terrified, startled look on Banks's face. He was staring at her, tears pooling in his eyes.

"What's wrong?" she said. "What was that, some kind of countdown?"

"What was what?" Banks replied, still looking stunned.

"Never mind," Garland said. "Are you OK?" It was a stupid question but it was all she had.

At first Banks didn't reply. Then he said, "I know who I am."

He grabbed her arms so hard she thought his fingers might crush them. When she cried out, he let go.

"I know who I am," he repeated. He got to his feet, and looked at his face in the window. He made a fist of his hand and smashed it into the plastic glass. His fist bounced back, bloody. He did it again, and again.

"I know who I am!" he shouted, and began to

batter both his fists against the door.

Garland wrapped her arms around him and pulled him back to the floor, where he sat, sobbing.

They stayed like that for a long time.

Interlude One

There used to be a boy called Peter.

. . .

When he was seventeen, Peter was called into the principal's office.

"You're leaving us today," the principal said.

Peter wasn't especially surprised. He seemed to spend most of his time in the principal's office, sent there by teachers who took his lack of interest personally. Peter didn't hate the teachers, he just found what they had to say dull, so dull that he would just get out of his seat and go and do something else. Sometimes he would get out a book and read that instead. Sometimes he would wander over to another student and start talking to them. Several times he accessed the school lesson program on his desktop computer (it was the kind of school where students had computers on their desk) and changed the lessons so they were more accurate.

Peter had discovered long ago that some of the things they were being taught were wrong. A lot of the science was wrong, like someone had misheard it or written it down incorrectly. There were big gaps in the language and literature syllabus, where books would routinely lose three or four chapters without comment, as if they had been stored on corrupted hardware. Worst of all, Peter found, was the history syllabus.

The history syllabus was pretty much nonsense. Events followed events with no explanation or apparent connection. Figures appeared and disappeared at random. Maps didn't make any sense. Facts contradicted themselves. Peter tried to correct the syllabus, but history isn't like science: it's hard to fill in the gaps just using logic and equations. When Peter got into the university computer, which had a backed-up archive, he was able to access a lot more information and correct the course to a greater extent, but there were still enormous gaps, sometimes where the information had just disappeared (an entire country had apparently ceased to exist about three years back) and sometimes where the information still existed but it had been placed behind an impenetrable wall.

Peter was about to break down the impenetrable wall when the principal called him to tell him he was leaving.

"Your talents, if we can call them that," said the principal, "will be better employed elsewhere."

• • •

Peter had no time to say his goodbyes. This upset him, as there were one or two people he would miss. There was a boy called Andro, and he had the best hair Peter had ever seen. Peter could look at Andro's hair the way other boys looked at sports shows or cars. It was absurd, there was so much of it, but it was beautiful.

One day Andro had said, "You like it so much, touch it."

Peter said, "I don't want to." But he did. In fact, there was a lot of Andro he wanted to touch, but he couldn't say that.

Andro sighed. "Here," he said, and shoved Peter's hand into his excessive hair. Peter pulled his hand away, then put it back. He dared not stroke Andro's head, but instead twisted his fingers around Andro's hair and then dug his hands in as if bathing them.

"That's enough," Andro said. "Someone's coming."

Later, Peter saw Andro talking to some other boys. He was sure, he didn't know, that they were talking about him. When Andro ran his fingers through his ridiculous hair, Peter was certain. He was a joke to them.

• • •

The car pulled away with Peter in the back.

"You going to help us win?" said the driver.

"I beg your pardon?" Peter said.

"Fucking ponce," the driver replied, and after that neither of them said anything at all until the car reached the big house.

• • •

The house was the oldest thing Peter had ever seen. There were stone pillars in front, holding up a porch with a triangular roof, and the statues on the lawn had noses and hands missing like petrified lepers. Even the front step was dented like a pillow from years of people walking on it. Inside the house were carpets that smelt of dust and paintings of people with round eyes and no chins. The men wore armour and the women and children wore dresses but apart from that they all looked the same, a defunct race of globe-headed, globe-eyed people who liked being painted.

The driver shoved Peter into a room with a very long table in it and left, closing the door behind him. At the end of the table was a man sitting at a laptop computer and, improbably, smoking a pipe. When he saw Peter, he stood up.

"Come here," he said. "Look at this."

Peter looked at the laptop. On the screen was a film. In the film, ropes of different colours tangled themselves around a cartoon bear. The more the bear struggled, the more the ropes tangled themselves.

"I can't do these things," said the man.

Peter sat down. He looked at the keyboard, tapped a few keys tentatively, and having got the measure of the puzzle, untangled the ropes.

"Good Lord," said the man. "I've never seen that happen before. Although," he added, "the aim of the game is not to *free* the animal."

He hit a key, and the ropes snapped back into place. They snaked and coiled around the bear, until they were so tight that the bear's eyes popped out like those of the people in the paintings, and then burst.

"There we go," he said, and extended a hand. "Call me Mister Denning," he said. "And welcome to Park."

· · ·

Park was where Peter lived and worked now. Every day after breakfast he left his bedroom and was taken to a large room in a building at the back of the house. The room was full of desktop and laptop computers, each one operated by a young man or woman. Nobody spoke, and Peter had no idea what anybody else was doing. He himself was assigned different tasks, the amount depending entirely on how much he could get done throughout the day.

There were only two constants. The first was that he was never told what to do. Peter might find a map on his screen: having no idea where it was or what he was supposed to do with it, it took him a few minutes to work out that some of the places on the map were connected, and by clicking on the names of the places he could make them vanish. He might find a series of abstract and random images, which he would then divide into groups; he might be given a scientific document whose errors he would then correct. He had no idea if what he was doing was wrong or right. No encouragement or discouragement was ever given.

The other constant was the bear and rope puzzle. Once every two or three days, one of these puzzles appeared on his screen. They were always easy to solve once it was grasped that the point of the puzzle was to kill the bear, not to free it. Sometimes for his own entertainment Peter would free the bear, but when he did the same puzzle always reappeared the next day, as if waiting for him to do it properly this time, so after a while he grew bored of setting the bear free and just killed it with the ropes to free up time for his other work.

· · ·

After lunch, which was always under his desk in a plastic box, Peter and the others worked until the evening, when they were allowed to socialise. There were limits to this: nobody was allowed to talk about their work, or even refer to it. As Peter had no idea what he was doing, this was not a very onerous demand. Much harder was the pressure of socialising. Peter had no idea who anyone was or where they had come from, but to a man or woman they were all shy, quiet and far from chatty. Peter, who had considered himself a loner at school, began to realise just how gregarious he had actually been.

School at least had forced people together in clubs, in hobbies and with games. No such distractions were encouraged at Park. Sometimes people might disclose a former interest in model-making, or football, or films, but there was simply no way of indulging these interests at Park, short of carving twigs or making a ball from old clothes. Even reading was not an option, as there was no library. And, at the end of each working day, nobody really had the energy to do anything but watch television.

Soon Peter had fallen into the evening routine of making his way to the TV room after dinner, sitting in an old armchair and letting the television's selection of nature shows and incomprehensible soap operas wash over him. He had the feeling that every animal and person in these programmes was long dead, but he didn't care. This was his new life.

· · ·

One evening, when Peter was about to nod off during a particularly old programme about sloths (Peter knew it was old from the blurred quality of the film and the fact that the white people in it were wearing khaki shorts and knee socks), he felt a sharp dig in his ribs.

A voice said: "I've seen this. They capture the sloths and take them away, but we never find out where."

He stirred. A young man he'd never noticed was sitting in the chair next to his, a chair normally occupied by a fat boy called Lamb.

"Where's Lamb?" said Peter.

"Over there," said the young man, and Peter saw that Lamb was perched with difficulty on a small stool by the window. "I told him I was allergic to draughts and he gave me his seat. He's a very kind boy."

"No, he isn't," said Peter. "He farts in his hand and puts it over your mouth."

"Well, he might do that for you," said the young man, giving Peter an amused look, "but it's not really my sort of thing."

"I didn't mean I asked him to –" Peter began, then stopped. "Who are you?" he asked.

"Hatch," said the young man. He extended his hand. "And you're Peter."

Peter looked at the hand. "Hello," he said.

Hatch seemed not to notice his lack of enthusiasm.

"Listen," he said, nodding at the TV set. "It's coming up."

Unsure what Hatch was talking about, Peter looked at the television. Two sloths had been trussed up and were being hoisted up on poles.

"The mission has been a success," said the fruity voice-over. "And now the sloths will be taken to —"

Peter didn't hear where the sloths would be taken to because at the exact moment the narrator spoke, an elephant trumpeted.

"See?" said Hatch. "They took the name out."

"It was just an elephant," said Peter.

"An elephant," said Hatch. "In South America. Right."

"Excuse me," Peter said. "I have to go."

"OK," said Hatch. "I'll tell Lamb he can have his seat back."

• • •

The next night, Lamb sat next to Peter. Peter pretended he wasn't disappointed.

• • •

The night after that, when Peter went into the television room, he found himself scanning the room for Hatch. He saw him, sitting on a couch with a boy and a girl. Hatch caught his eye and, to Peter's horror, patted the arm of the sofa. Peter turned away and went to his normal seat.

• • •

Denning came to see Peter at work.

"Is everything all right?" he asked.

"Yes, fine," said Peter. "Why?" he added, although he didn't really need to. His concentration had not been great recently and he'd found some of the games and puzzles less obvious than usual.

"Nothing," said Denning. "Only sometimes we find the environment here doesn't suit everyone."

"It suits me fine," said Peter. "Really."

"Good," said Denning. "Just checking."

• • •

That evening, Peter decided to avoid the TV room entirely. He stayed in his room, staring at the ceiling, trying to make the cracks turn into ropes and strangle the light fitting. "Fuck you, Hatch," he said suddenly. He got up and went downstairs.

The TV room was full. Hatch was sitting in Peter's chair. He smiled when he saw Peter come in.

"I think there's something wrong with my washbasin," he said.

"You need the caretaker," Hatch replied.

"I can't find him," Peter said.

Hatch sighed and got up.

"Come on then," he said.

• • •

An hour later, Hatch left Peter's room.

"We should do this again," he said.

Peter couldn't tell in the dark, but he was sure Hatch was smiling.

• • •

And so Peter's life began. He never said so, even to Hatch, but he dated the beginning of his existence from the moment that they met. He couldn't prove that Hatch felt the same way, of course, because the way they were together was another thing that could not be discussed, but he knew, inside himself, that they were meant to be together.

Certainly life smiled on them. Denning took them both

from the obscurity of the computer pool and put them into smaller, more intensive workrooms, where the puzzles Peter worked on were more opaque, more abstract and – judging by the pleasure Denning expressed when Peter solved them – more important. There were new privileges associated with working in the smaller rooms, too. Better food, more access to the grounds – which turned out to be huge – and even visits to a nearby village which, while small, had a shop and even a pub, both of which took Park scrip.

• • •

It was on one visit to the pub, about two years later, that Hatch, setting their half pints of bitter down on a copper table, said:

"Do you think this is it for ever for us?"

Peter nearly blurted out that he hoped it was, when he realised that Hatch was not talking about the two of them.

"I mean," he continued, "the war, of course."

Peter looked shocked.

"You're not supposed to talk about –"

"I know. But there's nobody else here, and besides, it's ridiculous. There *is* a war, and we're in it, same as everyone else. In fact –" and Hatch did at least lean in and speak quietly, "– I think we're the ones winning it."

"What do you mean?" Peter took a sip of his bitter nervously.

Hatch laughed. "You don't think we're just playing puzzles and games all day, do you? We're part of the war effort, Peter."

"I still think you should be quiet," Peter said.

"No," said Hatch. "I'd have to do something really bad

to get into trouble. Last year Sorensen in Room 12 came to work drunk and pissed himself at his desk, and nobody said a word."

"Pissing yourself isn't treason," said Peter, and felt foolish even as he spoke.

"Nor is this," said Hatch, sharply. "Peter, I don't know what we're doing or how it helps the war, but it *does* help and we're the ones doing it. One day they'll give us medals, believe me."

And with that they finished their drinks and left.

• • •

Things changed shortly after that. Men and women didn't come into work and were never seen again. The puzzles weren't – not difficult, but *unreasonable*, somehow, as if it was asking too much of Peter to solve them. They were sloppier, harder to follow and – most annoying of all to an expert puzzle solver – badly put-together, as though whoever was making them had lost interest in their work. The only constants were the rope and bear puzzles, which never varied. Ropes continued to writhe and strangle, and bears' eyes continued to burst.

The worsening situation bothered Peter, but it didn't seem to worry Hatch.

"We're safe here," he told Peter one night in his room. "So long as we keep solving the puzzles, everything will be fine."

• • •

A few weeks later trips to the pub were banned ("There's no beer anyway," said Sorensen, morosely.) A few weeks after that, everyone was confined to Park for their own safety. There were blackouts – these didn't affect the computers, which had their own backup generators as well as batteries – and sometimes there was no food. The TV programmes began to get more and more repetitive, too. The sloth programme, in particular, seemed to be on every evening.

• • •

"I wish they'd get some more tapes," said Hatch.

"This programme means a lot to me," Peter said.

"That's because you are a bloody sloth," Hatch replied.

Peter turned to him.

"What do you mean?"

"I've had Denning on my back. Apparently he thinks I have some influence over you," said Hatch, tightly. "He says you're slacking."

Peter was confused and angered by everything Hatch was saying.

"I've been working as hard as ever," he said.

"Plodding is one thing," said Hatch. "Results are another. I don't want this to reflect on me."

• • •

After lights out, Peter waited in his room until it got so late he decided to go to sleep. But he couldn't sleep.

• • •

Hatch took to avoiding Peter. Sometimes they didn't speak for days. Peter worked hard in the computer room to avoid thinking about him, but the puzzles were now so sloppy and incomprehensible that he could only effectively work on new rope and bear puzzles.

I want to throw myself into my work, he thought, *but my work keeps throwing me back out.*

• • •

One day Peter woke up. He thought about Hatch, and he thought about work, and he decided it wasn't worth getting up.

About lunchtime, when nobody had come for him, he got bored and went into the computer room. Despite his unshaven appearance and the fact that he was wearing his dressing-gown over his pyjamas, no one even seemed to notice he was there. In fact, there were very few people in the room at all.

• • •

This went on for a week or so. Peter hadn't spoken to Hatch for months now. He hadn't spoken to anyone but, he noticed, people in Park had pretty much given up on talking anyway.

• • •

Towards the end of the winter, a winter without heating or much electric light, Peter was woken by a banging on the door. Before he could sit up, he was pulled out of bed by two figures in dark blue jerseys and jeans. They dragged him, not protesting at all, down the corridor and up a staircase. At the top of the stairs was an open door into a small room.

He was taken into the room and tied to a chair. Some sort of metal ropes were wrapped around him. Peter had never seen them before, but they looked familiar somehow. At the front of the room was a glass window, behind which he could just make out a face. The face was Hatch's.

As the ropes gathered around Peter, he tensed. A smaller rope was tightening itself about his neck. He found it hard to breathe. Despite this, he kept his head up, eyes on Hatch. Hatch didn't return his gaze: he was too busy pressing keys on his laptop.

Hatch wasn't as good at the puzzle as Peter, but it still took him less than three minutes to envelop the bear in six or seven ropes. As the last rope coiled into place, the bear's expression turned to one of alarm.

A few seconds later and it was over. A team removed the body and cleaned the window.

There used to be a boy called Peter.

• • •

"Hatch is useless now," Denning said to the woman on the screen.

"You told me he was first percentile," said the woman. "You told me he was essential."

"No one is essential," said Denning. "Except yourself, of course," he added quickly.

"He turned in the degenerate," said the woman. "He performed the removal himself. And then…" She looked disgusted.

"What shall I do with him?" asked Denning.

The woman said nothing. Unaware she was doing it, she put her hand over her throat, as though feeling for a missing necklace.

"He's human waste now," she said. "Take his face and let him go."

· · ·

They took Hatch's face and gave him someone else's. The operation hurt so much he could only bear the pain by making number patterns.

· · ·

Seven.

· · ·

They were doing something to his eyes.

· · ·

Thirty-two.

· · ·

He was strapped down and his shirt was cut off.

· · ·

Seven. Nine. Fourteen. Seventy-eight.

· · ·

His chest was open.

· · ·

When they stopped, he was still in pain. It hurt so much he didn't wake up for a month.

· · ·

When he did, he was on a train.

TWO

"So now you know," said Banks.

"That wasn't you," said Garland.

"It was," Banks said. "A different name doesn't make you a different person. A different face doesn't change you."

"I didn't mean that," said Garland. "You're not him. What you did was awful but it changed you. Not your name or your face, but you."

She held him. He was bony and difficult to hold. Outside, lights flashed and rainclouds burst.

"You're not Hatch," she said. "I'm sorry about Hatch too, but Hatch is dead."

Banks looked up at her.

"I can still remember, though," he said. "What I did."

"Look where we are," Garland said. "Look where they put us. Whoever they are, they're not good people. They didn't have to make you choose between Peter and your own life. They didn't have to kill him —"

"I killed him," said Banks.

"They killed him too," said Garland. "And they killed us."

She stood up.

"I think," she said, "that we really need to have a word with the driver."

• • •

As Banks picked up his cans and put them back into the kitbag, he said, "How do you even know this is the right way?"

"What do you mean?"

"Well," said Banks. "When you woke up back there, you just opened the first door you found and headed in this direction. For all you know, we could be going towards the back of the train."

Garland frowned.

"You're doing that thing with your hand again," said Banks.

"When I woke up," she said, moving her hand, "I was sure there wasn't another door in the carriage. Which has to mean it was the last carriage on the train. The end carriage."

"You didn't check?"

"I wasn't inclined to, no. It was more like a cattle truck than a carriage. It was dark, and there were chains."

"Doesn't mean anything. Half the carriages on this train don't look like each other. There's one up there that —"

Banks stopped. Garland gave him a look.

"I thought you said you'd been in your carriage the whole time," she said.

"I did," said Banks. "I was. Only –"

He put down the bag.

"In the early days, sometimes I'd hear noises. From the other direction – your direction. So I'd move away, up the train."

"You've been here before? And you saw the cage, too?" Banks was on the defensive.

"I hardly knew you. You could have been a trap."

"OK. Sorry. But tell me – is there anything up there I should know about?"

Banks shook his head. "This is pretty much as far as I got."

"Pretty much as far, or exactly as far?"

"Just as far as the game," Banks said.

"What game?" said Garland.

"I'll show you," Banks replied.

• • •

They made their way through a carriage which was unremarkable except for the fact that everything in it was broken. Seats, tables, luggage racks: even the unbreakable windows were cracked and bowed.

"Something angry was in here," Banks said. He reached under a smashed table and pulled out something. A can of peaches.

"Maybe it couldn't open cans," suggested Garland.

They came to the doorway of the carriage. The door had been peeled away like the skin of a fruit and lay ripped in half on the floor.

"I don't know," Banks replied. "Seems like it can open things just fine."

He stepped over the broken, flattened door and into the next carriage.

• • •

The lights were out. Banks found the torch. He turned it on and let it sweep around the carriage.

"Fuck," Garland said.

"I wish you'd stop saying that," said Banks.

• • •

The carriage they were standing in was full of graffiti. All kinds of graffiti. Some of it was, Garland supposed, modern graffiti, words painted in almost abstract blobs, garish spurts fighting for space in clouds of colour. The effect was to make the inside of the carriage look like an old subway train (but from where? And what was a subway train?) Some of the graffiti was, frankly, incompetent, just scrawls and drawings in black by some person or persons who had no artistic talent whatsoever. Some of it was writing. Screeds of random-looking words, not all of them in any alphabet Garland recognised: political slogans of the vaguest sort (CONTINUE THE STRUGGLE!) and dramatic personal boasts (I COULD HAVE ANYONE OF YOU). There were painted animals, and cartoon figures. Caricatures of people Garland didn't recognise.

And, all over one now-blind wall, where someone had simply sprayed right over the compartment window, one enormous painting.

"What is it?" said Garland.

Banks said, "I think it's a map."

He peered at it.

"Those are roads, or rivers, and I can see mountains, I think."

He pointed at a grey tangle.

"That could be a forest."

"It could be," agreed Garland. "It could also be a gorilla."

She took a step back.

"If it is a map," she said, "it could do with something to let us know where we are. YOU ARE HERE, something like that."

"We're on a train," Banks said. "We're here, and we're everywhere."

"Everywhere and nowhere," Garland said. "Shine that over there."

The torch's light fell on something. It was a table, further down the carriage, an ordinary kitchen table with two chairs on either side of it.

Banks and Garland sat in the chairs. The table was strewn with odd items, some squat, some square, and some tall and white.

"Candles," said Garland, grabbing them. "Useful."

Banks swept the table with the torchlight.

"Look," he said.

Some of the objects on the table were on a board. The board was an irregular grid of coloured lines and shapes, and the things on the board – while different to one another – were clearly games pieces. About half of them were black.

Garland picked one up.

"It's a tower," she said. "And that one is a knight."

"Chess," said Banks. "I remember now."

Garland shook her head. "I know chess," she said. "It's not chess."

"What is it, then?"

Garland made a face. "I don't know. But –"

She picked up another piece. It was a human finger, painted black.

"I don't like it."

Banks took the finger from her. He licked it.

"It's not real," he said.

"Well, thank goodness for that," said Garland, looking round at the painted chaos. "That would have spoiled the entire evening."

"I wonder if there's a set of rules anywhere," said Banks.

"You serious?"

"Got to have rules," said Banks. "You can't function without rules."

He stuck his head under the table, banged it, cried out, and then said something Garland couldn't hear. He emerged with a booklet.

"Rules," he said.

"I don't believe it," Garland said, as Banks flicked through the booklet.

"It's interesting," Banks said. "I mean, most of the pieces are missing, but it's a good game."

"I'm glad to hear it," said Garland. "Maybe you can teach it to me. I mean, when we have more leisure time."

"Weird," Banks said, not listening to her. "The idea of the game isn't to win."

"Is it to lose?" Garland replied.

"No," said Banks. "You just have to keep moving."

"Good advice," said Garland. "We should do the same."

Suddenly Banks cried out.

"Fuck!"

The finger on the table was bleeding.

"I thought you said it wasn't real," said Garland.

"It isn't," said Banks.

"And," said Garland, "I thought you didn't like that word."

"Can we go now?" asked Banks.

"Happy to," said Garland, and got up.

• • •

As they headed to the next door, Garland heard something. She made her way over to where the luggage rack should have been and put her ear to the wall. Sure enough, she could hear a faint rhythmic sound coming out of a painted-over grille.

"It's music," she said.

"Like before," Banks replied.

"Not like before," she said. "Listen."

• • •

A laconic voice was singing over a lazy-sounding backing track:

> *… and they screamed and begged,*
> *"Please let us go,"*
> *But the Devil was driving*
> *And he said, "No!"*

"Cheery," said Banks. "I wonder if we could find a news station instead."

And the train took the people to their awful fate
As the Devil drove on through Hell's foul gate

the voice sang and faded out.

• • •

"Let's get out of here," said Banks, and on they went.

• • •

"How many carriages?" asked Garland as they found themselves in another, relatively normal carriage and Banks dropped the kitbag onto a table.

"On the train?" asked Banks, pulling out cans and drinks.

"So far," said Garland, taking a drink.

Banks thought.

"Counting yours," he said, "eight."

Garland stuck a straw in her drink.

"And we've been moving for what?" she said. "A few hours?"

Banks nodded.

"We could be at the front of the train before nightfall," she said.

"How do you know it isn't nightfall already?" said Banks.

Outside, something erupted.

"I don't," she replied. "It just feels that way."

"Another thing is," Banks pointed out, "we have no idea how long the train is."

"Can't be too long," said Garland. "It's a train. A regular train. Something up there is pulling these carriages and it can only pull so many."

"So you say," Banks said.

Garland was about to reply to this when there was a red flash.

"Close your eyes!" Banks shouted.

"Why?" said Garland.

• • •

She was immediately blinded. Garland fell to the ground, covering her eyes. *A bit late now*, she thought, but she was wrong, as through her closed eyelids she could still sense another flash, yellow this time.

"What's happening?" she shouted.

"We're coming off the bridge," Banks shouted back.

"How do you know?"

"Because of the flashes," Banks shouted. "Every time the train comes off a bridge, there are the flashes. There should be another one —"

There was a yellow flash, rinsing Garland's closed eyes like toxic gold.

"I think it's a warning system," Banks said.

"Warning about what?" Garland said, slowly opening her eyes. The wash of colours began to fade.

"That," said Banks.

In front of them, the train curved round a bend away from the explosions below and towards a sheer rock face. Carved into the rock, barely visible in the clouds of smoke around it, was a tunnel.

"That doesn't look big enough," Garland said.

"Oh, all the tunnels are quite narrow," Banks replied.

Just then their carriage hurtled into the tunnel. It tilted as it turned, throwing Garland and Banks into a table. The tilt was so severe that the top of the train scraped the side of the tunnel. Sparks flew and metal screamed.

"Perfectly safe," said Banks as they picked themselves up from the floor.

• • •

The tunnel had three features. It was narrow, it was long – and it was cold.

"Typical," Garland said. "When it's cold outside, it's even colder in the train."

She looked out of the window. Water-streaked outcrops of jagged rock looked back.

"Why is it so cold?" she said.

"I expect we're inside a mountain," Banks said. "Deep inside."

"Oh," said Garland. "Good job I'm not claustrophobic."

"I'll say," Banks said. "I have a feeling we're getting deeper."

Garland grimaced. The roof of the carriage screamed again.

"And," said Banks, "I'm not sure, but I think the tunnel is getting narrower."

"Shut up," Garland said pleasantly.

• • •

The train screeched its way through the tunnel. Banks slept for a few minutes. When he woke again, Garland was scribbling away on a piece of paper.

"What are you doing?" he asked.

"Making a map," she replied.

"A map," he said. "We're on a train. I don't think a map is going to help us."

"That's the pioneer spirit," Garland replied. "I'm trying to remember all the places we've been."

"We've been on a train," said Banks.

"A moving train," Garland said. "We crossed bridges and fires and now we're inside a mountain. That's a lot of landmarks."

"But we can't get off," said Banks.

"That's where the other map comes in," Garland said.

"What other map?" Banks replied, but Garland had already flipped the paper over. On the back she had drawn a series of rectangular boxes.

"Each one of these is a carriage," Garland explained. "And each carriage is unique – this is where I woke up, this is the carriage of the fifteen dead, this is where I found you, this is the buffet car… and so on."

"Very impressive," Banks said. "I imagine it would be pretty useful if we got lost in the maze of interconnecting doors and – oh, that's right. We're on a train. We can only go back or forward."

"I'm trying to make sense of everything," Garland said. "Not burying my head in the sand. Don't make assumptions."

"All right," said Banks. He took the pencil from her.

"What are you doing? Give me that."

Banks got up and smashed a plastic window on the wall. From behind it he pulled out a piece of card covered in, Garland supposed, safety information. He turned it over, sat down, and began to copy Garland's map out.

"You draw like a horse," he said, sketching out neat boxes and labelling them.

"Nice writing," said Garland.

• • •

They looked at the train map for a while.

"There doesn't seem to be any system at all," Garland said.

Banks yawned.

"I'm going to the bathroom."

• • •

The bathroom, or rather the toilet, was back at the other end of the carriage. Garland walked slowly. She hoped Banks's yawn meant he was going to sleep. She hoped so: she was in need of some time to herself. As she approached the end of the carriage, she was rewarded with a low rumbling grunt, signifying that Banks was asleep. Garland exhaled. It was an odd thing to say to herself, here, on a train full of death and blood, hurtling through stone and fire to God knows where, but it was nice to finally have a bit of peace and quiet.

The toilet door was jammed shut. Garland tugged at it, but it was stuck fast. Then she shoved against it. It didn't budge. Garland thought about finding a different bathroom, but this seemed unwise especially (although she hated to admit it) without Banks. She considered going back the way they'd come, but this was a sort of defeat. So, with a deep intake of breath, she hurled herself at the door and, using her full weight, slammed into it.

This time the door gave way, so quickly that Garland's own momentum sent her flying into the tiny room, and knocked her to the floor. She was about to struggle to her feet when she saw something. The bathroom was not empty. Sitting on the toilet was a young girl. She was holding a teddy bear. The teddy bear was missing its head, and seemed to have been dipped in something sticky and red. The girl had short red hair, which looked like she had cut it herself, and was wearing the same clothing as Garland and Banks were.

The girl fixed Garland with a furious stare.

"There's someone *in* here," she said.

• • •

Garland got up off the floor.

"I'm sorry," she said absurdly.

"I locked the door and everything," the girl said. Garland could see she was more of a young woman than a girl.

"You should have said something."

"If the door's locked, that means someone is using the toilet," said the girl. "Everyone knows that."

Garland nodded at the teddy bear. "What happened to your bear?"

The girl looked sad. "He had a fight," she said.

"A fight?" Garland took a step closer to her. She hunched up, clenching the bear to her.

"They ganged up on him," said the girl. "Teddy only wanted to play."

Garland reckoned the girl was in her early twenties.

"Did they hurt you?" she asked, gently.

The girl shook her head. "No," she said. "Teddy fucked them up."

She looked down at the headless bear. Then she smiled at Garland.

"Come and see," she said.

• • •

Garland followed the girl down the train towards the next carriage. They stopped by Banks.

85

"Is he dying?" asked the girl.

"Just snoring very loudly," said Garland.

"I'm glad you told me," the girl said. "Otherwise I might have put him out of his misery."

Garland was silent for a moment. "You wouldn't get Teddy to do it?" she asked.

"Of course not," she said. "He's a teddy."

She prodded Banks with the bloodstained and headless toy. Banks woke with a start.

"This is Teddy," said the girl.

Banks looked at Garland, and then the girl.

"Who are you?" he said.

"Oh, thank you for asking," said the girl, casting a look at Garland. "My name is Poppy." She indicated her name patch. Someone had scraped off the original owner's name and scrawled POPPY in large black letters there instead.

"She was in the toilet," said Garland. "With Teddy."

"Is that blood?" Banks said.

"Teddy fucked some people up," Garland explained.

"Silly," said Poppy. "They weren't *people*."

And she walked off down the carriage.

• • •

"Tell me everything," Banks said quietly.

"There's not a lot to tell," Garland replied, "I only met her two minutes ago."

"Did she say anything about herself?"

"No, but you need to watch out for Teddy," Garland said.

"He seems harmless enough," Banks said.

"I think she's using him to cover for someone."

86

"I got that impression, too."

They were at the door to the next carriage.

Poppy turned to look at them.

"It is quite scary in there," she said. "But don't worry, me and Teddy are here."

She was about to open the door when Banks stopped her.

"I think it might be better if I go in first," he said. "You stay here with Garland."

Poppy considered this.

"All right," she said. "If you find Teddy's head, can you bring it back here please?"

"Of course," Banks said. He smiled.

Poppy didn't smile back.

"Just make sure it's *his* head, that's all," she said.

• • •

Banks returned a few minutes later. He looked strained.

"What is it?" Garland said.

"See for yourself."

Garland nodded at Poppy. "I imagine she's hungry."

"Have you got anything to eat?" Poppy said eagerly. "I'm starving."

"Sure," said Banks. He looked at Garland. "When you go in, don't look up straight away."

• • •

Garland opened the carriage door and went in. The lights weren't working properly: they flickered on and off randomly. She took Banks's advice and looked at the floor, which was slick with brown tracks, as though something had been dragged through it. The carriage, she noticed, bore out

87

Banks's alternating theory in that it had no seats or tables, just a single strip of carpet running through it like a blue road.

She decided to look up. Two luggage racks ran along each side of the carriage and Garland wondered what they were for, there being nowhere for anyone to sit. Then she noticed firstly that the racks were somewhat wider than usual, big enough to put some large objects on, and secondly that there were indeed some large objects on the racks.

Before she could take a closer look, the lights flickered out. They flashed back on for a second, letting her see something flap over the side of the rack. With nothing to stand on, she was unable to get closer. But then the train lurched to one side in the tunnel as the lights came back on, and something heavy and wet flew from the rack into her chest. Garland staggered backwards and let out a shout as the thing that was heavy and wet landed at her feet.

It was a dog, probably. Or a very large cat. Garland couldn't tell without getting close to it, and she didn't want to get close to it. Whatever it was, it was covered in blood, and now so was Garland. She took a deep breath and knelt down next to the animal.

The mouth lolled open, and Garland could see the animal had very big teeth, but very few of them. It was as if it had been designed to tear but not to eat. The claws were also long and thick, but – she prodded the tip of one with a finger – very sharp. The fur was thick and surprisingly abrasive, more like steel wool than actual hair, and the tail heavy – she lifted it – like a stick. Garland took a deep breath and pulled back one of the creature's eyelids. She wished she hadn't: the eye was coloured a deep green and had no visible pupil or iris.

Garland walked along the carriage. The racks contained more of the creatures, about four or five in total. They were all dead, and all clearly the victims of some kind of powerful assault. One or two were missing body parts. She turned to go back to the others and stumbled on something. She bent down and picked up the object, round and sticky in her hands.

It was Teddy's head.

"You are one hard bastard," she told it.

• • •

Back in the other carriage, Poppy was delighted to see the teddy bear's head. She began cleaning it at once.

"I'm glad someone's happy," Banks said. "What do you think happened in there?" he asked Garland.

Garland shrugged. "I don't know," she said. "If I'm honest, I don't think it was the bear." She looked at Poppy, who was jamming Garland's pencil deep into the bear's neck.

"Really?" said Banks.

"Most likely option," Garland replied, as Poppy crammed Teddy's head back on.

"Fixed!" she shouted. Teddy wobbled his approval.

"You haven't eaten anything," Garland said, looking at the untouched can in front of Poppy.

Poppy shook her head.

"Sugar's bad for you," she said. "Besides, I know where there's a fuckload of food."

"I wish people would stop using that word," said Banks.

"Food," Garland said. "You mean like cans and so on?"

89

"No," said Poppy. "Not like cans. Food."

She stroked Teddy's bloody fur.

"Real food," she said.

· · ·

This time Poppy led them through the carriage of dead animals.

"Stay close," she said.

"We're with you," Banks replied.

"I was talking to Teddy," Poppy said.

· · ·

Garland took the opportunity to study the carriage again. She could see now that the animals had not been so much placed in the racks as thrown into them.

"Who did this?" she asked.

"Too many questions," Poppy replied. She made Teddy's head shake in disapproval.

Garland looked at the marks on the floor. Most of them were clearly streaks of blood from something heavy being dragged about, but one or two could be footprints. It was hard to tell. Then she felt Banks grab her arm. She looked up, and saw what he saw.

In front of them was a door, but not the same kind of door as the other carriages had. This door did not belong in a train at all. It was enormous, filling the entire end of the carriage. It was made of some kind of thick metal and instead of a handle, it had a large wheel at its centre. Twin bolts kept it firmly shut.

In two sharp movements, Poppy slid back the heavy bolts.

"Give me a hand," she said to Banks, and began to turn the wheel.

"I'm not sure this is —" Banks began.

"Oh, what could possibly go wrong?" said Garland, and pushed him aside.

Garland and Poppy began to turn the wheel, which was as stiff as if it had been glued into place. Banks joined them, and slowly the wheel loosened.

"Get back," said Poppy, and they moved aside as Poppy first twisted and then spun the wheel.

"Get *back*," she repeated. Banks and Garland moved further away. Poppy span the wheel again with an annoyed jerk and they started at a loud hydraulic hiss from the door.

Poppy heaved at the wheel and the door began to open. Clouds of white steam flowed from behind it. With her free hand, she carefully placed the teddy bear inside her jacket and grabbed the kitbag from Banks.

"Be careful," she said. "It's quite cold in there." And she yanked the door open.

• • •

Enveloped in white clouds, Garland and Banks followed Poppy into the carriage. Poppy was right: it was cold in the carriage. Thin rimes of mist covered the windows, which looked almost cracked from their webbings of ice. Their breath sat in the air, lumpy clouds of silver.

"There goes your theory," said Garland. "The alternating carriage thing."

Banks looked around the carriage. There were no seats or tables. Instead, the carriage was full of tall, wide metal cabinets, each bigger than a man. He opened one. Inside it was the frozen body of an animal, possibly a cow.

"I told you," he said. "Buffet cars don't count."

• • •

Poppy had produced a knife from her jacket and was hacking at a carcass.

"This is good meat," she said. "Much better than your cans."

"I like my cans," said Banks, sounding hurt.

"A varied diet is best," Garland said. She opened another cabinet, this one full of small, frozen packs of something.

"There's certainly plenty of meat. But it's too big and too frozen to microwave. How do we cook it?"

Poppy gave her a look. "With fire," she said. "How do you normally cook meat?"

She strode on, opening cabinets and throwing packets of meat into Banks's kitbag.

"Fire?" Garland said.

Banks shrugged.

"Just go with it," he said.

• • •

The carriage seemed very long, and it was only when the train reached a bend and the carriage bent with it that Garland saw that it wasn't one carriage at all, but a series of carriages.

"How long is this thing?" she asked after they had been walking for several minutes, each minute colder than the last one.

"The larder?" said Poppy. "Quite long. Which means plenty of food for us."

She was right. Garland estimated that they had passed at least fifteen metal cabinets, each one of which contained a few carcasses or a collection of meat in packets or boxes. Nothing was labelled, which was not ideal, but on the other hand nothing seemed to be particularly weird. It was all fine, she decided, unless you didn't eat meat. Garland wondered briefly if some of the cabinets contained vegetarian options, but after thinking about what she had encountered so far on the train she decided that this was unlikely.

• • •

"Here we are," said Poppy, stopping suddenly at another massive steel door.

Banks and Garland helped her turn the wheel, and they stepped into a normal carriage. Poppy dumped the kitbag on a table and sat down.

"This should keep for a few days," she said.

"Have you done this before?" Banks asked.

"Yes," she said. "You mean you haven't?"

"I just got here, I think," Garland said. "And Banks was happy back there with his cans."

Poppy wasn't listening.

"I'm hungry," she said.

She pulled a large haunch of meat from out of the kitbag.

"Can I have my supper now, please?"

• • •

Garland hacked a few chunks of meat into reasonable-sized pieces. Poppy reached into her jacket and pulled out some crumpled paper plates and a fistful of plastic knives and forks.

"Nice," said Banks. "But all a bit cold."

"I told you," Poppy said. "We just need fire."

"I've got this," Garland said, holding up her lighter.

"Don't need it, thanks," Poppy said.

She got up and stood in the middle of the carriage.

"Stay where you are," she said.

"What are you doing?" Banks asked.

"Getting fire," Poppy said.

Suddenly she balled her fist and punched the carriage floor. Her fist went through it as if it was made of water.

"You'll lose your hand –" Banks began to say, as Poppy's arm disappeared through the floor.

She grimaced for a second. Her arm flexed as if she was groping for something and then, with a sudden wrench of muscles, came back up.

In her hand, Poppy held a tangle of cables, fizzing and sparking with electricity. She ripped the cushion from the seat opposite her and plunged the wires into it. It sent out smoke that reeked of plastic foam, and then caught fire. Poppy dropped the cables, which spasmed and sparked across the floor, and threw the meat onto the flaming seat cushion.

"Fire," she explained as Garland and Banks covered their faces.

• • •

After a few minutes, during which they almost got used to the stink of the burning seat cushions, Poppy pulled the chunks of meat off and dropped them onto the paper plates.

"Back in a minute," she said, and carried the burning cushion into the toilet. They heard a hiss and then Poppy returned.

"All done," she said. "Tuck in, everyone."

• • •

It was, so far as she was aware, the weirdest meal Garland had ever eaten, but it was also pretty good once she let her brain delete the strong odour of burning foam. She could have done with some vegetables, but the meat was hot, and filling, and tasted entirely of beef and not, say, something from a nightmare. Afterwards she sat back and felt comfortable for the first time since she had woken up.

"You haven't eaten your meat," Poppy said to Banks.

"I have a few reservations about this meal," Banks said.

"I don't care," said Poppy, and crammed Banks's portion into her mouth.

"I'm sure we'll find some more cans soon," Garland told Banks.

• • •

After everyone who was eating had finished eating, and Poppy had tidied up by taking all the debris of the meal away and putting it into the toilet, Garland said:

"Do you know anything about what happened to you?"

Poppy frowned.

"I don't want to think about it," she said. "It might make me unhappy."

"When we found you, you were hiding in a toilet with a bloodstained teddy bear," said Garland. "Were you happy then?"

"I don't know," Poppy said, and she almost pouted. "I don't want to think about that either."

"It's OK, we won't press you," Banks said.

"Good," Poppy said. "Because then I might get cross."

She smiled and stroked Teddy's head. Garland shivered slightly: after what she'd seen, she had a feeling that making Poppy cross would not at all be a good idea.

• • •

After a while, Poppy fell asleep.

"She looks quite angelic like that," Banks said quietly.

"That's because she doesn't snore," Garland said. "When you sleep, it's like you're having an argument with yourself."

"When I snore," Banks said, "it's because the armies of the night are moving through my soul. Also, because my nose is blocked."

They contemplated Poppy for a while until she stirred in her sleep, let out a sharp cry, and settled again, Teddy clasped in a firm grip against her chest.

"I think," said Banks, "that I'm a bit scared of Poppy."

"I think you'd be stupid not to be," Garland said.

"Can't we just leave her here?" Banks said. "That was a joke," he added.

"Was it?" Garland said.

• • •

Time passed. All three of them slept, so deeply that nobody was woken by Banks's snoring.

They didn't hear the noise from above them either, as something crashed across the roof over their heads, backwards and forwards, seeking a way in.

· · ·

Banks slept a dreamless sleep, as though even his dreams had been deleted.

· · ·

Garland slept deeply. She dreamed she was standing in a small room. Outside she knew, but didn't know how she knew, a large crowd was waiting for her. She looked up. In front of her was a mirror. Garland studied her reflection approvingly. She looked good; confident, poised and ready for anything.

Her reflection looked back at her and extended its hand to shake. Garland took it. She shook hands with her reflection for a moment, and then turned to leave the room and address the crowd.

· · ·

Poppy slept, and dreamt the dream she always dreamt.

· · ·

In the dream, she is skiing –

Interlude Two

In the dream, she is skiing.

The snow is deep and endless and it seems to her, as she races across it, that the slope of the mountain has shaped itself to her skis. She barely has to turn, and there it is, waiting to take her further on. It's almost like a moving carpet under her, sensing which way she wants to go, letting her choose her own speed.

There is nothing in the dream but her, and the snow. The mountain is bare, and there are no people. This suits her. In the dream there is nothing else, but in her other life, the waking life, there are too many people. She puts this thought from her mind, and skis.

She can ski as long and as far as she wants in the dream. There is, after all, nobody here to stop her.

She feels the air around her, cold and powerful, urging her on. The wind is chill but not sharp, and she can almost see it enfolding her and pushing her on. The whistle of the wind blends in with the noise her skis make on the snow, every sound adding to the speed with which she moves.

A bump in the snow is a launch pad to send her racing through the air. A sudden dip only adds momentum to her flight. The wind is at her back and no matter how far she skis, the ground only seems to move downhill for her. She remembers an old saying: *may the road rise with you*. Here the snow road seems to both rise and descend for her simultaneously.

She moves like a bird, like a shark, like a fox. Nobody can stop her, and nobody will. She is alone and she is in control. On she skis, barely aware of the sticks she is holding, the sunglasses over her eyes, the gloves on her hands. There is nothing but speed, and snow, and her.

• • •

After a while the dream, as dreams sometimes do, becomes aware that it might be only a dream. Her mind starts to look for cracks in the story, flaws in the logic. She has been skiing downhill for a long time; longer than normal, surely? She never gets out of breath, she never feels tired, her muscles do what she asks without complaint. All this is possible, but is it likely? She isn't hungry, or thirsty, or even bored; and yet all she has done for hours is ski. Her mind tries to reject the doubts, but they keep coming back. Where is she? Why does this mountain never end? Why are there no trees, no rocks, no people? For the first time she loses her rhythm, skis too close to a snowbank. She regains control easily, but her confidence isn't the same afterwards.

And then she sees, below her, the town.

...

The town is not like the mountain. Where the mountain is clean, and white, and bare, the town is a dirty grey mess. Where the mountain is simple, the town is chaotic. And where the mountain lets her fly like an arrow, the town looks jealous, like it would crowd in on her and happily see her fall.

The town is getting nearer, and she can't see a way to ski away from it. The mountain is turning into foothills now. She remembers another saying: *first there is a mountain, then there is no mountain, then there is a mountain.* The town looms up at her now, and she can see individual, grim houses. She can see cars, filthy with grease, steaming down narrow roads. And people, hunched, pushing grubby wagons. She can see, somehow, that the wagons are full of scrap.

She very much doesn't want to go towards the town, but she finds she cannot stop. Almost the skis have a mind of their own, racing eagerly towards the town, towards –

– towards the road.

...

She is skiing towards a road, and she cannot stop. She tries to brake, to twist the skis to one side, even to make herself fall: nothing works. She is skiing towards a road and she cannot stop.

...

She flies, improbably, into the air, like a brave stunt girl attempting an insane jump. But there is nowhere to jump to.

First there is a mountain.

A truck hits her first, side on, so she is only thrown across the road. Then she is hit again, by a car coming the other way, and this time she slides underneath it.

Then there is no mountain.

When she wakes up, she cannot move. She tries to move her arms, then her legs. Nothing works. Nothing seems to be there. Nothing is there.

Then there is a mountain.

When she wakes up again, there are doctors around the bed. She assumes they are doctors, anyway, because they have white coats and glasses and clipboards, and they are smiling. Clearly they are all top-flight medical professionals who have come to tell her the good news.

"You have made a complete recovery," one of them will say.

"In some ways, you are fitter than before," another will add.

"Your teammates are insistent that you join them in training immediately," says a third.

• • •

None of these things happen. Instead, the doctors – who are, for reasons she never quite understands, not really doctors, but some kind of scientists – explain to her that, against all odds, she has survived her accident, which they insist on referring to as "the realistic simulation". It seems that her mind was correct about the dream and she had not been skiing at all, but – she can just remember now, underneath the pain and the fear – testing out a new and, yes, realistic training program for the forthcoming games. She was an expert skier who believed herself to be at the very top of her ability, but there were those in the government who felt that this was not enough, to be at the top of her ability, and that she could do better.

As a consequence, normal training was not enough for her, and she was placed in machine simulations, which replicated part of her training with computer-generated imagery, and part with physically demanding recreations of actual movement. This had the edge over other simulations in that it gave the mind the illusion that it was skiing and as a consequence ensured that the body had no outside distractions. As far as mind or body were concerned, they were skiing down a mountain.

But something had, as things do, gone wrong, and when her mind had begun to doubt that it was really doing what it thought it was doing, the program had not known what to do, and had tried to convince the mind that it was in a realistic scenario by showing it something realistic, in this case a dirty old town.

This had worked to some extent, but had not taken into account the fact that, while the mind was coming to terms with the new information (or "lies"), the body was strapped into a very large, very heavy harness designed to ensure that it performed at the extreme limits of its abilities. This harness was naturally also equipped with fail-safes and escape mechanisms so its failure would not cause its occupant to be, for example, crushed or mutilated or maimed. But these fail-safes had failed to activate. As a consequence, the body in the harness had been subjected to impossible stresses and, essentially, broken.

"Like a twig?" she said.

"Like a bundle of twigs," said one of the scientists, before apologising.

• • •

She lay there, because there was nothing else she could do, wondering when she would find out why they were really smiling.

• • •

Some days later, a man in a suit came to see her. He smelt of pipe tobacco, which she found interesting as both pipes and tobacco were illegal, and he was carrying a teddy bear and a blue cardboard folder.

"This is for you," he said. "Someone to talk to."

He put the teddy bear on the cabinet by her bed, then looked down at the folder.

"I know," he said. "Here we are, put a man on the moon, computers in every front room, and here I am with a cardboard folder."

"I didn't know we put a man on the moon," she said.

"Figure of speech," the man said casually. "I brought this because – well, it seemed more personal than a tablet."

She had no idea what he was talking about. Then again, she had had no visitors apart from the scientists for a long time. So she said:

"What's in it?"

"I'll show you," the man said, and pulled out what looked like sheets of paper but were actually photographs. She had never seen photographs printed out like this, half shiny, half glossy, and decided they must be very expensive.

"Now this is you," said the man, and held up to her eyes a picture showing some X-ray images. The images showed what must once have been limbs, but were now just flat, floppy collections of bone fragments.

"Nasty," he said. "But what's done is done. Now this is what you could be." He corrected himself. "What you *will* be."

The next photograph was of a naked woman. The face of the woman was hers, but the body wasn't.

"Bit of artistic licence," said the man. "But I know you ladies don't mind flattery."

He let her study the photograph.

"You're an athlete," he said. "Fit, healthy, a machine. Well, you were. And you can be again. Would you like that?"

She would have shrugged if she could.

"Silly question, I know," said the man. "I'll take it as read that your answer is yes. Who doesn't want a second chance?"

He gathered up the photographs before she could reply.

"Thing is, it's not really up to you," he said. "Wasting your time pissing about on skis? This is a good thing. Now we can use you."

He walked out, leaving her and the teddy bear to stare at one another.

· · ·

The operations were painless, which surprised her. Perhaps there just wasn't enough left of her to actually hurt.

· · ·

When she awoke again, she found that she was lying, not in a bed, but in a bath of gel. The gel was red, which was somewhat disconcerting, as it made her feel like she was in a bag of blood. The rest of the room was black, which didn't help, but next to her on a chair was the teddy bear. She laughed at this. They'd done so much to her, but they thought that giving her a stuffed toy would make it better. Then she was filled with an overwhelming urge to pick up the bear and hold it. She sat up without thinking. Red gel slid off her body as she reached out for the bear. She picked it up from the chair and held it in her arms.

It took her a moment to notice that she had arms.

· · ·

She was still sitting up and holding the bear when the scientists came back in. This time they weren't smiling.

"She's supposed to be lying down," one said.

"She's supposed to be unconscious," said another.

"No way is that bear sterile," said a third.

She looked at them all. It clearly wasn't a look that they liked.

"I want ice cream," she said, surprising herself.

· · ·

For the next few days she stayed in the red gel, eating ice cream. From time to time a scientist or two would come in, hover at the back of the room, and make notes on a tablet.

She would tire easily, and lie back in the lukewarm embrace of the gel, having first placed the teddy on its chair.

• • •

They gave her tests to do. Puzzles with pegs and holes, metal rings to slip over other metal rings, that sort of thing. After a while she noticed that they weren't concerned with her mental state or her intelligence, but only seemed interested in whether she could manipulate physical objects. If she dropped something, or broke it, they were full of encouragement, but if she found something too difficult, they didn't seem to care. It was as if they were training her not to learn, but to do tricks.

The tricks grew more involved. She was asked to undo knots and untangle wires. She was encouraged to fold paper into artistic shapes, and even to see if she could use a needle and thread. Her manual dexterity was excellent, but every time she performed a task, she felt she was holding something back.

In the second month, they gave her some light physical exercise, small weights for lifting and so on. Again, she found that once she had mastered this sort of activity, she was aware that she was not operating at her full capacity. She wondered what that capacity was.

In the third month, they let her sit up, in a chair. Two large men lifted her up and she found that, despite her long inactivity, she could stand and even walk a little. It was tiring, though, and she was glad to lie down again.

• • •

The tests continued. Now they were clearly strength-related. She bent things, punched things and on occasion was asked to tear a large directory in half.

She looked at the scientists.

"You do it," she said, and closed her eyes.

• • •

After a while, she was placed in a bed again. A few days after that, they gave her a wheelchair. Then, after she crushed the wheel rims trying to get around in it, they gave her another, stronger wheelchair. Then steel crutches and, shortly after, a walking stick.

And finally, after they were certain that she could walk normally, they strapped her to her bed.

• • •

She woke up to discover that once more she could not move, except this time she was immobilised by metallic bands crossing her body.

"Why have I been tied down?" she asked one of the scientists, an annoying man with glasses and straggly hair that she longed to tie back. The man said nothing, just continued to stand a few metres away and make notes on her tablet.

When the man had left, she flexed her limbs and was about to test her bonds when she saw the camera above her bed. She went to sleep instead. In the night she woke again, flexed her arms and legs, and was not surprised to feel the bonds protest. The next day she made a mental inventory of where everything was in the room that she might need. She knew that she would have to be quick.

• • •

She was quick.

• • •

Breakfast was a paste sucked from a tube. The moment she was left alone in the room, she sat up and freed first her arms and then her legs. As she got out of bed, alarms began to screech and ring. She ignored them, reaching for a thin medical gown and slippers she knew were stored in her bedside cabinet. She threw her water jug at the camera, smashing its eye, and opened the door of her room.

She was about to step out into the corridor when she remembered the bear. She went back into the room, retrieved it, and headed off down the corridor.

Her knowledge of the building was scant, but her memory was excellent. She located the staff lockers three doors down, broke in, and put on someone else's clothes. Striding now, she made her way towards a large glass sliding door. It had been locked shut. Behind the door, some of the scientists stood. They looked more nervous than usual.

She began to kick the sliding door, and on the third kick the glass collapsed entirely. Stepping through, she grabbed the man with the straggly hair.

"Get me out of here or I'll break your neck," she told him. The man nodded.

"Follow me," he said.

• • •

They walked quickly towards an elevator, which took them from a level called B13 to the ground floor. When the doors opened, the man had time to shout, "Help me, for fuck's sake," before the soldiers waiting outside opened fire. As she stepped over the man's body, she noticed that bullets just bounced off her arms, which was handy. She rendered the soldiers harmless, and ran past a crowd of orderlies and staff towards the main door of the building.

She pulled the door open – strictly speaking, she pulled it *off* – and went outside. Instantly she was cold. The air was full of snow and there was ice on the ground. She was in the mountains.

She stepped into the road. A truck came towards her. Impossibly, it was the truck from her dream, the simulation. She just had time to wonder how this could be when the truck hit her for the second time.

• • •

When she woke up, she had been placed inside some sort of casing that resembled a mummy's sarcophagus. Even her head was unable to move.

She heard voices now.

"The simulation was entirely predictable," said one voice. She couldn't see who was speaking but she could smell tobacco. "I knew this whole thing was a waste of time."

"We can run more tests," said a second voice.

"No point," Denning said. "Strip this one for parts and put the rest in a furnace."

• • •

They moved her like furniture, first by hand and then, when her weight became apparent, on a gurney. After a journey whose only landmarks were the strip lights above her head, she was left in a cold loading bay with some machine parts. Whoever was moving her had clearly decided to take a break before the next stage of her terminal journey.

She flexed her toes. She moved her hands. She balled

her fists. She kicked a little, and something cracked. She punched downwards, and the sarcophagus split. Rolling her shoulders, kicking and thrusting, she smashed the casing around her. She sat up, hunching debris off her body.

There was still nobody around. *Perhaps this is another simulation*, she thought. She opened a door into a room full of boots and coats and shoes − and skis. She found some clothes that fit her, dressed, and took a helmet and skis.

Outside, she pulled goggles over her eyes. In front of her, a few yards from the road, was a snow-laden mountainside.

If this is a simulation, she thought, *at least this time I'm going to enjoy it.*

The snow was smooth beneath her skis, and she moved in silence through the cold night. Gaining speed, she easily avoided the trees dotting the mountainside and, even though she had no idea where she was or where she was going, she knew no pursuer had a chance of catching up. So long as she could keep moving, she was unstoppable.

The mountain rose with her and descended with her. The wind seemed to be always at her back as she sped across the snow. She could hear them now, in their clumsy vehicles, trying to catch her. Sometimes a bullet whined past her, or nicked the snow ahead of her. It didn't matter: she was faster and stronger than anything.

As she approached the edge of the mountain, she saw the one thing that might have killed her.

• • •

It hurtled through the night, oblivious of the mountain above it. It screamed through the darkness, huge and relentless. The train was about to go into a tunnel and disappear into the mountain.

• • •

She didn't know if she could do it, but at the same time she was certain that she could. She crouched down, gained more momentum and *aimed* her body at the train. Below her, she could see a gap between carriages. The whole thing was, in theory, impossible, like firing an arrow through a keyhole from the back of a motorbike. But she was going to do it.

She raced over a cliff edge, which threw her up into the air. Her poles fell away, freeing her hands, and she crashed into the dark gap. Her hands, flailing, found something to hold. She was nearly shaken free by the sheer force and speed of the train, but she managed to hold on.

She just had time to see her pursuers try and stop at the edge, and fail, and fall, before the train hurtled into the tunnel.

• • •

First there is a mountain. Then there is no mountain.

• • •

She wrenched open the connecting door between the carriages. Inside it was dark, and smelt bad. Something in her clothes seemed to be nudging her. She reached into her jerkin. It was the bear.

"Hello, Teddy," she said. She heard a sound, and looked up.

They thundered towards her, teeth and claws and impossible eyes.

• • •

Then there is a mountain.

• • •

When she woke up, they were dead. Teddy was covered in blood, and his head was gone. She was incredibly tired and she just wanted to rest, and to be on her own, with nobody looking at her, or testing her, or trying to kill her.

Poppy wandered the train for a while, found some things of interest and other things that were just unpleasant. She suddenly felt very tired indeed, so she went into a bathroom, locked the door behind her and, with Teddy tucked into her jacket again, fell fast asleep.

THREE

Garland woke first. She tapped Banks gently on the arm.

"What is it?" he said.

"Nothing," she replied. "I just think we've slept enough for now."

Banks was about to reply when he let out a belch so deep and long it distorted his face.

"Goodness," said Garland.

"Excuse me," Banks said. He looked at Poppy. "You can wake her," he said.

"Coward," said Garland, and regretted it at once.

"It's OK," Banks said. He leant over towards Poppy and gently stroked her arm.

"I don't think that's going to do it," Garland said.

Banks tapped Poppy on the shoulder.

"Are you going to tell her this is her stop?" said Garland. "Here, let me."

She clapped her hands in the air. Poppy's eyes opened instantly.

"Where am I?" she said, then, "Oh, yes. Hello, everyone."

"Did you sleep?" said Garland.

"I slept," said Poppy. "But not enough."

She got up.

"I think we all need a nice rest," she announced.

Banks belched again. "Sorry," he added.

"I'm a lady, so I didn't hear that," said Poppy. "It's this way."

"What is?" asked Garland.

Poppy gave her the kind of look she might reserve for a simpleton.

"The nice place, of course."

. . .

"I am starting to wonder just how long this train is," Garland said as they entered their fourth carriage (two stripped out, one with seats and tables intact, one with nothing in it but a single metal table studded with deep, low dents).

"Not far now," said Poppy.

"I'm more worried that it might loop round and eat itself," said Banks.

"Seems unlikely," said Garland. "Where would the engine be?"

"Maybe there is no engine," said Banks.

"There's got to be an engine."

"Maybe not. Maybe the whole thing is a simulation – ow!"

Poppy released her grip on Banks's arm.

116

"Just don't say that, please," she said.

"Sorry," said Banks. Poppy walked on. Banks raised an eyebrow at Garland, who shrugged.

• • •

The fifth carriage was clearly the one. Poppy stopped outside with a broad grin on her lips. She took Teddy out and kissed him.

"Here it is," she said. "The nice place."

"Are you sure?" said Garland. "This train has been notably short of nice places so far."

"If you don't ask, you don't get," said Poppy gnomically. She pulled open the door like it was made of rice paper, and went in.

The fifth carriage was not at all like the other carriages. Garland had never seen anything like it before.

For a start, it was divided into different compartments.

For a start, there was a dark blue carpet running down the middle.

For a start, each compartment had windows on the inside.

• • •

All the windows were decorated with curtains that matched the carpets, and all the curtains were closed. There were of course doors to each compartment, and Poppy opened one now.

"Come in," she said. "For a minute, anyway."

Garland and Banks followed her into the compartment.

"What the fuck," said Garland.

• • •

The compartment was a bedroom. *More of a boudoir*, thought Garland. The walls were decorated with embossed purple wallpaper, all stripes and little ribbons. There was a small dressing table in the corner, with an ornate mirror and a round stool to sit on. Hairbrushes and compacts festooned the table. The rest of the compartment was taken up by the bed. This was covered with a mauve bedspread that frothed out in all directions like a purple silk ocean. By the headboard was a collection of what Garland could only think of as too many cushions. These too were various shades of purple.

• • •

And that was pretty much it. On the wall were some round pictures of goggle-eyed people in old-fashioned clothes (she noticed Banks didn't like to look at those) and in the corner was a tall, thin closet made from the same kind of painted wood as the dressing table. Garland opened the doors but there was nothing inside.

Poppy threw herself and Teddy onto the bed. It protested audibly as Poppy sank into the coverlet like a softly drowning doll.

"This is my room," she said. "You can get your own."

• • •

Garland and Banks went out into the corridor again.

"I'm not that sleepy," she said.

"I am sleepy," said Banks, "but no way am I sleeping in one of those."

"Are they an affront to your masculinity?" asked Garland.

"No, of course not," said Banks. "Yes," he added, a

second later. "Besides, those beds are quite short. I'd have my feet on the dressing table."

"I can see how that might be embarrassing when the maid comes in," said Garland drily, and opened the nearest door.

• • •

Her room was, fortunately, not quite as purple as Poppy's. Garland removed her boots with some difficulty, found some wipes in a drawer on the dressing table and cleaned her face, and then – first checking under the coverlet (for what? Snakes? Tiny robot assassins?) – lay down and covered herself.

Judging by the sounds coming from the next compartment, Banks had changed his mind about trying to sleep in a small bed, and was busily engaged in knocking everything off the dressing table with his boots.

• • •

Garland closed her eyes, and found she could not sleep. She found herself instead making an inventory of – was it really only a day? – the day.

What did she actually know about the event she was experiencing? She was on a train, that much was obvious (discounting simulations, which she was sure would be a great deal less messy). She had met two people, both of whom – Poppy especially – were not quite normal. But then, Garland had to admit, she herself was not quite normal. When she had woken up in this place, she'd been unable to read, an ability which seemed to be coming slowly back to her. Then there was the fact that she could not remember who she was (she had to remind herself that Garland probably wasn't her name, just a patch on her clothing).

And finally there was the business with the world outside. While she had little or no memories to draw from, Garland was pretty sure that, last time she'd been able to check, the world had been in a lot better condition.

Clearly things were falling apart, like the poem said (*what poem?* she wondered) and it was up to her to see what she could do about it.

She was just trying to work out why she thought it was up to her to do something about it when there was a massive crash outside, and Banks started screaming like a maniac.

Garland slid off the bed, pulled her boots on in record time, and threw open the door. What she saw was hard to believe.

Standing on all fours in the corridor, one enormous paw on Banks's inert body, was some sort of bear. It was taller than a bear, and its fur was hard and sharp, and its snout was non-existent, but at some point in its ancestry it had been a bear. It was making a horrific noise, not so much a growl as an endless scream.

"Banks!" shouted Garland. "Wake up!"

If Banks could hear her, he gave no indication. Instead the bear thing, which was so much taller than a real bear that the top of its head was flattened by the roof of the train, turned its awful flat face to her – its nose as well as its snout being flush with its eyes, making its head look like a kind of horrible hairy plate with teeth – and screamed, this time a hissing, wet scream that sounded even angrier than before.

"Easy," said Garland, in a softer voice. The bear thing

120

hiss-screamed again. It arced its arms out in a semi-circle, the claws pointing directly at her.

"Banks," Garland said, quietly, "can you hear me?"

There was a silence, then:

"Of course I can fucking hear you," Banks said, quietly but angrily. "I'm trying to play dead."

"Sorry," she said. She looked the bear thing in the eye. Doing so was discouraging: its eyes stared at her so wildly that she was convinced the animal was insane. She had no way of predicting what it would do next.

Banks was silent again. Garland eased a foot backwards. The bear thing seemed to relax a little. Garland eased another foot backwards, and to her relief the animal did the same. It turned its head and sniffed the air. Perhaps it wasn't interested in them at all.

She slid her foot back quietly again. And then the bear went crazy.

• • •

It slammed its right paw into the wall beside it. The wall was thin, made of some kind of hardboard, and the claws went right through it. Enraged, the animal pulled its paw out, shook off some splinters of fake wood, and screamed again, this time with a raw, terrifying fury. Now it smashed its other paw into the wall, but hit a light fitting and the paw came back red from the glass it had smashed.

The bear thing screamed long and hard. It kicked Banks's prone form backwards with one iron-hard heel and stepped forward, hissing spit and heat at Garland. And then it lunged. Garland felt teeth on her neck, about to lock in and sever her head from her body. She smelt the animal's boiling breath, and felt its harsh metallic fur. Then she was crushed against the wall of the compartment and then –

Then the animal was no longer on her. Screaming, it tumbled backwards towards the outside wall. Its arms flailed as it seemed to be pulled back somehow, sucked into an invisible hole. Now it was on the ground, its thrashing legs almost touching Banks's immobile body.

"Get up!" Garland shouted. "Get up!" Banks opened his eyes, saw what was next to him, and scrambled away from the bear thing.

"What the hell is happening to it?" he asked.

They stared at the bear thing as it thrashed some more, screaming, its saliva bubbling in its mouth, its head twisting from side to side. Garland felt sorry for it in its death agonies: it could have no idea what it was or why it was dying.

Finally it was silent, no longer twitching. Then, in one sudden move, it seemed to throw itself aside, its carcass landing in the debris of the smashed compartment. From a slick pool of its blood that had gathered where the animal lay in its death agony, something red stood up.

It was Poppy. She was covered in the bear thing's blood and in her hand she held part of its spine.

"I came out when I heard you screaming," she said.

"I wasn't screaming," said Garland.

"Whatever," said Poppy. She dropped the handful of spine and looked across at the matted corpse.

"Don't tell Teddy," she said.

• • •

They stood for a while by the animal's body. Banks got down on one knee and looked over the corpse.

"What are you looking for?" asked Garland.

"I don't know," said Banks. "Clues, I suppose."

"Clues are the one thing we've got plenty of," said Garland. "This place is full of clues. It's answers we want."

"Nothing," said Banks, standing up. "It's just your average mutated giant killer bear."

"Shall we eat it?" said Poppy.

• • •

One of the compartments turned out to be a bathroom, the kind where the word "bathroom" is usually prefixed by the word "private". It was a bit fluffy, but it contained a functional shower and bathtub.

"I'll go first," said Poppy. Banks and Garland looked at her, drenched in blood and some guts.

"You're going last," said Banks.

• • •

After everyone had showered, they cleaned their clothes as best they could and, while they couldn't cook and eat the bear, they used the debris from the smashed compartment to build a fire back in one of the stripped compartments and ate some more of the slowly defrosting meat. Poppy had washed and shampooed Teddy and now she dried him over the fire. Teddy smelled slightly singed afterwards but nobody said anything.

• • •

"That's it?" said Poppy. "That's your plan?"

"What's wrong with it?" asked Garland.

"Nothing," said Poppy. "Because it's a nothing plan."

"I don't think that makes sense," Banks frowned.

"I don't think you make sense," said Poppy. She held the teddy bear's paw and tapped it against her palm.

"Did you just high five yourself with a stuffed bear?" asked Garland.

"No," said Poppy.

"We'll continue this conversation when you're not feeling so childish," Garland said, and began to pick up the debris of the meal.

"I think you've hurt her feelings," said Banks.

"Well, it's a stupid plan."

"That's not the point. You don't have to keep saying it."

"Oh," said Garland, "does this mean you think it's a stupid plan as well?"

"No," Banks said hastily, "I meant – I don't know what I meant. I was just trying to defend you."

"I don't need defending," Garland snapped.

"Tell that to the bear," said Poppy.

"Fuck off!" Garland shouted.

Poppy burst into tears.

"Our enemies must be trembling in their beds," said Banks.

• • •

Later, Poppy went to find Garland in her bedroom compartment.

"I'm sorry I said your plan was stupid," she said.

"I'm sorry I told you to fuck off," said Garland.

"The thing is –" Poppy said.

"Please don't say it's a stupid plan again."

124

"I wasn't going to. I was going to say that it's – it's quite a simple plan."

"We're on a moving train. It's full of weird monsters and dead people. We don't really have the luxury of evolving a complicated plan."

"All right. But what do we do when we get – where are we going anyway?"

Garland looked at Poppy.

"Wherever," she said. "We're going wherever we have to."

"The front of the train?"

"Yes," said Garland. "We're going to find the driver, or whoever is in charge."

"And then what?"

"We're going to make them stop."

"How?"

"Well, we could have a little chat," Garland said. "Or you could hurt them. I'm not really fussed either way."

"All right," said Poppy. "But might it not be better to keep going?"

"We don't know where we're going."

"We don't know anything," Poppy said. "For all we know, where we're going is better than where we are now. It might be the city, or the country, or the seaside."

"I don't think we're going to the seaside," Garland said. "I think – look, I woke up here and I'd been chained up. Banks was being taken somewhere, too. I don't know how you got here, but I'm pretty sure I was going to jail, or worse."

Poppy thought.

"I got here on my own," she said. "And I'm going to leave on my own."

"What? But we need you."

"I'm tired of being needed," Poppy said. "I killed the bear thing, I showed you how to cook, I don't owe you anything. I'm leaving."

"This is – you can't leave."

"I'm out of here. Laters! TTFN," said Poppy.

"You're not making any sense," Garland replied.

"Like you said, you're on this train to be punished. Banks is too. But I'm not. I'm young –"

"Thanks," said Garland.

"I'm fit. I mean, incredibly fit. And I've had my dinner. I can do anything."

Garland shrugged. "All right then. We could have used you but I'd rather you were gone if you're going to be in the way," she said. "When are you leaving?"

Poppy frowned. "I don't know," she said. "I'm just waiting for the right opportunity."

Banks walked in. He looked excited about something.

"Look out of the window," he said. "Look out of the window!"

Garland drew back the curtain.

• • •

The train was no longer inside the mountain. It was outside again, speeding through a night-time blur of darkness and sudden light. But the light was no longer random; instead, it was coming from enormous, regularly-spaced lamps.

"Where are we?" said Garland.

"Are we slowing down?" Poppy asked.

"I think we are," Banks said. "Look!"

• • •

Beneath the windows, they could see other tracks running alongside them. Further away, more lamps. Then, incredibly, low banks of concrete.

"Are those platforms?" Garland said.

"I think they are," Banks said. "I think we're coming into a station."

"Fuck," said Garland. She looked at Poppy.

"I think the right opportunity just came along," she said.

• • •

Music came from the speakers again.

A song where someone was talking about days.

They hardly heard it.

It was a sad song, as though the days were never coming.

But it was only a song, and the train was slowing.

• • •

The train was slowing down, and making a lot of noise about it. Sparks flew on either side, and the rails groaned and roared.

"This thing must be incredibly long," said Banks. "I hope it doesn't overshoot the platform or we've got a lot of walking to do."

"Walking?" said Garland. "We're not getting off."

"I am," said Poppy. "I was thinking of ripping out a door and jumping, but this is much better."

"We have to get off," said Banks. "Don't we?" he added uncertainly.

"We have to find out what's going on," Garland said. "We need to find someone in authority."

"I expect there'll be someone on the station we can ask," Poppy said. "There might even be an information desk."

Garland gave her a look.

"I don't think an information desk will have the answers I need," she said.

"No, but they might have a number for a taxi," said Poppy. "Joking."

"We're still not stopping," said Banks.

"Oh no," said Poppy. She tried to get a better look out of the window.

"Maybe we're slowing down for another reason," Garland suggested. "Letting another train pass."

Banks looked out of the window again. There was nothing out there but lamps and low concrete platforms. None of the other platforms had trains beside them, or people waiting for trains, or any signs of activity whatever.

"Another train?" he said. "I'm not sure that there are any other trains."

• • •

"Are we stopping or not?" Garland asked, a few minutes later.

"Why don't you ask the driver?" Poppy said, a bit snappily.

Poppy pulled the kitbag up from the floor.

"I'm going to need this," she said.

Garland grabbed the strap.

"It's not yours," she said. Poppy snapped it out of her hands.

"He's coming with me," she said, indicating Banks. "So should you."

"I need to find out what's going on!" Garland shouted.

"You can find out what's going on when we get out there," Poppy shouted back.

Garland muttered something.

"What did you say?" asked Banks.

"She said," Poppy answered, "that she's not going out there."

• • •

Garland slumped to the floor.

"I can't get off," she said. "I can't face – whatever. I just can't."

"OK," said Poppy, shouldering the kitbag. "You stay here, we'll go out there. Worked out fine, didn't it?"

"Wait," said Banks. He put his hand on the bag.

"What?" said Poppy.

"I'm not saying she's right –"

"Oh great."

"– but we don't know what's out there."

Poppy sighed heavily.

"We don't know what's in here, either," she said. "I mean, apart from the mutant killer animals. And the weird rooms full of blood. And – oh yeah, the carriage full of dead people. Hey, maybe we should stay on the train. It's great."

"Go," said Garland.

"We're going to," said Poppy. "No permission required."

Banks looked at Garland.

"Go," she said again.

Banks shook his head. "I can't leave you here," he said.

"You don't owe me anything," Garland replied.

"You heard her, you don't owe her anything," Poppy said. "Let's go."

"Sorry," said Banks. "I've had my fill of leaving people behind."

"Your funeral," said Poppy. She stuffed Teddy further into her jacket and pushed past them into the corridor.

• • •

There was a door at the end of the carriage which faced onto the platform opposite. Poppy stood by it, grasping the handle in readiness.

"What if it doesn't open?" Garland said.

"I'll pull it open," Poppy replied. "Or off."

She drummed her fingers impatiently on the side of the corridor. Little dents appeared in the metal.

"I think we're stopping," Banks said.

"Finally," Poppy said, and curled her fingers around the door handle.

• • •

The train was stopping. With a slow scream of metal on metal, it bumped and hiccupped and whiplashed until every carriage finally settled.

"Is it still moving?" said Poppy.

"No, just feels that way," Banks said. "We've been moving for so long it's going to take a moment to get our –"

"– land legs," said Garland. She looked out of the window. Banks was right. Even though the platform couldn't possibly be moving, it swam about in her eyes like it had loosed its moorings.

"Well, it was nice knowing you," said Poppy. She looked, for a moment, lost and sad. Then she rapped Teddy's head with her knuckles and grinned.

"Adventure time," she said, and pulled the handle.

Nothing happened. Poppy pulled it again.

"Perhaps there's a button," said Garland.

"There isn't a button," Banks replied.

Poppy pulled again.

"Aaah!" she shouted. The handle came off in her hand, as well as some of the door.

"Shit," she said, dropping the handle. "Fuck this for a game of soldiers."

She punched the glass in the door, hard. It gave a little, but didn't break.

"It's not even cracked," observed Banks.

Poppy forced her fingers into the edge of the window and pulled. The frame didn't move. She kicked the door, and it didn't bend.

"The outside door seems to be stronger than the inside ones," said Banks.

"No shit," said Poppy, and began kicking the door as hard as she could. It dented a little but was otherwise fine.

Now Poppy began to punch the window, and then the door, again and again.

"You'll hurt yourself," said Garland.

"Fuck off!" shouted Poppy, and thumped the window so hard that her fist recoiled and she fell over.

"Told you," said Garland.

Poppy grabbed her by the jacket. Garland raised an eyebrow.

"Just open the door and you'll be rid of me," she said.

"I don't want to be rid –" Poppy said, then stopped.

"Shit," she said. She walked down the corridor and began punching a window. Just like the other window, it didn't so much as crack.

"FUCK!" she shouted. "How do I get off this fucking thing?!"

She crouched down and began punching a hole in the floor.

"That's going to take a while," Banks pointed out. "And you've got all the chassis and gubbins underneath to take into consideration."

"Chassis and gubbins?" queried Garland as Poppy punched on.

"I'm not an engineer," Banks said.

Poppy stood up, her fists clenching and unclenching in frustration.

Just then, a whistle went off.

"I don't believe it," Banks said. "That's a train whistle."

"That's *our* train whistle," Garland said. "I think we're moving again."

"No!" Poppy shouted. "Fuck shit no! I have to fucking get off!"

There was a rumbling from below.

Poppy looked around wildly.

The train began to move.

"Shit the FUCK!" she shouted. She pulled herself upright, and began to punch the ceiling.

"I am not!" she yelled, punching. "Staying! On this! Fucking! TRAIN!"

A small hole appeared in the ceiling. Poppy kept on punching. Wires tumbled out. She kept punching. Some debris fell out.

The train began to gather speed. Poppy kept punching. The hole got bigger. The train sped up. Poppy punched, and punched. And then she gave up.

She collapsed into the seat below her and slumped back.

"It stopped," she said, in tears. "It stopped."

Garland sat next to her. Banks sat opposite.

"You gave it your best shot," she said.

"Yeah," said Poppy.

She began to laugh, even while she was still crying.

"First prize, getting off the train," she said. "Second prize, not getting off the train."

The hole in the ceiling made it quite cold, so they wrapped themselves in bedding. Poppy went into the bathroom and locked the door.

• • •

After a few minutes, Garland knocked.

"Fuck off," Poppy said through the door.

"You really should stop using that word," said Garland.

"You use it all the time."

"I'm not the one with a teddy bear stuck down my top."

The door opened.

133

"Do you think Teddy can understand swearing?" said Poppy.

"Nothing surprises me any more," Garland said. "I wouldn't be that shocked if he was behind all of this."

"Don't be silly," said Poppy. "He'd tell me if he was."

• • •

Garland sat on the ledge by the sink.

"I suppose getting off the train was as important for you as staying on it is for me," she said.

"Except you want to stay on the train for the same reason as Banks. Because you're scared."

"No, Banks is scared, I just want to get to the front. I want to know what's going on."

"Whereas I don't give a – I don't care what's going on. I just want to get away."

"You think you can? Get away, that is."

"I don't know. But at least if I get off this thing, I can decide where I'm going."

Poppy sat up and looked at Garland.

"Now get out," she said.

Garland raised her hands.

"Sorry. I was just having a conversation," she said.

"Yes, so was I, and it was very nice," said Poppy. "But I want a wee."

Garland got out.

• • •

"Is she all right?" Banks said.

"She'll live," Garland said.

"I suppose that's the thing," Banks replied. "We all live. It's keeping living that's the issue."

"You should do inspirational posters," said Garland. "You'd make a fortune."

• • •

Poppy appeared. She had washed her face, and Teddy's fur.

"I'm ready," she said. "Ready for what, I have no idea."

"Right," said Garland. "Let's get the fuck out of here."

"Not in front of Teddy," Poppy said.

• • •

They left Banks's compartment and were immediately confronted by the corpse of the bear thing.

"We should move it," said Garland.

"I killed it, you move it," said Poppy.

Banks crouched down by the body of an animal that wasn't a bear.

"Poor thing," he said.

"Easy to sympathise now," said Garland.

"Yeah, now I've killed it," Poppy said.

"Did you kill it?" said Garland. "You never said."

"It's like us," Banks said. "It was harmless – well, fairly – and then they did something to it, and now it's a monster."

"A monster that I killed," said Poppy.

"Take a photo and stop going on about it," said Garland. "Please."

Poppy leant down and pulled out one of the bear thing's teeth.

"Better than a selfie," she said.

• • •

They had a snack and some juice in the wreckage of Banks's bedroom. Poppy put a counterpane over the animal's body, then took it off again.

"It looks silly with a blanket on it," she said. "I don't want it to look silly."

They walked on down the carriage.

• • •

There were no more compartments in the carriage, just empty sections which looked as though they were waiting to be completed. The carpet also stopped abruptly, a few metres before the end of the carriage, as did the wallpaper and the fancy paint.

"It's like the edge of a video game," said Banks. "Like they couldn't be bothered to finish it off properly."

"'Video game,'" said Poppy. "Are you from the olden days or what?"

"Says the girl with the teddy bear," Garland pointed out.

Poppy stroked Teddy's head with a finger.

"I am not a girl," she said. "Now, are you going to open that door or shall I pull it the fuck off?"

"I'll open it," said Banks.

• • •

The door opened easily and Banks and Poppy stepped through into the next carriage. Garland closed it behind her.

"Oh," she said.

"Oh is right," said Banks.

"Wow!" said Poppy. "Stuff!"

• • •

The compartment was lined with shelves from wall to ceiling, and the shelves were crammed with things. There were books, and handbags, and shoes, and vases, and bottles, and belts, and watches, and books, and music players, and boxes. In fact, the majority of things on the shelves were boxes. There were big boxes, and small boxes. There were cardboard boxes, and metal boxes. Glass boxes and plastic boxes. Functional-looking boxes and decorative boxes.

"This is like a treasure trove!" said Banks.

Garland pointed at a large cash register.

"Or a shop," she said.

"That too," Banks agreed.

They walked up and down the carriage, mesmerised.

Banks said, "I've never seen so much –"

"Stuff," Poppy finished for him.

• • •

Garland reached out and pulled down a book. It had no writing on the cover or, she found when she opened it, inside. Just photographs. She laughed.

"Funny book?" Poppy asked.

"Look at it," she said. "It's just pictures of –"

She gestured.

Poppy shrugged.

"It's a catalogue," she said. She picked up a tiny jewelled egg.

Garland bristled a little. "Where's the prices?" she said.

"I think," said Banks, "if you can afford to shop in here, you don't need to ask the prices of things."

"Whoops," said Poppy, as the tiny egg fell to the floor and smashed. They stared as its contents spilled out over the floor.

"Are those sweets?" said Garland.

Banks picked one up. "Only if emeralds are sweets."

"What the fuck kind of place is this?" said Garland.

"Out of my price range," said Banks. "I wonder if there's anything to eat."

"Keep an eye out for hampers," said Garland. "Might be some caviar, I suppose."

"I think there might be something in there," said Banks, pointing at a squat metal box. "Poppy, give me a hand."

Poppy didn't reply.

"Poppy?"

Garland turned to see Poppy sitting on the floor. She had a magazine on her lap, and she was crying.

• • •

Garland crouched down. The magazine lay in Poppy's lap and Garland picked it up. It was printed on absurdly thick and shiny paper and, while it was not entirely wordless, was mostly composed of photographs. Fully half of the photographs were of watches and perfume bottles, so it fit right in with the rest of the shop. But some of the photographs were of people. Most of the people were wearing the watches and holding the perfume bottles, but some of them were photographed in more candid situations, such as at parties and outdoor events.

One of the outdoor events was clearly a sports competition. There were pictures of athletes taking part in winter events, like skating, and ice hockey. In the middle of the photo spread was a picture of a young woman, smiling and holding a medal on a ribbon up for the camera to see. The woman was Poppy.

138

"They took it from me," Poppy said. "They took everything."

• • •

Garland sat with Poppy for a few minutes. Every so often, Poppy would pick up the magazine and look at the photograph of her with the medal, then when she began crying, Garland would take the magazine away again.

"I was so good," said Poppy. "I loved it. When I was out there, I never wanted to stop. And it was all me."

She looked down at her hands that weren't her hands.

"It was all me," she said.

• • •

Banks came over.

"Is this a good time?" he asked.

Garland and Poppy started laughing.

"Please stop," he said, but they didn't. "Please stop it now," he went on. "I really don't like being laughed at," he added.

"We're not laughing at you," said Garland, trying to control herself.

"Yes we are," said Poppy, spluttering.

"This is the most exceptional fun," Banks said, as they continued to snort with laughter. He looked down, and saw the magazine.

"Is that you?" he said.

"For fuck's sake," Garland said. "Sorry, Teddy," she added, before she and Poppy fell once more into convulsions of laughter.

"I can wait," said Banks.

139

"Just as well," Poppy managed to say, "I think we're going to be some time."

• • •

Finally, when some time (a great deal of time, it seemed to Banks) had passed, and Poppy and Garland had reduced their output to the odd giggle and some sniffling, Banks assumed a dignified expression.

"Are we done now?" he said.

"Wait," said Garland.

"Yes," said Poppy.

"Good," said Banks. "I need you to help me open this box."

• • •

"I don't see why that's funny at all," Banks said, a few seconds later.

• • •

The box was small, but heavy.

"Do you want me to rip the whole thing apart or just snap the padlock?" asked Poppy.

"Just the padlock," began Banks, but Poppy gripped the lid of the box and pulled it off like paper on a bar of chocolate.

"Sorry," Poppy said, throwing the lid across the floor, "I needed to let off some steam."

They looked into the box. It was full of closely packed banknotes.

"Money," said Garland. "Useful."

Banks removed the notes from the box. Underneath were some tiny jars. Banks took one out.

"Caviar," said Garland. "Told you."

"I love caviar," said Poppy, snatching the jar from Garland. She unscrewed the lid and scooped out the contents of the jar with a finger. She crammed the gloopy lump into her mouth.

"Salty," she announced.

"You're sure that was caviar?" Banks said to Garland. Garland shrugged.

"Very funny," said Poppy. She reached into the box and came up with some tiny bottles with red labels.

"Vodka," Garland said. "Anything else."

"No," said Poppy, then, "Wait. There's something else."

She reached into the box and came out again with something small and shiny. A key.

"That's one thing we don't need," said Poppy. She was about to drop it back into the box when Banks took it from her.

"You never know," he said.

"I do," Poppy insisted. "I'm not a big key person, really."

"Nevertheless," said Banks.

He took one more look around the carriage.

"Take whatever you need from here and let's move on," he suggested.

• • •

A few minutes later, having opened boxes of chocolates, and jewellery, they decided that there was pretty much nothing else useful in the shop.

"Let's go," said Banks. He zipped the key into a side pocket, and led the way to the end of the corridor.

Garland was about to open the door when Poppy said,

141

"Stop." She said it so quietly that at first neither of them heard her.

"Stop," she said again, and this time Banks and Garland turned.

Poppy was standing at the door of a closet. The door was open and she was looking – no, staring – into the closet.

"I don't believe it," she said.

Inside the cupboard was a complete set of skiwear. Boots, goggles, trousers, jacket, helmet and –

"Skis," said Poppy and took everything out of the cupboard.

"I'm ready," she said.

• • •

Behind them, the movement of the door caused a small breeze to flow across the floor of the carriage. The bundle of banknotes slid across the floor and a few notes flew up. The notes were the same as banknotes the world over: a collection of complicated lines and curves, a denomination and a bland face staring into the middle distance.

There was, however, one difference between these banknotes and all the others: the face on these banknotes was one that Banks, Poppy and Garland would once have recognised immediately.

• • •

At first, the door to the next carriage would not open.

"It's wedged," said Banks.

"I can see that," said Garland.

"No," Banks said. "It's wedged because it's badly made. Like it doesn't fit properly."

"Let me try," said Poppy. She passed the skis to Banks.

"Skis," said Banks.

"Be quiet," Garland said.

Poppy pulled. The door came away in her hand.

"Much better," she said. "Oh," she added.

Behind the door was something quite unexpected. A narrow doorway, containing two thinner, smaller doors.

"That is ridiculous," said Garland.

"I've certainly never seen anything like it before," Banks agreed. "Were they trying to save space or something?"

"Never mind the philosophical discussion," Poppy said. "Which one do we go through?"

"Oh, what?" Garland said. "This is even more ridiculous."

• • •

They stood and looked at the two doors for a minute longer.

"We could split up," suggested Banks.

"That's a terrible idea," Garland said.

"It's just a door," Poppy said. "Two doors."

"Two very narrow doors. I don't like it."

"All right," Poppy sighed. "Let's pick one and go in together."

"OK," said Garland. She indicated the left-hand door. "That one."

She stepped forward. Poppy moved in front of her.

"I'll go first," she said. "Just in case."

She put her hand on the door and tried the handle.

"Open," she said. "Makes a change." She grabbed her skis. This time Banks raised a large eyebrow.

"What?" she said. "These are really good skis."

143

She gently slid the skis through the door and went in after them.

. . .

The door shut abruptly behind her.

. . .

Inside the door, Poppy turned to open it again.

Outside the door, Garland grabbed the handle.

. . .

"It's not opening," said Garland.

"Let me try," Banks said, and pulled. The handle didn't move.

After a few seconds' struggle, Banks gave up.

"Why did you stop?" Garland asked.

Banks said, "Look."

The door was shaking, imperceptibly.

"That's her," Banks said. "She's trying to open the door."

"Are you sure? It's hardly moving."

"That would be my point," Banks said, drily.

. . .

Poppy shook and shook the door, but it didn't seem to move at all.

"Fucking doors!" she shouted, and battered the door with a few kicks.

. . .

"What are we going to do?" Garland asked, once the door was entirely still again.

"This," said Banks. "Hello!" he shouted. "Hello! Poppy, can you hear us?"

No response.

. . .

"Garland!" Poppy shouted. "Banks!"

Nothing.

. . .

"She can't have gone," Garland said.

"She's still there," Banks said. "She just can't hear us."

"That's ridiculous. She's only on the other side of the door. There's just a few centimetres between us."

"She's there," said Banks.

. . .

"Can anyone hear me?!" shouted Poppy. "They've gone and left me," she told Teddy.

Teddy said nothing, but Poppy fancied he looked doubtful.

"Well, if they haven't left me," she said, "then why aren't they doing anything to help me?"

She studied Teddy's face.

"Oh," she said. "Right. Shit."

Poppy sat on the floor, the better to think.

. . .

"Let's be logical," said Banks.

"Oh, let's," said Garland.

"She's behind the door. She's probably not dead –"

"Nice."

"– so now she's given up banging on the door or shouting for help –"

"How do you know she has?"

"We did, so she will."

"OK."

"She's not going to hang around. She can't open the door she came in through, so she's going –"

145

"– to find the exit."

"Exactly."

"Which means…"

Banks looked at the other door.

"We have to go through this door. Which was the plan in the first place."

Garland looked at the other door.

"We don't know what's in there."

"We didn't know before. Nothing's changed."

"All right." Garland took a deep breath, then:

"You open it."

"Thanks very much."

Banks opened the door.

• • •

Poppy sat and thought.

"There's no way back," she told Teddy. "So we go forward."

She stood and, for the first time, looked around. The corridor was, understandably, fairly narrow, being only half the width of a regular train carriage. This half of the carriage was also empty, and dimly lit. There were no seats, or racks, or tables. The windows, too, were blacked out, so only the noise and the constant shaking gave any indication that she was still on a train.

She now saw that the carriage wasn't entirely empty. A few metres ahead of her was something bulky, and square.

Pushing Teddy safely inside her jacket, Poppy moved forward.

• • •

Banks and Garland looked through the doorway but couldn't see anything. The carriage was narrow and not well illuminated.

"There's nothing here," said Garland. "It's just a carriage."

"No," Banks replied. "It's been divided in two, and that means it's not just a carriage."

"There's no need to be pedantic," Garland said.

They went in. The door slammed behind them immediately.

Banks rattled the handle.

"Just to be sure," he said.

The handle didn't move.

"Locked in?" Garland asked. Banks nodded.

"Let's go then," she said.

• • •

Poppy approached the large object. It reached from floor to ceiling, and it was made of some kind of plastic. The plastic was glossy, and dark. Poppy felt along the front of the object – *it's a box*, she thought – and could find no seams or handles. She tried the sides, and her fingers brushed over a small protuberance. She felt it gently. It was round, and almost set flush into the wall.

"It's a button!" she said, and pushed it.

Immediately she was blinded.

• • •

Garland and Banks made their way down the narrow corridor. The carriage was poorly lit, and seemed to be empty.

"This is weird," said Garland.

"Which makes it normal," Banks pointed out.

"Ooh, paradox," Garland said.

She stopped. In front of them was a large, box-like structure.

"What's that?" she said.

"Whatever it is," Banks said, "I don't like the look of it."

• • •

When her eyes had returned to normal, Poppy realised that the light which had blinded her was coming from inside the room. The button was a light switch, and the room, which she had thought was opaque, was in fact made of some kind of transparent plastic. The plastic was scored with scratches and dents and bumps: she felt the outside, which was entirely smooth, and saw that the damage was all on the inside of the room.

Inside the box, something was lying on the floor.

It's not a room, Poppy thought, *it's a cage*.

• • •

Garland and Banks approached the structure. It was made of a thick, dark plastic and seemed to be all of a piece.

"I vote we ignore this and move on," said Garland.

"It might be important," Banks said.

"True," said Garland. "It might also be dangerous. In fact, given that everything – and I do mean everything – that we have encountered so far has been dangerous, I'd be very surprised if it wasn't dangerous."

"All right," said Banks. "But –"

"But what?" Garland replied, testily.

Banks pointed at a nub on the door.

"These open the doors, if you know what to do."

"And do you know what to do?"

Banks grinned.

. . .

Poppy looked at the inert form lying on the floor of the cage. It had been crumpled into a vaguely foetal position, but she was pretty sure it was human. She couldn't see any fur, and besides, as far as she was aware, killer mutant animals didn't wear shoes.

After a while, when she was absolutely certain it was a human being, of average size and, presumably, strength, she rapped on the wall.

The figure stirred.

. . .

"Oh fuck," said Garland.

"Key," said Banks. He indicated a tiny hole in the side of the structure. "And – keyhole."

"No way," Garland said.

"Aren't you even curious?"

"Yes, but not in any way which would make me want to open that door."

"We don't know what's in there."

Garland looked at Banks.

"That," she said, "would be my point."

. . .

Poppy stood back. She watched the figure move its legs, put its hands on the ground to steady itself, try and get upright. It seemed to be broken in a couple of places, and she waited to see if it could stand.

It pulled itself across the floor, put its hand on what looked to Poppy to be some kind of small plastic object with straps, like a cool bag, pushed the bag away, and tried to stand again. Eventually the figure managed to get to its feet. It put a hand against the wall to steady itself, then, using the wall to balance, began to turn around.

There was a crackle from above Poppy's head. She looked up to see a speaker in the ceiling that she hadn't noticed before. Inside the cage, the figure coughed into its fist, and the cough echoed out of the speaker.

Poppy wondered if the sound worked two ways.

"Excuse me," she said. "Can you hear me?"

The figure looked up at the speaker in the roof of the cage. Then, as if understanding, it turned around to face her. Its eyes scanned the wall, but didn't alight on her face. Poppy realised that while she could see it, it could not see her.

"Who's there?" said the figure, and at that moment Poppy recognised the voice. The face was different – bruised, unshaven, one eye swollen – but the voice, cracked and dry as it might be, was the same.

Instinctively, she took a step backwards.

"Who's there?" said Denning again.

• • •

"We're not opening it," Garland said.

"OK," said Banks. "I concede that it might be dangerous. As you say, everything here is dangerous. It is the nature of this place to be dangerous. And I concede that there are other things we could be doing."

"*Should* be doing," Garland corrected. "Like just walking past these things, and getting out of here and finding Poppy. And the whole making our way to the front of the train to find out why we're here and escaping bit."

"Sure," said Banks. "But what if whatever is in *there* is the key to the whole finding out why we're here bit?"

"Here?" asked Garland.

"Yes," said Banks. "Why not?"

Garland considered the idea.

"I suppose I just assumed that the important stuff would be at the front of the train," she said. "I mean, it normally is."

Banks looked at her. "That's trainist," he said.

After a moment, Garland said, "That was a joke, right?"

"You are making a majorly big assumption," Banks said.

"I know," said Garland, "That's why I said 'assumed'. And it's not a big assumption. Whatever is driving this is going to be at the front of the train. That's where driving happens. Nobody drives from the middle of anything, do they?"

"Driving isn't everything," Banks said.

"What does that mean?"

"It means that whatever's in there could be, I don't know, an electronic brain. An archive. Something useful, anyway."

"In there?"

"Yes."

Garland sighed. "All right," she said. "What have we got to lose?"

"Attagirl," said Banks, and put the key in the lock.

• • •

"Do I know you?" asked Denning.

"No," said Poppy, unconvincingly.

"I do know you," said Denning, and even on the bruised and battered face she could see the cunning in the man still intact. "Say something else."

Poppy said nothing.

"Well," said Denning. "There are plenty of people who don't want to talk to me, so that doesn't really narrow it down. But your voice – it's very familiar."

He looked directly at Poppy, so directly that she found it hard to see him.

"This material, it's very clever," he said. "You can see me, but I can't see you. It's a one-way mirror, I suppose, but stronger."

He held up a hand. The nails were ragged and bloody.

"A lot stronger," said Denning. He exhaled.

"Let me think," he said. "A woman's voice. Young, too. Which narrows it down a little. Well spoken. But the odd thing is –"

Denning stopped. After a moment, he said:

"The odd thing is, I know your voice from hearing it, I mean, hearing it in person, but also from somewhere else."

He put his bloody finger on his chin and looked thoughtful.

"I have it," he said. "You were someone I worked with – or on – but you were also *famous*. Well known in the outside world, when there was such a thing."

Poppy found that she was holding her breath. She tried to exhale as quietly as possible.

"This is quite a fun game," said Denning.

He began to pace, frowning as he thought. He paused for a moment to gaze at the small bag on the floor, as though the answer might be inside it.

"Wait," he went on. "There was someone – she escaped. They think she –" and he began to giggle. Denning giggling was not something Poppy had ever expected to hear, and she didn't like it much.

"They think she caught a train!" said Denning.

Suddenly he walked up to the wall, up to where Poppy was standing. He thrust his face right up to hers.

"Poppy," he said. "Welcome to hell."

• • •

Banks turned the key in the lock and the door opened. Instantly the space was flooded with light.

"Ow," said Garland.

"Bright," confirmed Banks.

They stood in the doorway for a moment and looked into the room. It was empty.

"Well, that was useful," Garland said.

"Over there," Banks said, and pointed.

By the wall was a squat white bag. It was made of plastic, and had two carrying handles.

"Not empty at all," said Banks.

He turned to Garland. "You hold the door open, and I'll get the bag."

"Sounds reasonable," said Garland. She curled her fingers round the edge of the door and gripped it hard. Just to be doubly sure, she wedged her foot in the gap between the door and the wall.

"We are go," she said.

Banks looked at her. "'We are go'?" he said.

She shrugged. "'Attagirl'?" she replied.

"Fair point," said Banks.

He walked across the room and squatted down next to the bag.

"What is it?" said Garland.

"It's a bag," replied Banks.

"I'll walk out of here and close this door on you," Garland said.

"I don't want to open it in here," Banks said. He grabbed the straps and lifted the bag up. He looked puzzled

"Heavy −" he began, but got no further as Garland yelled and fell to the floor, holding her spasming hand. The door slammed shut. Banks dropped the bag and ran over to her.

"It electrocuted me," said Garland. She was shaking uncontrollably. "When you lifted the bag, it electrocuted me."

"It's OK," said Banks. He looked at her hand. "Does it still hurt?"

Garland sat up. "No," she said. "The door's closed," she said.

"No shit," said Banks. He looked back at the bag. "I think this was a trap," he said.

"As you say," Garland replied, "no shit."

• • •

"Hello," Poppy said, after a while.

"Ah, lovely," said Denning. "It's always nice to know

who you're talking to. It's also," he said, leaning against a wall now and wincing, "nice to know that you're fine."

"I wouldn't say I was fine," said Poppy. "And go fuck yourself," she added as an afterthought.

"That I think I have already done," said Denning. "As you can see from our relative positions. I imagine this is pleasurable for you, seeing me in here for once."

"Do you," Poppy asked cautiously, "know where you are?"

"Of course," Denning said. "I presume from your question that you do not."

"I'm on a train," said Poppy.

"Well, yes," said Denning. "A moron could deduce that. And that's it, is it? That's the boundary of your knowledge?"

"I'm on a train and I'm not in a cage," Poppy said.

"If you say so," Denning replied. "If you say so."

Then, to Poppy's surprise, he began to sing.

"You know this one?" Denning asked. "It's funny isn't it? That's what I did. I built a railroad and I made it run!"

And he laughed.

• • •

Banks and Garland stood in the middle of the room for a minute or two, occasionally turning round or lifting their heads to see if there were any gaps or seams in the room.

"Nothing," said Garland.

"There's never nothing," Banks said. He went over to the wall and ran his fingers over the plastic. "I'll go over every millimetre of this if I have to."

"Knock yourself out," Garland said. "Even if you do find

155

a crack, what are you going to do? Prise it open?"

"Make yourself useful," suggested Banks. "Look in the bag."

Garland squatted next to the bag and unzipped it.

"Interesting," she said. She stuck her hand inside and pulled out a fistful of small glass bottles.

Banks came over to look. The bottles were all unlabelled and filled with transparent liquid.

"Medical supplies?" he asked.

"Could be," said Garland. "Could be stock for the minibar. Seems unlikely, though."

Banks took a bottle and held it up. Then he did the same with a second bottle, and a third.

"No way of telling what's in here at all," he said. "They could all be the same stuff or they could all be different."

"Maybe someone should have labelled the ones we need DRINK ME," said Garland.

"Or DON'T DRINK ME," said Banks.

Suddenly he threw a bottle across the room.

"What the fuck!" shouted Garland. The bottle hit the wall, and bounced off.

"Just testing," Banks said.

"Well, don't," said Garland, going over and retrieving the bottle. "It could be anything in there. Acid, nitroglycerine…"

"Both of which would come in handy right now," Banks said. Before Garland could stop him, he threw two more bottles at the wall. As before, they bounced off and rolled to the floor.

As Garland picked them up again, Banks said, "You

know, someone wants us to open these bottles."

"What makes you say that?" she asked.

"No labels, can't break them," he said. "All designed to arouse our curiosity."

"Major cause of death in ninety-nine per cent of all cats," said Garland, placing the bottles back in the bag and zipping it up again.

• • •

When Denning had stopped singing, he leaned against the wall again and coughed.

"How long have you been in there?" asked Poppy.

"Long enough," said Denning.

"What – how are you staying alive?"

"Am I?" Denning asked. "Staying alive?" He laughed. "Mints!" he said.

"Mints?" said Poppy.

"Mints," said Denning. "I used to like mints. Or I didn't, but I smoked so they were useful. I forget. I sucked them anyway."

"There's someone else here?" Poppy said. "Someone in charge?"

"Oh, I wouldn't say that," Denning said. "Not in charge, no."

He came over to the wall again and smiled. Poppy could see that most of his teeth were missing.

"I don't suppose you could get me out of here, could you?" he said.

"Fuck you," said Poppy. "I'd rather die."

"I know *that*," said Denning. "But then, I know a lot of

things. In fact, I could be very useful to you."

There was a moment of silence.

"How useful?" said Poppy.

• • •

Banks was now moving his hands with painstaking lack of speed across the back wall. Garland sat on the floor, trying to clear her mind.

"You're not being terrifically helpful," said Banks, feeling his way along the wall.

"I'm trying to make room in my head," Garland replied.

"To do what?"

"To remember," said Garland.

She closed her eyes.

• • •

She was in a room. The room was a large cube, and it was full of light. Also in the room were some men in uniforms. The uniforms were covered in medals and badges and ribbons, and they had been made by skilled tailors, so that the size of the wearers' guts and backsides was concealed as much as possible.

They were, she now remembered, the generals, and they were to a man a vile crew of stupid old fuckers. She remembered the phrase – *a vile crew of stupid old fuckers* – because it was one she'd heard her father use at dinner. His dining companion had instantly hissed at him to shut up, but he'd laughed and said something like, *they can't do anything to me, they need me too much*. He'd been wrong about that, she reflected now, but that hadn't made the expression any less true, had in fact confirmed it.

So now she was in a room with no windows and a great deal of light with the vile crew of stupid old fuckers. Some of them, oddly enough, were rubbing their arms, and complaining about some sort of shot they'd been given earlier.

"Status symbol, old man," said one of the fuckers, and laughed. Then he looked around contemptuously.

"This is it?" he said.

"Nothing wrong with a decent windowless room," another general said cheerfully, a man whose breath was so foul Garland was surprised it hadn't rotted his tongue. "Put 'em in ranting and raving, bring 'em out all quiet and helpful."

"This is much more than a room," said a voice, a voice she knew well. She didn't need to turn her head to see him or even listen to his voice: the smell of pipe tobacco from his clothes and skin was quite enough. "This is the Disposal."

"Like waste disposal?" snorted a general.

"Very much," agreed Denning. "Bring him in," he said.

The generals parted like a sea of shiny shit (her father's voice again) as two guards brought in the prisoner. The last time she had seen the prisoner, he had been wearing a general's uniform, which may have been why his former comrades looked away from him when he came in.

"Yan!" cried the prisoner. "Collini! It's me! Prout!"

If any of those men were in the room, they said nothing.

"I see you recognise a few old faces," said Denning to Prout. Denning liked to savour a moment, she realised, and this was a perfect scenario for Denning: he got to test his

159

new toy and at the same time put the fear of God into the people who, in theory, employed him.

"This way, gentlemen," he said. "There's a green room."

· · ·

In the green room there was again a lack of windows and a good deal of light, but there was also a trestle table covered in wine bottles and little bowls of nuts. The generals consumed both with extraordinary speed as Denning's team set up a monitor. After some fiddling with the remote control, one of the scientists nodded to Denning and he clapped his hands for attention.

"Gentlemen," he said. "I trust you have enough to eat and drink."

"I could do with a whisky," said one general, and the others laughed.

Denning smiled tightly. "I'll see what I can do," he said. He left the room and the team followed. A second later, realising she was still in the room, he returned.

"This way," he said. "I'm not leaving you in there with those fucking perverts."

"Thank you," she said, surprised.

"Not at all," said Denning. "Whisky," he said contemptuously. "Like I'm the wine waiter."

He closed the door of the green room and, turning to one of his team, said, "Take Prout back to his cell."

"But I thought —" she began.

"Yes," said Denning. "So did they."

He pressed a switch on the wall that she hadn't seen. The door clicked.

• • •

Inside the room, one of the generals, who had been about to go and find a toilet, saw the door apparently lock itself.

"Did you see that?" he said. "The buggers have locked us in."

"Probably for our own protection," said his companion. "Health and safety and all that rubbish."

"Where's my whisky?" another general said, and everyone laughed, and laughed, and coughed, and choked, until their guts ran out of their softening throats and they suffocated on their own lungs and hearts.

• • •

The door opened. Denning looked around. There were tiny broken bottles all over the floor, among other things.

"Effective," Denning noted.

He moved his foot.

"Oh dear," he said. "I've stood in General Yan."

• • •

"The bottles," said Garland. "I remember them."

"Is that all?" said Banks, massaging his fingertips.

"Be quiet," she told him. She stood up and looked around. "Get me on your shoulders," she said.

• • •

"How useful?" Poppy repeated.

"Very," Denning said. "You know who I am, Poppy."

"Not really," she said.

"You know I was important."

"And now you're in a cage."

A look of impatience appeared on Denning's face. He made a visible effort to quash it.

"I know everything," he said.

"Like I said, and now you're in a cage."

"Maybe I'm in this cage because I know everything."

"Or because you know everything apart from how to stay out of a cage."

Denning made no effort to conceal his impatience now.

"I can save your life, you silly cow," he all but hissed.

"Going now," said Poppy. "Bye."

She began to move down the corridor. Then she stopped, and waited.

"Poppy!" Denning called.

She walked back to the cage.

"What is it?"

"I can get you off this train," Denning said. "I can get you off this train and to safety."

She thought for a second.

"No you can't," she said finally.

"Yes I can!" Denning shouted, desperately. "There's a door – there's a station – a stopping point."

"Go on."

"If we can stop the train there, I can – there are people we can reach. They'll look after us."

Poppy looked down at Teddy. His button eyes looked back at her.

"All right," she said. "Stand back."

There was silence for a moment.

"What are you doing?" Denning said.

"I'm going to get this door open," Poppy replied.

"You can't," said Denning. "This one doesn't have a key.

162

It's an upgrade and –"

She ignored him and began kicking the door, as hard as she could.

It opened, and she stepped in.

"You did it," Denning said. "I'm impressed."

He moved towards her suddenly. Startled, she stepped back.

Something crunched beneath her feet.

A vial.

Denning looked at her, aghast.

"You stupid fucking bitch," he said. "What have you done to me?"

Before she could reply, Denning clamped his hand to his mouth. He stared in horror as yellow fluid gushed over it, then grabbed his stomach and vomited gouts of half-digested food.

"What's happening?" said Poppy, but Denning was too busy staggering about and crying to reply. He stood up suddenly and frowned.

"My skin!" he shouted. "Jesus Christ!"

He struggled with his jacket and, finally getting it off, started frantically scratching his arms. Poppy stared as Denning's nails scraped deep furrows in his arms.

"Don't scratch!" she shouted. "It'll make it worse!"

"Fuck that!" Denning shouted back, gouging skin and blood from his forearm. Then he doubled up again.

"Oh no," he said. "Oh no."

He grasped his stomach, which seemed to be writhing. Then he vomited again, and this time something fibrous and spongy flew out. It spattered on the window in front of Poppy and she jumped back.

"What was that?!" she shouted.

"I think…" said Denning, struggling for breath. "I think it was a kidney. Oh God, oh God, this is shit. Fucking balls!" he added, spitting out more.

He screamed now.

"This is it!" he shouted. "This is me fucked!"

And to Poppy's horror, he began to melt.

• • •

"What are we looking for exactly?" asked Banks.

"Stop wobbling," replied Garland. "There it is," she said.

She dug her nails into the ceiling and found a grille. Garland twisted it until it dropped onto the floor, and shoved a finger into the hole where it had been.

"What's that?" Banks asked.

"Comms," said Garland. "Communication system."

She poked around with her finger and found a small, nipple-sized bump. She pressed it.

The air was filled with screams.

• • •

Poppy screamed as Denning screamed. Her scream was a lot clearer than Denning's as his face and mouth had begun to collapse.

He was turning into a kind of soup.

• • •

"What the hell?" shouted Banks over the screaming.

"Poppy!" Garland yelled.

The screaming stopped.

• • •

Denning's hair ran down his face. His shoulders sagged as his arms lengthened and his fingers began to drip. He began to stagger around the cage, moaning now, as his clothes started to slip from him.

"Unf," he said, insistently.

Poppy closed her eyes and listened to Denning bump into the walls as his remaining bones and muscles fought for control of his liquefying body. She opened her eyes again and watched, transfixed now, as what was left of Denning seeped out of his clothes and began to pool on the floor.

Soon it was over. Denning's nails and even his teeth were liquid now, and there was nothing left but a sticky mess.

Poppy sighed. "Goodbye, Mister Soup," she said.

• • •

And then she heard the voice coming from the grille. It was calling her name.

"Garland?" she shouted.

• • •

"Poppy!" Garland shouted back. "Are you all right?"

• • •

"I think so," said Poppy. "How about you?"

• • •

"We're trapped," Garland said.

• • •

"Let me guess," said Poppy. "Are you trapped in a large, windowless plastic cage?"

• • •

"How did you know?" Garland asked. "Don't tell me," she said. "Just concentrate on getting us out."

165

There was a pause, then Poppy said, "I don't know if that's a good idea."

"What do you mean?"

• • •

Poppy stepped over the human broth on the floor and picked up the cool bag in the corner. She opened it.

• • •

"What do you mean?" Garland repeated.

• • •

Poppy rifled through the bag. There were three small bottles. Two were sealed and full of a clear liquid, but one had no lid, and most of its contents were missing.

She looked up towards the grille.

"Is there a bag in there?" she said. "A bag with little bottles in?"

• • •

"Yes!" Garland shouted. "Why?"

• • •

"Do not on any account open them," Poppy said.

• • •

"Told you," said Banks. "Can you get down off my shoulders now?" he added.

"In a second," said Garland irritably. "We haven't opened them," she shouted at the grille.

• • •

"Thank fuck," Poppy said. "I think they create a chemical reaction when they're opened. Denning opened one and –"

• • •

"Denning?" said Banks. "Is Denning there?"

• • •

Poppy looked down at her feet. Soup was seeping towards her boots.

"In a manner of speaking," she said.

• • •

Banks helped Garland down from his shoulders.

"Did you hear what she said?" Garland asked.

"Yes," Banks said.

"Of course it's all hypothetical since, firstly, the bottles are still sealed and, secondly," he pointed out, "we can't get the door open."

• • •

"I'm going into my corridor," said Poppy. "Stand back."

• • •

"What did she say?" Garland asked Banks.

Seconds later they heard a tremendous battering.

• • •

After a few seconds, a crack appeared in the wall. Encouraged, Poppy continued her barrage, until a hole appeared at the bottom the size of a giant mousehole. She bent down, thrust her hand in and started to pull at the wall, first tentatively and then, as it began to crack further, ripping out great chunks.

Soon she had a hole big enough to crawl through.

• • •

"I'm outside," she called. She could see Banks and Garland in their cage. "Are you still standing back?"

"We don't have anything else to do," said Banks.

• • •

"Hi!" Poppy said as she stepped into the cage.

Suddenly the entire train lurched to one side. Poppy was

thrown back against the door, which slammed closed, and then opened again.

"Everything OK?" asked Garland.

"Fine, thanks. I met a man called Denning and he melted when I broke one of these bottles," said Poppy.

"Denning?" said Garland.

"One of *these* bottles?" Banks said nervously.

"Yes, he turned to gloop in front of my eyes," Poppy went on, "but it didn't affect me."

"So maybe it only kills men?" suggested Garland.

"Oh good," said Banks.

"We should probably go now," Poppy said. "Just be careful where you put your feet."

• • •

They tiptoed out of the cage and down the corridor.

• • •

"Do you want to have a look?" Poppy asked. "At Denning, I mean."

Banks shook his head. Garland thought about it.

"No," she said. "I mean, he's soup. He's definitely dead."

"He's not coming back from that," Poppy agreed.

"Let's focus on getting out of here," Banks said.

• • •

The next carriage was extremely normal, except that it smelled quite strongly of boiled eggs.

Banks, Garland and Poppy sat down at a table, and Banks rifled through the kitbag for food and drinks.

Banks looked at Poppy's skis, which she had managed to fit into the luggage rack.

"When did you fetch those here?" he asked.

Poppy shrugged.

"Just slid 'em along the corridor as I went," she said. "You never know when they might come in handy."

"No, I do know when they might come in handy," Banks said. "Which is never."

"We're getting low on cans," said Garland.

"Not a problem," Banks said. "By my reckoning, we should be due a buffet car soon, and if nobody else has beaten us to it there will be more cans."

"So long as it's not soup," said Poppy.

• • •

"The only thing I don't understand – well, not the only thing," Poppy began, "is the bit with the air meeting the stuff in the bottle."

"Because the air inside was the same as the air outside?" Banks interrupted. "Easy – Denning was a senior official, so he had been injected with an anti-radiation agent for his own protection."

"I didn't –" Garland began.

"– but the agent was also designed to react with the poison, fatally," said Banks.

He sat back and looked smug.

"That wasn't my question," said Garland, a little tersely. She turned to Poppy.

"I mean, I get that it did for Denning, that was fairly clear. But I don't see why I didn't soup up as well."

"*Soup up?*" said Banks, disapprovingly. "That's not an expression."

"It is now," Poppy replied. "So how come I didn't soup up?" she repeated.

Garland shrugged. "Could be a number of reasons," she said. "Limited field of effectiveness, like you'd have to be standing next to him to be affected as well. Or the air inside was mixed differently, so someone standing outside or in the doorway wouldn't be souped up as well."

"Not a real expression," Banks muttered. Poppy gave him the finger. Garland gave him two. "Or," she continued, "your own immune system – who knows what's inside you? You could be crawling with nanites or something."

"Lovely," said Poppy. "Now I feel itchy."

"Now what?" asked Banks.

"Finish our lunch, then on we go," Garland shrugged.

"But first," said Poppy, and took out the bottles of clear liquid from the chamber.

"Shit!" shouted Banks. "What the fuck?!"

"Anyone got any paper?" Poppy asked. Garland gave her some tissues and bits of newspaper. Poppy carefully wrapped the bottles and put them in her pocket.

"If you hear a crunch," she said, "run for it."

• • •

The train rounded a bend, lurched to one side, and threw them back in their seats.

Banks gave Poppy a stern look.

"Relax," she said. "What could possibly go wrong?"

"Put them back," Banks said. "Throw them away. Drop them down the toilet."

Poppy said, "But they only work on someone who's

had the jab. And we haven't."

"We don't know that," Garland said.

"We don't have any other weapons," Poppy said. "No guns, no knives, nothing. Just these," and she thumped the table with her fists. "So if something happens to me, you two flesh bags are buggered."

"Nice," said Garland. She sighed. "She has a point," she said.

"Too right I have a point," Poppy said.

They finished eating. Banks cleared up the debris.

"Why do you do that?" asked Poppy. "Tidy up after?"

"Because it's messy otherwise."

"But nobody cares."

"I care."

"This place is full of dead bodies, blood, guts and all kinds of stuff. A few packets and cans won't make any difference."

"It makes a difference to me," said Banks. He found a bin behind a table and shoved the rubbish into it. He put the kitbag over his shoulders.

"Ready?" said Garland.

Banks nodded. Poppy patted her pockets.

"Ready," she said.

"Don't do that again," said Garland, and set off down the carriage.

• • •

Behind them, far enough away to be inaudible under the noise of the train, there was a thump, then another, then a third. Something was on the roof, and it was getting nearer.

FOUR

The next carriage was a buffet car.

"See?" said Banks. "I was right."

He put down the kitbag and began opening cupboards.

"Cans!" he said, his eyes glistening. "Look!" he said, holding up a can.

"More purple," said Poppy.

"This isn't purple," Banks said, "it's mauve."

"What kind of food is mauve?" asked Garland.

"Guess we're going to find out," Poppy replied.

Banks tore open the can, stuck in a finger and licked it clean.

"Blueberry," he said.

"Blueberry what?" Poppy asked.

"Just blueberry," said Banks.

"My favourite," said Poppy.

Banks opened all the cupboards. They were crammed with cans, and juice boxes, and packets of dried food.

"Wow," said Garland. "We hit the motherbuffet."

• • •

"We just ate," Poppy said, as they sat down to a table covered in food.

"I know, but we can't carry all this. Besides," Banks said, his mouth full, "blueberry."

Poppy shook her head.

"I'm going to the bathroom," she said. "Nobody touch my skis."

• • •

In the bathroom, Poppy washed her face. After a moment's thought, she drank some water from the tap. It tasted fine, so she drank some more.

"What does not destroy me," she said to the mirror, "makes me want to pee."

Just then the light went off.

• • •

"Hey!" she shouted. "Turn the light back on!"

Then she remembered that there was no light switch. She went to the door and turned the handle but it didn't open.

"I'm stuck in here!" she shouted.

• • •

In the darkened car, Banks swore as he got up.

"Banged my head," he explained.

Garland got to her feet unsteadily.

"Did Poppy leave her coat?" she asked. "The bottles."

"On the back of her seat."

"Good."

"What are you doing?"

"I'm not sure," Garland admitted. "But I think I should go and find Poppy."

• • •

"I can't get out!" Poppy shouted.

"There must be a short circuit in the lock," said Garland.

"Must there?" shouted Poppy. "Who needs an electronic lock on a toilet anyway?"

"I'll file a complaint," Garland said. "Can't you smash the door?"

"Why is it always me who has to smash doors?" Poppy asked. "Don't say anything, I know the answer."

And she balled her fist.

• • •

"Banks! What are you doing?"

"Putting the cans back in the kitbag."

A pause, then Garland said, "Why?"

"Because they're rolling around in the dark."

"Could you perhaps do that later? I need you here."

"What for?"

A sigh in the dark.

"Just. Come. Here."

• • •

Poppy's fist hit the door. There was a flash of light, and a sharp pain through the top of her arm into her shoulder. Her chest jolted and she fell to the floor.

• • •

Garland heard the thump.

"Poppy?" she shouted. "Get this door open!" she told Banks.

"I'll need a lever."

"Get a fucking lever then."

"I really hate that word."

• • •

There was a lot of clanking and banging, followed by some hissing, and then Banks was beside her again.

"Here."

"What is it?"

"Heating pipe."

Garland found the edge of the door. She was about to stick the end of the pipe in when she accidentally touched the edge of the doorway. An electric shock jerked the pipe away and she grabbed her hand.

"The door's electrified."

"But the power's out."

"Yes, I can see that. And the door's electrified."

Garland thought.

"It must be a separate circuit," she said.

"Or a fault."

• • •

Poppy lay on the floor. Her head was bleeding and her eyes flickered in their sockets. She was conscious but she could not move.

Outside, she could hear the others talking.

• • •

"We need to shut off the power to the door frame."

"We need the lighter."

A few seconds, then Banks's face illuminated by a flame. Banks stuffed paper and cloth into a juice container, and lit it.

176

"There have to be cables somewhere," he said, getting down on the ground.

"That panel," said Garland. She pointed down at her feet and handed Banks the pipe.

"OK," said Banks. He set down the flame and began to prise the panel off. The pipe snapped.

"I thought you hated that word," said Garland.

• • •

Poppy tried to move. She could feel the muscles tense and flex in her shoulders and at the top of her legs, but her limbs refused to move.

I've been short-circuited, she thought to herself, and wondered if that was possible.

• • •

"We need more pipe," said Banks.

"We need more light," Garland corrected him, as the flame guttered out. "What's that?" she added.

Further down, back the way they had come, something loud was happening.

• • •

Poppy felt it more than she heard it, a rattling thunder of movement.

• • •

"It can't be," Banks said.

"Can't be what?" asked Garland.

They listened to the clatter of approaching feet. It was heavy, and determined.

"Soldiers," said Banks.

. . .

Poppy could hear them now, shouting, running in step. She tried to move towards the door, but her limbs were dead weight.

She flexed a muscle in her back, and felt her body shift.

. . .

"How can there be soldiers here?" Garland said.

Banks thought. "The station," he said.

"What, the doors opened back there and a load of troops got on?"

"The train must have stopped for some reason."

Garland was silent.

"Poppy!" she shouted.

. . .

Poppy inched towards the door, every muscle in her thighs and shoulders and back straining at every millimetre of territory gained. She could see nothing, but she estimated that her feet were now almost touching the door.

Kill or cure, she said to herself, and with every ounce of her remaining strength she forced her muscles to push her dead legs at the door frame.

. . .

"I can see them!" Banks said. He grabbed the pipe.

. . .

There was a burst of flash from the door frame and Garland recoiled, showered in sparks. The door fell away.

Poppy, dragging herself to her feet, put a hand on Garland's shoulder.

"Reversed the fucking polarity," she said.

"What does that mean?"

"I don't know, exactly. I shocked the system more than it shocked me, I think."

"You could have been killed."

"Well," said Poppy, "that's life."

She stepped out unsteadily into the compartment.

"Bit dark, isn't it?" she said.

• • •

They stood there, in a train carriage with no light.

"Where's my jacket?" said Poppy.

"On the back of a seat," Garland said. "Not sure it's much use against a platoon of soldiers."

"Platoon?"

"At least."

"Fully armed, presumably," said Banks. "And keen to get on with it, by the sound of them."

The sound of running men was a lot closer now.

"What have we got?" asked Poppy.

"You, and a metal pipe," said Banks.

"Could be worse," Poppy said.

"How?" replied Garland.

• • •

They braced themselves as the noise got closer.

"How many of them are there?" Garland asked.

"Platoon," Poppy reminded her.

"I don't know how many that is."

"It's enough," Banks said.

• • •

They could hear shouting now, words in a language none of them recognised. They could see lights, torches probably.

"Any second now," Banks said, gripping his metal pipe tightly.

• • •

The door of the carriage was flung open and a soldier marched in, shouting.

Then the lights came back on, startling them and the soldier who stood in the carriage. He stepped forward, hand covering his eyes.

"Security ch –" he began.

There was a terrible noise behind him, like meat being crushed. There were shouts, and screams, and some guns went off.

The soldier turned round and ran back to join his comrades. The door slammed behind him.

• • •

Poppy stepped forward. Banks grabbed her arm, and she shook him off. Garland followed her to the door. They stood behind the glass, trying to see what was happening.

A hand slapped against the glass, covered in blood. It slid down in its own red trail and vanished.

Silence.

• • •

They waited a full half-hour before opening the door.

• • •

"Remember, there's always one who isn't dead," Banks said.

"Not this time," Garland replied.

The soldiers were in a terrible mess. Most of them had

been killed quickly and efficiently – a severed head here, a punctured chest there – but some were less lucky, and had been battered against bulkheads, or partly cut in half. It was as if a very angry whirlwind or a small gang of chainsaws had barged its way down the carriage. This impression was not disproved by the path the thing that killed the soldiers had literally cut through them, a path that ended suddenly at the end of the previous carriage.

"Where did it go?" Garland asked. "And by 'it'," she added, "I mean 'whatever the hell that was'."

Poppy pointed at the ceiling.

"Up," she said.

There was a large ragged hole in the ceiling. It was covered in hair and blood, like a demon's plughole.

"Which way did it go?" Banks said.

"Let's worry about that later," Poppy answered. She bent down over a dead soldier. "Look at this," she said, lighting the soldier's face with his torch.

"Definitely dead," Garland noted.

"And this one," Poppy said, shining the torch on another dead man.

"Oh," Garland said.

The two soldiers were identical. So, they soon discovered, were the two next to them. And the next.

"They're all the same," Banks said. "Same faces, same eyes, all the same."

Garland thought of a hand reaching out of a mirror, and said nothing.

"Let's get out of here," she said.

"First, let's ransack their corpses," Poppy replied. "Give me that kitbag."

Banks handed her the bag. "Practical," he said. "I like it."

Poppy searched the pockets of the nearest soldier. They were empty. She moved on to the next soldier.

"No money, no ID, no house keys," she said. "No food, no concert tickets…"

"I expect they have lockers," said Banks.

"No pictures of sweethearts, no lucky charms," Poppy went on, moving to another soldier. "No dog tags."

"Can we go?" Garland said. "This place is creeping me out."

"Plenty of torches, though," Poppy said. "Wait, this one doesn't have a torch."

"You've done him already," said Banks.

"Sorry," said Poppy. "They all look alike to me."

She stood up.

"Guns," she said, and began to gather up the dead soldiers' weapons.

. . .

Back in the buffet car, they inspected their haul.

"We don't need all these guns," Banks said. "There's only three of us."

"Strength of ten men, me," said Poppy, loading a couple of rifles over her shoulder.

Garland looked at one of the guns. It had a recess in its side, like a shell.

"That's a thumbprint," she said.

She picked it up, aimed it back down the train and pulled the trigger.

Nothing happened. Garland tried again with another gun, then another.

"Personalised weapons," she said. "The rifles will be the same."

Poppy dumped her guns on the floor.

"At least we have lots of torches," she said.

. . .

"So how come the power came back on?" Banks asked, when he'd finished packing the kitbag.

"The soldiers must have had access to the electrics," Garland suggested.

"Maybe they just pulled a fuse out," said Poppy.

Banks's face took on a thoughtful look. He said, "If they did that, they must have had a —"

"Manual?" said Poppy.

"Map," said Banks.

He ran back into the other corridor.

. . .

"I've searched them all!" Poppy called to him. "I really am good at ransacking," she told Garland.

. . .

Banks found a soldier with more rank badges than the others.

"I've found the commander," he said.

. . .

"I did him too!" Poppy shouted. "I looked in all his pockets!"

. . .

Banks rolled the officer over. He was lying on a crumpled sheet of paper.

• • •

"You should have looked under him," said Banks, returning to the carriage.

• • •

"No one likes a smartypants," said Poppy.

• • •

Garland spread the map out on the table.

"Well, this makes no sense," she said.

"Yeah," said Poppy. "I was expecting something that was more of a, you know, map of the train. Not –"

"What is this?" Banks said.

The map was a collection of seemingly unrelated symbols arranged in the rough shape of a figure of eight. The symbols were unfamiliar, and bore little or no resemblance to one another. Some were pictograms, but part of no language they could recognise. One or two were numbers, quite a few were letters of the alphabet, and one, bizarrely, appeared to be a photograph of a cat.

"This is fucked up," Poppy declared.

Garland flipped the map over.

"That's more like it," she said.

On the back of the map was a schematic drawing of a train carriage, showing the wiring, the heating pipes and the ventilation ducts. They could see the audio grilles, one or two plug sockets, and a small drawing of a box, highlighted in red.

"There," said Banks. "Fuse box."

"Great," Poppy said. "If we ever need to change a fuse, we can."

Garland folded up the map and put it in the kitbag.

"You might as well throw that away," Poppy said.

"Maybe we'll meet someone who can explain it to us," said Garland.

"If we meet someone," Poppy said, "then we're not going to need a map, are we?"

Garland ignored her.

"Next carriage, anyone?" she said, and strode off down the carriage.

• • •

They stood at the door of the next carriage. It was a perfectly normal carriage door, but Banks hesitated before opening it.

"Get on with it," Poppy said.

"I was just thinking about whatever it was killed those soldiers," Banks said. "It might have gone in there."

"It might have," said Poppy. "It might not have. There really is no way of telling."

Banks still hesitated.

"I'll open it," Poppy said.

"No," said Banks.

"What is it?" Garland said.

"It's just – the more carriage we go into, the greater the risk," said Banks.

"That's showbusiness," Poppy replied. "Now get out of the way."

"Every carriage we enter," Banks said, "the danger is

worse. I think we should —"

"What? Ask someone what's in there?"

"Obviously not," said Banks. "But I don't think we should go rushing in."

"There is," Poppy said heavily, "no danger of that happening."

And before Banks could stop her, she shoved the door open and went in.

• • •

A moment later, she was back. She looked terrified.

"You're right," she said to Banks. "We should have waited."

Banks went pale. "Oh God," he said. "What's in there?"

"I can't say," said Poppy. "It's just —"

"Stop it," said Garland, as Poppy collapsed into giggles.

"Great," Banks said. "You got me."

"There really was no need for that," Garland said, as Poppy went a sort of purple.

"Sorry," said Poppy. "It's been a long day."

"So what is in there?" Garland said.

"Come and have a look," Poppy said. "It's really nice."

Banks looked at Garland.

"Nice? I'm not sure I can handle nice."

But he followed them anyway.

• • •

The next carriage was long, and bright, and its walls rippled with blue and silver light. It smelled, somehow, of rose petals and it was pleasantly warm. As they entered they went up a small flight of steps, because the entirety of the carriage was raised up on a platform. The reason for this became apparent immediately: most of the space in the carriage was taken up by a long, and shallow, pool. The sides of the pool were tiled and here and there were small baskets of something.

They walked around the edge of the pool and stood there, looking in.

"Is it a swimming pool?" Banks asked.

"I don't think it's deep enough," said Poppy.

"Oh God," Banks said. "It's a shark tank."

"Again," Poppy said, "not deep enough."

Garland crouched down.

"Oh my," she said.

Looking back at her from inside the pool, its head peering out of the water, was a very small turtle. Garland reached a hand into the water and picked it up.

"Careful," Banks said. "It might take your hand off."

"It's a baby," said Garland. She stroked its head with her finger. "And I think it's hungry."

She reached into one of the baskets and brought out a small packet, similar to the juice boxes in the buffet car. Garland tore open the packet and poured its contents into her free hand. The baby turtle snuffled around and began to peck her palm.

"Not taking my hand off yet," she said.

"Look at its shell," said Poppy.

Under the dappled light of the pool, the turtle's shell seemed to be glowing.

"It's…" Banks was searching for a word.

"Iridescent," said Garland.

"Like a rainbow," Poppy said.

"Both of those things," Banks agreed.

• • •

More baby turtles swam up to the side of the pool. Poppy and Banks opened more packets of food. Banks tipped his into the water. Poppy scooped up a couple of turtles and fed them in her hands.

Garland studied the schematic.

"You're looking at that now?" said Poppy.

"I want to try something."

Garland walked to the central part of the carriage. She slid back a panel in the wall.

"Nobody move," she said, and reached a hand inside the panel.

A moment later, the lights went out.

"What did you do that for?" said Banks.

"Shh," said Poppy. "Look."

They looked.

• • •

The pool was full of tiny shining objects.

"They're glowing," Poppy said.

The baby turtles swam in the dark, their shells giving out pearly rainbows of light.

"Over there," Garland said.

A larger light was moving slowly towards them. The smaller lights began to swim towards it.

"No one turn the light on," Poppy said. A second or two later, there was a small splash.

"What's she doing?" Banks said. "Oh," he added, as he

heard something move through the water.

• • •

Although the pool was shallow, Poppy found she could swim in it. With a packet of food in her teeth, she made her way to the mother turtle. Slowly she sat up in the water, filled her hands with food, and chuckled as the turtle, shell glowing in the dark, nibbled her hand. Then she dropped the remaining food in the water, lay back and let the turtles swim over her.

• • •

"Don't give them too much to eat, it's bad for them!" Banks called out.

"Be quiet," said Garland.

Banks grumbled into silence and they watched the turtles swim around Poppy, making patterns like tiny swirling constellations in the water.

• • •

"I don't know what to make of this," Garland said, as Poppy and the turtles circled one another. "I don't mean the last few hours, the blood and the mess, I mean –"

She waved an all-encompassing hand at the carriage.

"– this," she finished.

"*This sudden beauty*," Banks said, as if quoting. "I know."

"It's from nowhere," she said. "On this thing."

"You know how trains got their name, right?"

"I'm sure you're about to tell me."

"It's 'train' as in 'train of thought'," Banks said. "As in a load of things being pulled along, one in front of the other. Or behind."

"If this is a train of thought," said Garland, "it's a train of particularly horrible thought."

"With something beautiful in it," Banks said. "The pearl in the oyster."

Poppy waved goodbye as the mother turtle began to nudge her babies away from her.

Garland corrected him. "The pearl in the monster," she said.

"That makes no sense," said Poppy as she climbed out of the water.

• • •

When Poppy was dressed, they made their way to the end of the carriage. Poppy turned before Banks opened the next door.

"Bye, turtles," she said. "Stay safe."

• • •

The next carriage was ridiculous. It was just a train carriage. In fact, it was so much like a train carriage that they felt uneasy.

"This is like being in a museum," said Banks. "Or a reconstruction."

There was nothing odd at all about the carriage. It had a full complement of seats, and tables. It didn't smell of anything unusual, and it was averagely clean.

Poppy clambered onto a seat to put her skis in the luggage rack. Garland explored a bin.

"Look at this," she said, holding up a paper coffee cup and sniffing it. "Cold," she said.

"Anything else?" asked Banks. Garland shook her head.

"Wait," said Poppy, still standing on the seat. She reached into the luggage rack and pulled something out.

It was a book.

• • •

They sat down at a table and read the book.

"I thought you couldn't read," Banks said to Garland.

"I couldn't," said Garland. "But now I can. Some things, anyway."

"Books are boring," said Poppy.

"No they're not!" Banks said, shocked.

"Name one good book," Poppy demanded.

There was a pause.

"I can't think of any books," said Banks.

"Exactly."

"No," Banks said. "I mean at all. I can't think of any books at all."

"Neither can I," said Garland. "That's not good."

"And you two are book fans," said Poppy. "I don't believe I've ever read a book," she added with dumb satisfaction.

"I'm sure I've read hundreds," said Garland.

"Well, you can read this one then," Poppy said unsympathetically.

• • •

Garland opened the book. The first page she turned to began with words in bold type.

"*Make-up is a skilled creation*," she read out.

"I'd agree with that," said Poppy. "Go on."

"*It is the role of the actor whether in cinema or elsewhere to show the emotions and mental processes of a character*," Banks

191

read, "*as well as that character's look.*"

"Wow, boring," said Poppy. "Are there any pictures?"

"No," said Garland with satisfaction. She read on. "*The outside and the inside, the look and the content, thus must interweave to be a successful portrayal.*"

"Stop there," Poppy said.

"I'm with her," said Banks.

Garland sighed and closed the book.

"It might be a clue," she said.

"It might be a murder weapon," Poppy replied. "And you still can't name a good book."

Garland wasn't listening. She pulled out the map again.

"You think this will get us to Narnia?" said Poppy.

"What's Narnia?" Garland said.

Poppy looked abashed.

"It's a book, isn't it?"

"It's in a book."

"Same thing."

"Not."

Garland shook her head and spread the map out on the table. Then she fished out a pencil and began making marks on the paper.

After a while she stopped and said, "There are at least forty symbols on this map and I can't make head or tail of them."

"Then how do you know it's a map?" asked Banks.

Garland stared at him. "Because that's what it looks like," she said. "See here, where the two loops of the figure of eight cross over? That's obviously a bridge. And there –"

She pointed to a wobbly blue line.

"– that's a river."

"It's a line."

"A line representing a river."

Banks made a face.

"Or a border. Or a road."

"You agree it's a map then."

"Not much of a map, without a bit where it says 'You Are Here'."

Garland shook her head and pushed the map at Banks.

"You find it, then."

"Woah," said Banks.

"That was a bit harsh," agreed Poppy.

"No, I meant, we're going uphill," Banks said. "I can feel it in the pit of my stomach."

"It's getting steeper," Poppy said. "I can feel it too."

Banks stood up.

"I wonder if I can see anything," he began, just before Poppy pulled him back into his seat again.

"Look out!" she yelled, pulling him towards her.

"What is it?" Garland shouted.

Suddenly something fast and metal shot past them.

"It's –" said Banks. He stood up.

"Be careful," Poppy said.

"What *is* it?" repeated Garland.

"It's a buffet trolley," Banks said, and began to laugh.

• • •

The trolley was metal, about chest height, and had been on four small wheels, one of which was now broken.

They approached it with interest.

"Those are nuts," said Banks, indicating some small blue foil packets. "And those are pastries."

"They look pretty stale to me," Poppy said.

"Is that whisky?" Garland said.

Banks reached a long arm into the trolley and scooped everything out into the kitbag.

"This is more like it," Poppy said, grabbing a handful of miniatures. "Let's get smashed."

"No," Garland said.

"All right," Poppy said. "I'll get smashed. You stay boring."

"Fine," said Garland. "When whatever killed those soldiers turns up again, we'll run away and you can divert it by being eaten."

"Fuck," Poppy said after a moment. She dropped the bottles back into the kitbag.

• • •

They sat down and enjoyed their alcohol-free snacks.

"We're really high now," Banks said.

"Speak for yourself," said Poppy.

"High *up*," said Banks.

Poppy gave him a special look and turned to look out the window. Something silvery spattered itself on the glass.

"Snow?" Garland said.

Banks shook his head.

"Ash," he said.

• • •

Further down the train, where something had torn a hole

in the roof of the carriage, a freezing wind began to tunnel back in. Clouds of silver, glittering ash fell rapidly into the carriage.

The thing on the roof began to howl.

• • •

"It *is* snowing ash," said Garland.

"Good Lord," Banks said, "you're right."

"When I say it, it's not true, but when she says it, it is," said Poppy. "I might as well not be here."

"Be quiet and eat your nuts," Banks said. Poppy pointed up at her skis.

"I might put those on and get out of here," she said.

Banks ignored her and turned to Garland. "This is bad," he said.

"Your catchphrase," Poppy muttered.

Garland asked, "Why is it bad?" and Banks said, "Because giant drifts of ash and trains don't mix. We could break down. We could get stuck. There could be a power outage, which means we'd freeze."

"Or," said Poppy, "none of these things could happen and we could just carry on happily to our destination."

Garland leaned over and sniffed Poppy's breath.

"You've been drinking," she said.

"I only sneaked a couple when you were looking at your stupid map," said Poppy.

Banks looked in the kitbag.

"A couple?" he said. "You've had six."

"I'm fast," said Poppy. "Bit tired," she added, and passed out.

"Well, that helps," Garland said.

Banks said nothing. He had fallen asleep.

Garland made a face, took out her pen again and began making more notes on the map. After a few minutes she leaned over into the kitbag, gently pulled out the last whisky, and drank it slowly. Then she too fell asleep.

• • •

Outside, the silver ash fell more and more deeply by the minute. The thing on the roof, its systems frozen, went to sleep as well, which probably saved their lives.

• • •

Garland woke first. She remembered that she was on a train, that it was snowing silver ash, and that her name might be Garland. She looked out the window and saw the ash, deep in piles outside. The train wasn't moving any slower, so she presumed the tracks ahead were fine.

She took out her map and continued to make notes. After a while she stopped, because the notes were just lists that made no sense. She opened the book again, but this only made her sleepy again.

Garland was thinking of waking the others, partly to annoy them and partly to have someone to talk to, when she noticed that the train was going downhill again. She noticed this firstly when the buffet trolley slid past, hampered by its broken wheel, and secondly when she felt the acceleration of the train.

• • •

"We're picking up speed," said Banks.

Poppy woke up.

"Is it me," she said, "or is everything *wider*?"

"It's the ash," Banks said, and indeed the silver expanse outside the window did seem to make the world outside broader. "That, and the moonlight."

"A moonlit night," Garland said, wonderingly. "How long has it been that?"

"Night, or moonlit?" Banks said. "I'd say the moon has only just come up. But as for how long it's been night…"

He looked at them both.

"How long do you think it's been night?"

Poppy frowned. "I've only been awake a few hours… I think. But it's been night all that time."

"Me too," said Garland. "Banks, you're the veteran. How long has it been night?"

Outside, in the silver-lit night, something red exploded in the sky.

"As long as I've been here," said Banks. "Weeks. Months, possibly."

"Months," Poppy said. "You've been here for months."

"Maybe," Banks said. "Does it matter?"

Poppy shrugged. "I suppose it depends on what you want from a train ride," she said.

Another red burst went off in the sky.

"Fireworks?" asked Garland.

"Could be," Banks said. "Could be anything. Distress flares, explosions…"

"The end of the world," Poppy suggested.

"I think we'd know if it was the end of the world," said Banks.

Garland looked at the red flowers in the sky.

"Would we?" she said.

• • •

Time passed.

• • •

Garland shoved Banks on the shoulder.

"I was asleep," he said.

"Sorry," she began.

"And," Banks continued, "I was actually having a dream in which I wasn't being tortured, or torturing someone else."

• • •

"I think it's stopping," Banks said, a few minutes later.

"The train?" Poppy asked excitedly.

"The ash," replied Banks.

• • •

After that, nobody said anything for quite a while. Banks opened a pack of juice. Poppy practised scratching her name into the table, and Garland made notes.

• • •

"It's stopping," said Banks.

"You said that an hour ago," Poppy replied.

Garland stood up.

"Not the ash," she said. "The train."

• • •

Poppy clambered onto her seat and began to punch the ceiling.

"I'd wait a minute if I were you," Garland said.

Poppy continued to batter upwards.

"We're not fucking this up again," she said.

• • •

Garland and Banks remained in their seats, looking out for any signs of activity outside.

"The windows are clearing," said Banks. "I can see something."

"Buildings," Garland said.

• • •

Outside, in the distance, there were towers, somehow both tall and squat. The towers were unlit, and grey, and stood in fields of unbroken ash.

Poppy took a break from punching.

"Anything else?" she asked.

"Just towers," said Garland.

"Wait," said Banks. "I think I can see –"

• • •

A few metres away, parallel to them, something long, and brightly burning.

• • •

"– a train," Banks said. "A burning train."

"Looks like we're in the right place for once," said Poppy, and went back to punching the ceiling.

She paused to rip away some wiring.

"Nearly through," she said.

• • •

Now they had the burning train as a landmark, they could see that they were definitely coming to a stop now. As before, it was a long, slow stop. A platform appeared out of the darkness, thick with deep, undisturbed ash.

"Been snowing ash for a while here," Banks said.

"No footprints or signs of anyone clearing it," said Garland.

199

"Can you only speak when you see something interesting?" Poppy shouted, her body half in and half out of the roof. "It's really hard to concentrate."

• • •

The train was so covered in drifts of ash that it was hard to see anything at all.

• • •

"A sign!" shouted Banks.

Garland peered out. Banks was right. Visible through a gap in the rising mist was, not a sign as such, but a raised piece of stone with carved letters set upon it. Some of the letters were missing, others smashed beyond legibility, but most of them were intact. Intact enough to read, anyway.

"INGCOS," Banks slowly spelled out. "What's that?"

"Don't ask me, I don't even remember my own name," said Garland.

Poppy appeared from inside the ceiling, covered in grease.

"Ingcos," she repeated. "Never heard of it."

"Still, that's where we are," Banks said.

• • •

As imperceptibly as it had begun to slow down, the train stopped. One minute it was moving and one minute it wasn't.

• • •

They sat there for a moment, then Poppy jumped up.

"No time to lose," she said, burrowing back into the ceiling.

After a moment, she reappeared.

"Skis," she said.

• • •

"That's something you don't see every day," Banks said to Garland as they watched Poppy drag and bang the skis against the wall.

"Don't help," said Poppy.

"Back in a moment," Garland said, and she and Banks got up and left the compartment.

• • •

The door to the platform didn't budge.

"Which we expected," said Banks.

Garland put a hand on his arm. "There's a light flashing," she said.

"There was," Banks replied. "It stopped."

They looked at each other. Then Garland reached out her hand, gripped the lever, and pushed.

The door opened.

"Hold it there!" Garland shouted.

• • •

She stepped back into the carriage. Poppy wasn't there.

"Poppy!" she shouted. "Poppy!"

After a moment or two, Poppy's head appeared through the hole.

"You better not be telling me the door opened," she said.

"Sorry," said Garland.

Poppy swore, and dropped her skis back through the hole.

• • •

They all stood on the platform. Drifts of ash were heaped up everywhere, glowing faintly in the light of the high neon lamps that dotted the platforms. There seemed to be an endless array of platforms, spread out as far as the eye could see.

"We should split up and explore," said Poppy.

"We should get back on the train," said Garland.

"The door!" said Banks, and stepped back onto the train again. "You look around," he said. "If it looks like the train's about to go off again, I'll shout and hope you can hear me."

Poppy nodded. "Yeah, but what if you get, you know, ripped apart and eaten?" she said.

"I'll just hope you can hear that too," said Banks.

• • •

"I think we should have stayed with Banks," said Garland as they made their way up the platform.

"Look, a footbridge," Poppy said.

"We shouldn't get too far from the train," Garland said, but Poppy was already sprinting up the platform to a thin metal bridge that crossed the tracks.

• • •

Garland, slightly out of breath, joined Poppy on the top of the footbridge.

"Good God," she said.

"Pretty much," Poppy agreed. "Just look at it."

Below them, on almost every platform, were trains. Some were long and luxurious, plated in silvery chrome. Some were filthy and functional, stumpy tenders with great hooks or coal containers on the back. A few were relics from the past, some were futuristic, but most of them were just trains, lowering in the night.

"We've spent all our time in that one metal tube," said

Poppy. "And all the time this has been here."

"You've seen one train, you've seen them all," Garland said.

"Let's go and get a close-up view."

Garland shook her head.

"I really don't want to stray too far," she said.

"That's true," Poppy replied. "You don't."

And she leapt down the stairs, three at a time.

Garland suppressed a bad word, changed her mind, said the bad word, and followed.

• • •

"This one's got a thing," said Poppy, pointing.

"A destination board?" suggested Garland.

"That's the one." Poppy twisted round to the front of the train to look.

"Ingcos," she said, disappointed.

"Makes sense," said Garland.

"We need more names." Poppy strode up the platform.

"We haven't got time for this." Garland followed her.

"*You* might not," Poppy said. "*I* do."

They stood opposite one another. Garland found she had her hands on her hips.

Just then a voice came half-sliced on the wind.

"Quick!" shouted Banks.

Garland gave Poppy a look and ran for the bridge.

"It's not moving," Garland said.

"I know," Banks replied. "Come here."

Poppy followed them back into the carriage.

"What is −" she began.

"Listen," said Garland.

There was sound coming from the speaker grille.

"Music," said Poppy. "Great. Are they playing your request, then?"

"It's not like the other songs," Banks said.

"It's not a song," said Poppy.

The music was all bleeps and whooshes. There were odd drums that sounded like they were spinning.

"What's that?" said Poppy at one point.

"I think it's a guitar," Banks said.

"It's wonderful," Poppy said. "Now can I go?"

Garland looked at her.

"You can do what you like," she said. "I thought we agreed about that."

Poppy looked hurt. Then her face broke out in a broad grin.

"I guess so," she said. "You going to see me off or what?"

The music had faded out. Banks held the door open for them to get out.

"This is it, then," said Poppy.

"Wait," Banks said.

"What for?" said Poppy.

"A lot's happened since we last stopped."

"Like mystery killing machines and clone soldiers?" said Poppy. "I'm out of here."

"What about you?" Banks said to Garland. "Poppy's right, the train isn't safe."

Garland hunched her shoulders and looked around. "Where is?"

She touched Poppy briefly on the shoulder. Poppy flinched, but not much.

"I have to stay," she said. "I have to find out what happened. To me, to everything."

"I'm cool with that," Poppy said. She touched Garland's hand with her fingers.

"Who says 'cool with that'?" said Banks.

"Goodbye, Banks," said Poppy, shouldering her skis. "Goodbye, Garland."

• • •

Banks kept the door open as Garland got back onto the train.

• • •

Poppy hoisted the skis higher on her back and walked down the platform back to the footbridge.

Once back on top of the bridge, she was able to survey the surrounding landscape and consider her options. She quite fancied seeing the silver train close up first. She didn't know if she'd get on it though, just maybe have a look at it: she'd spent enough time cooped up lately. Maybe she'd just have a look and then head for the way out.

She heard a sound, like a hooter. It *was* a hooter, sounding back where she had come from. The train that Garland and Banks were on was giving off clouds of steam as its engines began to warm up again, sending flurries of glittering ash into the night sky.

• • •

"Now what?" Banks said, yet again.

"As we were," said Garland. "Sit down and wait for

this thing to start moving again."

"What if it doesn't? What if this is it?"

"It will. This isn't it."

They sat down. Banks found some juice.

"Got one for me there?" asked Garland.

• • •

Poppy watched as the train wheels began slowly to rotate.

"Nice knowing you," she said, giving the train a smart salute.

• • •

"You won't be able to see her, you know," said Banks, as Garland peered out of the window into the billowing mist.

"Maybe it's not her I'm looking for," said Garland.

"There's nobody else out there," Banks said, and sucked the last of his juice.

• • •

Poppy waited until the train was definitely moving out before she picked up her skis again. She could see the carriage they'd been in – the hole she'd made was leaking enough warm air to make the ash on the roof dance – and wondered if they could see her.

"Probably studying that fucking map," she said, and noticed that her voice sounded wistful rather than harsh.

She took one last look at the train, which was when she saw something move along the roof.

• • •

"I hope she's going to be all right," Garland said.

"She'll be fine. She can pull the ceiling out of a train,"

said Banks. "Which I wish she hadn't done, because it's getting cold in here."

"We'll be out of here in a minute," Garland said.

"Updating your map of where we've been?" Banks asked.

"Like she said," Garland replied. "You never know."

• • •

Poppy estimated it was bigger, and heavier, than a human being from the way it cleaved to the roof, keeping its centre of gravity flat and low. It was slow, hindered by the wind, but it was moving steadily forward. She estimated it would only be a few minutes before it got to the carriage Garland and Banks were in. The carriage with a hole in the roof.

She began to run towards the train.

• • •

The thing on the roof was not overendowed with intelligence but it had an excellent sense of smell, an almost industrial digestive system and teeth that had never known what it was like to not sever something at the first attempt.

It had no real emotions, in the more complex sense of the word, but it had basic needs and feelings. Right now it was hungry, and it was cold.

It wasn't particularly worried about this, however. It was sure that slightly ahead of it was the solution to both problems.

It crawled on.

• • •

Poppy ran so hard she could feel her feet jarring against the concrete platform.

• • •

"Did you hear something?" asked Garland.

Banks shook his head.

"I expect it's the wind coming through that hole," he said pointedly.

Garland gave him a look.

"Nearly done," she said.

• • •

The thing on the roof could smell them now. There were two, and they were warm, and they would provide hot blood and bones to break.

It began to move more quickly.

• • •

Poppy tried to keep pace with the train as it sped up but her legs, while powerful, were not designed for speed and she began to fall behind.

• • •

"I heard a thump," Garland said. "Just down there."

She got up. Banks stood as well.

"There's no need for you to come," said Garland.

"Nevertheless," said Banks, and went round her.

• • •

The thing could see the hole in the roof now, if 'see' was the right word, and it nearly was. It could detect the warmth of the carriage below, and its sense of smell, which was almost entirely weaponised, was almost in a frenzy at what waited for it down below. Sometimes its makers gave it frozen meat to eat, offal and old eyes, but this was better. Much better.

With renewed effort, it dragged its bulk closer.

• • •

Banks touched Garland's arm.

"I think," he said, "it's going to come through the hole in the roof."

"Run," said Garland.

They ran.

• • •

Poppy made a decision. She veered to her right, leaped blindly into space and let her hands grope the air. They met first with flat metal, slipped down for a moment, and then found a handle.

Half dragged, half flying, Poppy held on to the handle, raised a hand up and groped for another.

There wasn't one.

• • •

The thing found the hole and slid over it. Then it just let itself fall.

• • •

"Did you hear that?" shouted Banks as he grappled with the compartment door.

"Just get the door open," Garland said.

"It's stuck," Banks said.

"You're fucking joking," Garland said.

• • •

The thing got up.

• • •

Garland turned around. What she saw pushed the air from her lungs. She was looking at something her mind could barely process.

It was almost three metres tall and appeared to be

209

standing on all fours, except it didn't seem to have legs. It was covered in a brownish hide, hard rind-like plates stippled with tumps of hair and grey and green bumps that reached down to the ground. Where its head should be was a large mass of darker grey plates, under which something liquid like a black jelly moved.

Its mouth was easy to see, a wide collection of teeth set in a dark slash below the head. The teeth were yellow and long and some of them, improbably, were serrated like hacksaws.

None of this was pleasant, or comforting, but what distressed Garland the most was not the animal aspect of the creature. What upset her, down to the very core of her being, were the aspects of the creature that were not remotely animal.

There was, for example, something resembling a limb that extruded from one side of its body, long and muscular and ending in a cluster of sharp claws. This was worrying enough itself, but made worse by the fact that the limb and its claws did not appear to be entirely organic at all, but rather a kind of mash of metal and bone and raw muscle, as though someone had decided to create a part-machine animal, and had done so, not by grafting but by somehow *growing* metal and bone and muscle together.

Worst of all, though, were the parts of the creature which resembled nothing else at all. Near the top of its shoulder, Garland saw, was an area which at first she thought was made of some kind of shiny metal or plastic. It was not. As the creature moved, preparing itself, she saw the place by the shoulder ripple.

"It's liquid," she said. "Part of that thing is liquid."

"That's impossible," said Banks, "an animal can't be liquid."

The creature opened its mouth, or the place where its mouth was, and let out something like a howl. It sounded like amplified static. It sounded like frying steel. It sounded terrifying.

Garland said, "I don't think it's an animal."

• • •

The creature was moving now, slowly.

"It knows we're not going anywhere," said Garland.

Banks said, "We should run."

Garland said, "What's the point? It might not have any legs, but we can't outpace it."

"Are we just going to stand here and let it eat us?" asked Banks.

"You run, I'll try and stall it," Garland said drily.

"I'm not leaving you now," said Banks.

Garland looked at him. She smiled.

"I'll remember that," she said. "You know, in the last few seconds."

• • •

The creature opened its mouth wider.

"Oh, for fuck's sake," Garland said.

In the middle of the creature's mouth was something like a tongue. It was red, and soft, except for its edges, which were yellow, hard and sharp.

"A tongue with teeth," Garland said. "Now I've seen everything." She turned away from the tongue, which was now clattering itself against the creature's other teeth.

"I've changed my mind," she said to Banks. "Let's run."

They ran.

• • •

The creature reared up. It screamed static and metal.

• • •

Banks shoulder-charged the door but he couldn't unstick it.

• • •

The creature began to move slowly towards them, like an enormous armour-plated slug.

"Let me try," said Garland. She tugged at the door, but it didn't move.

• • •

"I think," said Banks, as the creature got nearer, "that this is it."

"I think you're right," said Garland.

"You don't sound scared," Banks said.

"No point," said Garland.

• • •

They faced the creature.

• • •

"Never did get to the front of the train," said Garland. "That's my only regret."

• • •

There was a thump. The creature turned slowly around.

• • •

"Never say never," said Poppy. "Ow," she added. "My fucking leg."

• • •

The creature hissed, and sprang at her.

FIVE

Poppy moved forward, limping slightly.

"What the fuck is that?" she asked.

"We were wondering the same thing," Banks said.

"Why are you here?" Garland said. "Get out now; it wants us."

"I don't think it's that fussy," Poppy said. "It wants to kill all of us. Probably could, too."

She made a chucking noise at it.

"It's not a puppy," Garland said.

"You never know," Poppy said. "Right," she added, pulling something out from her pocket.

The thing stiffened, and sniffed the air.

"What have you got?" Garland said.

"Meat," said Poppy. "Must have hidden it for a snack."

"That's not going to help us," Banks said.

"Nope," Poppy said. "But this will."

And she ran at the creature and kicked it hard in the face.

· · ·

The creature screamed, reared up, and moved across the floor in a loud, grating rush.

"Poppy!" shouted Garland.

But Poppy was gone.

· · ·

"Missed!" she shouted from the hole.

The creature looked up, snarling.

Poppy looked back down. She threw something at it.

"Torch," she shouted. "I've got loads."

· · ·

"Get back down here!" Garland shouted.

"No," replied Poppy.

"I hope she's got a plan," said Banks.

· · ·

Slowly, the creature lengthened itself.

· · ·

"Poppy!" Garland shouted again.

There was no reply.

· · ·

The creature almost seeped upwards, its plates rippling as it forced itself up into the hole again. With a great deal of effort, it began to climb up into the ceiling.

· · ·

"Now what?" Banks said.

"I am seriously going to fine you every time you say that from now on," said Garland.

"Yes, but seriously –"

"No idea," said Garland. "No fucking idea whatsofuck-ingever."

• • •

The creature curved and bent itself until it was once more on top of the roof of the train. It opened a black jelly eye and looked around itself. Glinting ash was beginning to fall again, and the furrows of the tracks it had made earlier were already covered.

In front of it stood Poppy, wearing skis.

"Hiya," she said.

• • •

The creature half-lunged, half-slid towards her.

Poppy kicked down, and skied away along the roof of the train.

• • •

"What's going on up there?" said Banks.

"Movement," said Garland. "Let's get that door open."

• • •

Poppy looked behind her for a moment and saw the creature, moving without grace but determined and fast, towards her. Her skis bumped and almost snagged on the roof, but the smooth ash kept her moving.

She came to the end of the carriage. There was a sizeable gap between it and the next one.

This definitely isn't a simulation, she told herself. *Nobody would be that stupid.*

She flew into the air.

• • •

The door slammed open.

"Oh fab," said Garland. "Now it opens."

"I heard another thump," said Banks.

They ran into the next carriage.

• • •

Poppy landed with a skid on the next carriage, almost twisted her ankle, regained her balance, and skied on. She cast a look over her shoulder and saw the creature slow down, rear back and then – somewhat sloppily, in her opinion – *throw* itself over the gap between carriages. Once landed, it moved towards her with increasing confidence.

She felt in her pocket as she raced on. Another torch, a wad of tissue paper…

The vials.

She shook her head. Throwing them here would be useless: they would smash on the roof and disperse in the wind.

Use the available resources, she told herself. And answered herself:

There aren't any fucking available resources.

• • •

"Wow," Banks said as they entered the carriage.

"No time," said Garland.

"There's some really interesting stuff in here."

"And our friend is on the roof being attacked by a monster."

Banks ran after Garland.

"I only meant maybe we could come back later."

• • •

Poppy had jumped to another carriage. It was good to be

216

moving, but her lack of a plan was worrying. As was the growing realisation that she had only one option.

Stand and fight.

. . .

"That was extraordinary," Banks said.

"Later," said Garland.

"I know, I'm just saying," Banks shouted as they ran.

"Don't," replied Garland.

. . .

Trouble is, thought Poppy, *it's hard to stand and fight when what you're fighting is essentially an armoured lump with teeth, and what you have to fight it with is nothing at all.*

Nevertheless, she stopped.

. . .

"I can't hear anything," Banks said.

"Maybe if you shut up talking," suggested Garland.

They stood in the middle of an empty carriage, looking up at the ceiling and listening.

. . .

The creature lifted its head and showed Poppy its mouth.

"Lovely," she said to it. "You can lick me and eat me at the same time. Very useful."

As if understanding her, the creature cocked his head.

"We don't really have much to talk about," said Poppy. "But if you kill me, I imagine you're going to go back and kill my friends. And that isn't on."

She took off her skis, one by one.

"So I'm going to batter you to fucking death," she said.

. . .

The creature advanced, then stopped. It seemed to be taking her in, like it was seeing her for the first time. It reared up, opened its mouth, revealing teeth, tongue and something else deep in its throat.

Poppy peered at it.

"A sting," she said. "In your own throat. No offence, but you were designed by a committee. Which means you might be a bit more shit than you think."

She lunged forward. The creature screamed static, and Poppy shoved a ski into its throat. Poppy pushed harder and the creature screamed more. She levered the ski downwards, trying to force it further and further inside, but then the creature lurched forward, bent its head down and the ski snapped.

The creature writhed and curled its neck, trying to get the ski out.

"I hope," Poppy said, pulling up her other ski, "that chokes you."

She lunged forward again, but the creature had learned to anticipate her and, with its limb of bone and metal, smashed down on Poppy's arm. The ski flew into the air and was blown away into the night.

Poppy turned. She didn't want to run – it was pointless – but she needed time to think. Then she saw it.

• • •

The next carriage wasn't a carriage at all. It was a flatbed car, long and wide with no sides, just a base made of planks.

• • •

Poppy jumped.

The creature followed.

Excellent, she thought. *That's exactly what I wanted you to do.*
Even to herself, she sounded unconvincing.

• • •

"There!" Banks shouted. He was pointing towards the door
at the end of the carriage.

Garland turned.

"Is that the end of the train?" she said.

"Just look," Banks said.

Garland went up to the door and looked through the
glass. At first she couldn't see anything, then it all came clear.

Outside the door was a long, flat car. On it were two
figures.

• • •

The ash was thicker here. Poppy was able to move through
it easily, but the creature, propelled by who knows what,
was less fortunate. It waded towards her, shrieking like a
rocket, its sting now protruding horribly from its mouth.

"Someone's awfully cross," observed Poppy.

She strode towards it, iron fists clenched.

• • •

Banks said, "Is that her?"

"What do you think?" Garland replied. "Here, help me."

"With what?" said Banks.

• • •

Poppy continued to stride towards the creature. It reared
up, sloughing ash from its body. She jumped, and thrust
her arms into its mouth. It screamed and its jaws began
to close. At that moment, Poppy's hands closed round its
sting, and wrenched it. The sting came away from the

creature's mouth, and it let out a gurgling roar of anger and pain.

Poppy fell backwards, the sting convulsing in her hand, and watched as something wet oozed out of its pores, burning her skin. She stood up. She had no idea what she was going to do, but she was going to do it until one of them was dead. Although, she reflected, it was probably going to be her.

• • •

"That's not going to be any use," Banks said as Garland ripped out a section of luggage rack.

"What do you suggest we do?" Garland said, handing him a plastic strip.

"I suppose we could try to attract its attention," Banks said.

Garland just looked at him.

• • •

Poppy braced herself. The creature's mouth was leaking venom and it was writhing in pain. She noticed that she was still holding its sting, and threw it over the side of the car, where it sank into the lake.

"Right, you wanker," said Poppy, and charged at the creature.

• • •

It hit her with the full force of its metal and bone limb. She staggered backwards, her chest heaving. She felt as though something huge had trodden on her ribcage. The creature advanced, shrieking.

This time Poppy ran at it, then, at the last minute, ran round it and leaped onto its back. Holding onto where its throat should be, she grabbed its lower jaw and began to tug at it. The creature drooled more venom onto her arms and she watched in horror as her skin began to boil and peel.

Poppy pulled harder, and harder. Then, with a sound like steel being ripped in half, the creature's jaw began to come loose. It roared now, as she used all her strength to tear whatever it had for muscles apart. The creature, jaw hanging at a crazy angle, tried to dislodge her, but she held on with one hand, battering its head with the other. She managed to get her arm under the plate covering its face, and started to bash the jelly of its eye.

The creature could not get to her with its limb, writhed and flexed to get her off, and then shrieked in agony as Poppy's fist burst its eye. She fell off its back, exhausted, trying to get her strength back. And then, as she was about to get up again for one last attack, the creature seemed almost to deflate. It collapsed, its plates shuttering up like a telescope, and it rolled over almost lazily onto her prone body, its enormous weight crushing her limbs.

Now it was Poppy's turn to scream.

• • •

Garland threw the door open and stepped out.

"I can't see a thing," Banks said as he followed her.

"There," said Garland, and they followed the creature's sunken trail.

"Is it dead?" Banks said.

"It isn't moving," said Garland.

"Where's Poppy?"

"I don't know."

"Oh no. She must have gone over the side."

"Or been killed and eaten."

• • •

"I am still here, you know," said Poppy.

• • •

Garland could just see her head, trapped under one of the plates.

"How are you even talking?" she said.

"Habit, I expect."

Banks crouched down next to her.

"Are you in pain?" he asked.

Poppy looked at him.

"Only when I laugh," she said.

• • •

"We have to get this off her," Garland said. "It's crushing her to death."

"Still here," Poppy said. "Also, it's leaking some kind of acid. I can see my skin melting."

Banks looked at Garland. "We're going to have to push."

• • •

They got behind the creature and shoved. It didn't move. They shoved again.

"I think you've actually pushed it onto me more," said Poppy.

• • •

Banks looked ahead silently.

"I think we're approaching a hill," he said.

He went back into the carriage and returned with the metal strips from the luggage rack. He gave one to Garland and stuck the end of the other one into the base of the car.

"Help me," he said to Garland, digging the end of the strip harder into the wooden floor.

•••

"Pardon me for asking," Poppy said weakly, "but what exactly are you doing?"

Garland stood back. "We've removed the planks behind it," she said.

"Behind it," Poppy said.

"The plan is to balance it just right so that when the train goes up the hill, the creature slides back down the car and into the hole, freeing you," said Banks. "Assuming, of course, that the gradient of the hill is steep enough, and you aren't crushed in the process."

There was a short silence.

"You're fucking kidding me," said Poppy.

•••

After a while, Banks and Garland had removed most of the planks behind the creature.

"I think it slipped back a little then," Banks said.

Poppy said, "It's crushing my pelvis a little more too."

"Getting a lot steeper ahead," Garland observed.

Banks leaned on his piece of luggage rack.

"All we can do now is wait," he said.

•••

The train climbed higher.

•••

The creature began to move.

•••

Poppy cried out in pain.

. . .

"It's moving!" Banks shouted.

They watched as the creature's body slid backwards.

"It's doing it!"

"Poppy? Poppy!"

. . .

Poppy opened her eyes. Instantly she was blinded, so she closed them. When she opened them again, she could see that she was inside a carriage. Garland and Banks stood over her.

"What happened?" she asked.

"It slid off you," said Garland.

"Went straight through the floor," Banks said. "Rolled right into the lake."

"What about me?" Poppy said. "Not to be, you know, selfish."

Banks said nothing.

"I don't appreciate silence," Poppy said.

Garland said. "It's hard to explain."

"Try."

Garland breathed in. "OK. First of all, you're fine."

Poppy exhaled. "You might have opened with that," she said.

"Your actual body, just some bruises. Your arms and legs, nothing broken that we can see."

Poppy sat up. The skin on her hands was holed and scorched. Underneath she could see patches of something colourless.

"Your legs are the same," said Banks.

"Could be worse," Poppy said. "I'll just have to wear gloves and long trousers."

"No," said Garland. "Wait. Look."

Poppy waited. She looked.

"Oh my," she said.

Slowly, almost invisibly, the skin on her hands was growing. If she closed her eyes for a few seconds she could see it as it returned, shrinking the discoloured area, becoming flesh-like again.

They waited for almost an hour until it had grown itself back.

"Well," said Poppy. "I didn't know I could do *that*."

• • •

"What are we celebrating?" Poppy asked.

Garland handed her a miniature of vodka.

"Just that we made it," she said. "So far, anyway."

"And by 'we'," Banks added, "I think she means 'you'."

Garland said nothing.

"Glad to be here," Poppy said.

"I'm going to get the food," said Banks, and shouldered the kitbag.

• • •

Poppy watched as Banks made his way to the door and then out across the flat car.

"What food?" she asked Garland.

"We ran through a lot of carriages," said Garland.

"Yes, but *what food*? Like cans? Juice boxes? What else did you see back there?"

Garland narrowed her eyes. "Incredible things," she said. "One carriage had a live shark in a tank in it."

"What? How did you know it was alive? Did it attack you?"

225

Garland laughed. "Got you!" she said.

"Fuck off."

"There was a shark, though."

"Fuck *off*."

"It just wasn't alive."

Poppy narrowed her eyes.

"Now I don't know if you're lying or not."

"There really was a shark."

Poppy was about to say something when Banks reappeared. He dumped the kitbag on the table.

"Have a look," he invited Poppy.

• • •

Poppy almost gasped. Inside the kitbag were apples, bananas, oranges and pears.

"They're cold," she said.

"Some sort of refrigeration process," said Banks.

"Is that fresh juice?"

"Yep," Banks said. "I prefer the wine boxes myself."

Poppy's eyes sparkled.

"Is there cake?"

"Maybe," said Banks.

"I'll pull your head off."

"Yes, there's cake."

• • •

A few minutes later, her face streaked with chocolate cake and sprayed with orange juice, Poppy sat back in her chair and released a belch of cinematic proportions.

"Lovely," said Garland.

"Fucking hell," Poppy said. "That was great. Thanks,

Banks." She giggled. "Sorry," she said.

"It's just a name," Banks said. "It's not even my name, really."

"Should we call you by your real name?" asked Garland.

"No," said Banks. "I think I'll stick with Banks. It's more me."

"Thanks, Banks," said Poppy, and snorted until chocolate came out of her nose.

"I'm going to have a nap," Banks said, when Poppy had finally stopped. "Some way over there."

• • •

Banks's snores faded into muttered grunts.

"A couple of things I don't understand," Garland began.

"Here we go," Poppy said.

"What?"

"After the action, the inquisition."

"I don't know what you mean."

"Yes you do," said Poppy. "This is like when I was – before. Whenever I came back from a race, even if I'd won – and I always did win – there would be the inquiry. The *questions*. The interrogation."

"I was just –"

"People always are *just*."

Poppy sighed. "Go on, then," she said. "The couple of things you don't understand."

"Let's leave it."

"Let's not."

A few seconds passed.

"All right then," said Garland. "First of all, the train was moving. How did you get back on so easily?"

"Easily?" asked Poppy. "I nearly lost a finger. I nearly lost a *foot*. With these things —" she held up her hands, "— a lot of things are possible. I could go through you like butter. But a moving train? I had to dig in. Run, and dig, and climb, and dig, and climb."

She shook her head. "'Easily'," she said. "There's gratitude."

"Oh," said Garland. "No. I'm not taking that. I am grateful. Banks is too. I can't tell you how grateful. But —"

"And now," said Poppy, in the graceful tones of a television announcer, "the *but*."

Garland ignored her.

"Back there," she said, "you could have died."

"No shit," Poppy said. "That thing was heavy."

"You know what I mean."

Poppy shrugged. "I could have died a lot of times. We all could."

"Yes, but all those other times when we could have died, it wasn't a choice. But you chose to engage that creature."

"I didn't choose," Poppy said. "I just went for it, without thinking. Lucky for you. If the train hadn't been moving, and I'd had a moment to think about it, I might not have gone back after it."

"You think so?"

"No idea," Poppy said cheerfully. "Anyway, it's done."

"It's done," Garland agreed. "You got back on the train, even though it was moving and there was a monster on top of it, and even though the last thing you wanted to be doing was getting back on the train."

"I wouldn't go that far."

"I would. Tell me –" Garland fixed Poppy with a look far steelier than usual, "– which was harder: attacking that creature, or getting back on the train?"

Poppy returned Garland's gaze.

"Like I said," she replied. "I didn't have a choice."

• • •

The sky was full of lights now, distant explosions of red and yellow that burst too far away to illuminate the night landscape.

"I wonder what's out there," said Poppy.

"It can't just be stations," Garland replied.

"I don't see why not. The world could just be stations, for all we know. No more cities, no more towns. Just stations."

Poppy unwrapped one last bar of chocolate.

"The stations of the cross," she said. "Or at least," she added, looking at the explosions blooming in the distance, "the very angry."

Suddenly, Garland sat up in her seat.

"Banks?" she asked. "Are you all right?"

Poppy turned, and saw that Banks was twisting and turning in his seat at the other end of the carriage, his face and hands flattened against the window.

"I think he can see something," she said.

"Too right I can see something," came Banks's muffled voice. "Come and look!"

They were on a long bend. The train was curving as it sped along.

· · ·

"Oh my Lord," Garland said.

Banks said, "I was starting to think there wasn't one."

"This window is filthy," Poppy complained. "I can't see anything."

Banks pulled her over.

"There," he said.

"Jumping fuck," said Poppy.

· · ·

Outside the murky glass, hard to see but just about distinguishable from the lights of the carriages, slightly ahead of the bend, was the front of the train.

· · ·

"How near are we?" Garland said.

"I'm trying to count the carriages," said Banks. "There's a lot."

"I bet some of them are buffet cars," Poppy said.

· · ·

After a while the track straightened out again and they sat down.

"I can't quite believe it," said Garland.

"It's just a train," Poppy pointed out. "It's got to have an end."

"Everything's got to have an end," agreed Banks.

"It's there. It's out there," Garland said. "We've spent so long getting here, and it's there. It's –"

"– attainable," said Banks.

· · ·

Poppy said, "The thing that got me was how ordinary it was. The front of the train, I mean. Does it have a name? Is it the engine? The tender? The puller?"

"It's not called the puller," said Banks. "I know what you mean, though. I feel like it should be more dramatic."

"Like maybe it should have had flags on the front, or horns," said Garland.

"Or teeth," Poppy said. "Huge metal ones, with blood on them."

There was a short silence after that.

"Maybe not teeth," Poppy conceded.

• • •

The train sped on through the night.

"This is where someone says we should all get some sleep because we've got a long day tomorrow," said Poppy.

"You say it, I'm exhausted," Banks replied. Garland merely continued snoring.

Poppy began to drift into sleep. Banks covered her with the edge of the kitbag.

"Thanks, Banks," she murmured.

Banks sighed.

• • •

"Banks," said Poppy, half awake, "was there really a shark back there?"

Banks replied with a long, gentle snore.

"I knew it," said Poppy, and closed her eyes.

• • •

Hours passed and they all slept deeply.

• • •

In the ceiling of the carriage, a small light came on, blinked red for a few seconds, and went off again.

· · ·

Further down the train, another red light came on. It too blinked red, but instead of turning off, it began to blink out a repeating sequence of flashes, finally attracting the attention of a light-sensitive monitor set into the wall. The monitor registered the series of flashes, and responded to the signal by accessing a series of cameras up and down the train. Some of the cameras were damaged, and others had been destroyed, but most were still working.

One of the working cameras was in the carriage where Banks, Poppy and Garland were now asleep. It began to film them as they slept.

· · ·

"Anyone hungry?" Banks asked.

Poppy shook her head. "Can you get a hangover from eating chocolate?" she asked, reaching for a bottle of water.

"The amount you ate, I'm surprised you're still alive," said Garland.

"Chocolate can't kill you," Poppy said.

"It can if you're a dog."

"Yes," said Poppy, "but I'm not a dog."

· · ·

Unseen by them, the camera continued to film.

· · ·

"Are we ready?" Poppy said.

"Unless you want the toilet again," Banks said.

"There'll be other toilets," said Poppy.

"Let's just go," said Garland.

Banks hoisted the kitbag onto his shoulders and they made their way down the carriage.

232

"How many carriages?" Garland asked again.

She sounded nervous.

• • •

The next carriage was so odd it almost seemed to be showing off. There were zebra-skin couches with platform boots for feet, old photographs hung upside down on the walls, a carpet made of repeating images of someone wearing a large crown, and an old bath painted gold and filled with rubber bats.

"It's trying too hard," said Garland.

"I know what you mean," Poppy agreed. "What's this?" she said, stopping by a garish block of transparent red and yellow plastic material. Its innards were visible and filled with black slices of plastic.

"It's a jukebox," said Banks. "Young people, I don't know."

He looked at the box. There was a typewritten list pasted to its front. Banks began to read out loud.

"'Downbound Train Chuck Berry Love In Vain Robert Johnson Rail Gaadi Chirag Pehchan Mangal Singh Morningtown Ride,'" he read in a monotone.

Then he jabbed at some small numbered and lettered buttons.

After a moment, he stopped.

"It doesn't work," he said, sounding disappointed.

"Of course it doesn't," said Poppy. "It's not even plugged in."

Just as she was pointing at a flex which dangled uselessly from the back of the box, one of the plastic slices suddenly detached itself from a metal arm and flopped down onto a column.

An awful tearing noise issued from the box. Banks kicked it, and it subsided into a crackle. Then music began to play.

"This is different," said Garland.

• • •

A thoughtful voice began to sing over a galloping beat. It was a beautiful voice, and it sang in a beautiful language.

• • •

"I can't understand it," said Poppy, frowning.

• • •

"Listen to the rhythm," Banks said. "It's a train song. They're all train songs."

• • •

"I know what he's singing," said Garland. "I don't know how, but I do."

She listened for a moment, then said:

"My princess, my princess is gone
Never to return
I have waited so long
I will wait for all time."

• • •

"Very nice," said Poppy. "I wonder what it means."

"Onwards," said Banks.

• • •

Garland stood there for a moment.

• • •

"I have waited so long," the song told them. *"So long."*

• • •

"Onwards," she agreed.

• • •

The next carriage was a buffet car.

"These people *really* love their food," Poppy said.

"It's good food," said Banks.

• • •

The next carriage was perfectly normal, except someone had painted it white.

"They even painted the carpet," Banks said, tracing a finger over the stiff white fabric.

"Onwards," said Garland, again.

"I hate to be the one to ask," Poppy said, "but are we nearly there yet?"

• • •

The next carriage made them gasp.

• • •

"This is beautiful," Banks said.

"It is," agreed Poppy. "I mean, the turtles were better, but this is pretty good."

"How long must it have taken?" Garland wondered.

• • •

They were looking at, of all things, a model railway. It was composed of several metres of miniature track, complete with trains, stations, forests and rivers. The trains and the station platforms were populated with tiny people and even animals.

"What's that?" asked Poppy.

"It's a dog," said Banks. "Honestly, young people."

"You don't remember dogs," she said. "You're not that old."

Banks changed the subject.

"Is this the train we're on, do you think?" he said, pointing down at a long, metallic-looking train with several carriages.

"It would be weird if it wasn't," said Poppy.

"A lot cleaner," Garland said.

"The whole thing's a lot cleaner," Banks said. "I mean, look at this landscape."

They looked at the landscape. It was an ocean of green rolling hills, verdant trees, sparkling blue lakes and even snowy mountains.

"Wait a second," Poppy said, bending over. "I know that mountain."

"Really?" said Garland.

"Yes," said Poppy. "It's a lot bigger in real life –"

She returned their stares.

"I mean, in scale it's a lot bigger," she said, tersely. "In relation to this landscape."

"Just checking," said Banks.

"But it's the same. Same shape, same slope."

"Look," said Garland, picking up a tiny figure. It was a skier, complete with skis and poles. "It's you."

Poppy shivered. "Don't say that," she said. "Put it back."

"Sorry," said Garland.

Banks crouched down and looked at the track. "Poppy's right about the proportions," he said. "This is the station we were at before, the first one, and it's not to scale at all."

"Probably couldn't fit it in the carriage otherwise," said Garland. "Wait," she added. "If this is a model of the train we're on, and this landscape is the places we know, then this is –"

She looked at the others.

"This is a map," she said.

"Oh great, another map," Poppy said.

"I don't think she shares your enthusiasm," said Banks.

Garland took out her paper map.

"It doesn't correlate," she said, shaking her head. "The tracks don't form a figure of eight."

"Maybe because this is meant to be old," said Banks. "Like this landscape is from the past."

"Hence why it's all green?" Poppy asked. "Like, when's the last time you saw a tree?"

"I've seen loads of –" Garland stopped. "I don't know when I last saw a tree."

"Me neither," said Poppy. "In a simulation, I guess."

"When I was at school, there were plenty of trees," Banks said.

"When was that?" Garland asked.

Banks looked confused. "I don't know," he said.

Poppy said, quietly, "How old *are* you, Banks?"

"I don't know that either," Banks replied. "I remember the school, and Park and – I remember it all like it was yesterday. But it wasn't, was it?"

He looked at the model landscape, and then at the window. Yellow stars burst in the sky.

"How long have I been on this train?" he asked.

Garland said, "Maybe longer than you think." She put her arm around him.

"I feel like I've been here for ever, I know that," said Poppy. She laid a hand on Banks's shoulder, as gently as she could.

• • •

Garland made drawings of the train layout.

"I wish I could just take a photograph," she said.

Poppy got down on her hands and knees and crawled about underneath the landscape.

"There's all wires here," she said. "Hang on."

She emerged from beneath the table.

"Lights," she said, as the model train began to illuminate itself from within.

"How is that happening?" Banks said. "It's not plugged into anything."

The tiny village in the mountains lit up too, as did the floodlights on the platform.

"It's going to start playing Christmas songs in a minute," said Poppy. She vanished under the table again and came back with a small brown box.

"What's that?" said Garland.

"I know," Banks said. "Controls. Can I have a go?"

"Wait your turn," Poppy said, teasingly. She pressed a switch and pulled a toggle. The train began to move, slowly at first, then picking up speed.

"Careful," Garland said.

"Please let me," Banks all but begged as the train accelerated.

"It's fine," said Poppy. "I'm in control."

The train sped up, racing towards the forest. Then it jarred against the edge of the track, flew free of the rails, and fell from the table onto the floor where it smashed, broke in half and lay there, sparking.

They looked at the broken wreck of the model train for a minute.

"Onwards," suggested Banks.

• • •

The next carriage was empty, and every surface was mirrored. They found it hard to keep their balance.

"This is like being in zero gravity, except I'm still heavy," said Banks.

"Please don't tell me I look like that," Poppy said.

Garland said, "OK then, I won't."

• • •

The carriage after that was locked.

"Means we're getting somewhere," Garland said.

"Not if we can't get in," Banks pointed out.

"Oh, we can always get in," said Poppy. She drew back her fist.

"Wait a second," Garland said. "We don't have to smash the place up every time."

"I don't see why not."

Banks and Garland searched around for a key.

"All right then," said Poppy. "Stand back, everyone."

Garland and Banks were about to step away from the door when they heard a rattle and a click.

The door opened.

• • •

A man was standing in the doorway. He was wearing a blue jacket with gold piping and had on a peaked cap to match. In one hand he held a silver whistle, and in the other some kind of mechanical device.

He beamed at them over the top of his gold-rimmed glasses.

"Tickets, please," he said.

• • •

"Excuse me?" Garland said.

The man beamed again. "Tickets, please," he said.

Poppy stepped forward.

"Do we look like we've got tickets?" she asked.

"Not for me to say," the man replied. "Nor is it for me to judge by appearances. I'm just here to see your tickets."

"We haven't got any tickets," said Banks, and he sounded regretful.

The man looked, if anything, slightly shocked by this information.

"Then how did you get on this train?" he asked.

"Oh fuck off," said Poppy. "This is a joke, right?"

"We don't know how we got on this train," said Garland. "We don't know where we are or how we got here."

"This is most irregular," said the man. "You'll have to come with me."

"What if we don't want to come with you?" asked Poppy.

"I want to come with him," Garland said.

"Nothing to lose," agreed Banks.

"That's the spirit," said the ticket collector.

"We'll see," Poppy said.

• • •

They barely registered the next carriage (buffet car, mauve interior) as the ticket collector led them into it. From time to time, he muttered to himself.

"That's it," he said, occasionally adding, as if to reassure himself, "He'll know what to do."

"Who's 'he'?" asked Garland. "The driver?"

"Oh goodness no," said the ticket collector. "Goodness me, no."

"Are you for real?" Poppy said. "Or just animatronic? Because you sound like you should be in a theme park."

"Sticks and stones," said the ticket collector. "Not far to go now."

"Have we met before?" Banks said to the collector.

"I don't believe so," he replied.

"You look really familiar." He turned to Garland. "Doesn't he?"

"Yes," Garland agreed.

"He's a clone," said Poppy. "Same as the soldiers."

"Let's just keep moving," the collector said, prodding Banks again.

"Are you?" asked Poppy. "Are you a clone?"

"I don't think that's an acceptable word," Garland said.

• • •

The rest of the walk passed in silence.

• • •

As they entered the next carriage the bursts of light in the sky were turning silver, and becoming more frequent.

"It seems to be getting brighter outside," Banks said.

"Blue skies are promised," said the collector. He looked confused by his own words. "Just electrical interference," he said. "Nothing to worry about."

• • •

The next carriage was extremely ordinary. The seats and tables seemed cleaner than usual, with new fabric on the

241

chairs and no scratches on the tabletops.

"Sit down, please," said the ticket collector.

"I don't believe it," Garland said, pulling something down from the luggage rack.

"It's another book," Poppy said.

"It's the same book," Banks noted.

"Please put it back," the ticket collector said.

"I intend to," said Garland. "It's unreadable."

"I really must insist," said the collector.

"She's doing it," said Banks. "He seems a bit rattled," he added.

"Well, it's just us and him," Poppy replied. "He's clone alone."

"That's enough," said the ticket collector, and there was a new harshness in his voice. He took something out of his coat. It was an electric cattle prod.

"Do you know what this is?"

Garland looked at Poppy.

"I told you to stop using that word."

"I bet it's OK if he says it."

"Just stop it."

• • •

Garland put the book back in the rack and they sat down, watched by the collector.

"We could disarm him," she said.

"With smiles and charm?" asked Poppy.

"With physical force."

"Can't be bothered," said Poppy. "Besides, we're going to find out what's going on soon enough."

"I suppose so."

"My," said Banks, "we *are* infused with the commando spirit today."

• • •

"I wonder how many of these tables we've sat down at," said Poppy.

"One or two," replied Garland. "Where's he going?" she added, as the ticket collector disappeared through a door.

Poppy leapt to her feet.

• • •

"This door's locked," she said.

"Of course it is," said Banks.

"I'm just saying."

• • •

Poppy sat down again.

• • •

"I mean, a conductor," she said after a while.

"He said ticket collector," Banks corrected.

"I think it's the same thing. Either way, it doesn't matter if he calls himself the Akond of Swat, he's clearly gone to get the boss."

"The driver," said Garland.

"I don't think it's the driver. Who'd be driving the train?"

"The conductor, then."

"He is the conductor."

"Let's not go there again."

• • •

Time passed, not quickly.

• • •

"This is it, then," said Banks. He didn't look happy.

"Whatever *it* is," Garland replied.

"Good," said Poppy. "I'm sick of walking through carriages, and meeting weird things, and… and buffet cars. I just want something to happen."

"I don't," said Banks. "I very much don't want something to happen."

"What about you?" Poppy asked Garland.

"I just want to get to the front of the train and meet the driver," said Garland.

"What for, though?" said Poppy. "You get to the front, you meet the driver and what?"

"Then I ask him," said Garland.

"Ask him what?" said a new voice.

• • •

The door between the carriages had opened, and the ticket collector had returned. Standing with him was another man. He was tall, and broad, his long blond hair streaked with grey and tied in a ponytail, and he was wearing a red shirt covered in images of blue parrots and faded pink baggy cotton pants that went down to his knees and were fastened with a drawstring. They stared at him for a few seconds.

"It's a look, I suppose," said Poppy.

• • •

"Come with me, why don'cha?" said the man. "Put that thing away, these people are our guests," he told the ticket collector, who reluctantly shoved his cattle prod back into his coat.

"Name's Lincoln," he said.

244

"Banks," said Banks. "Garland, Poppy."

"Yeah, I know," said Lincoln.

"Where did you come from?" Garland asked.

"I just blew in from the Emerald City," he replied.

He looked at them all and grinned.

"You hungry?" he asked.

"Always room for more," said Banks.

• • •

The restaurant car was entirely sumptuous. Wooden tables, bolted to the floor, were covered in blinding white linen tablecloths. Crystal glass and silver cutlery were laid at each seat, and across one wall was a bar stocked with a globe's worth of drinks.

"Take a load off," said Lincoln.

They sat down and he smiled.

"You're probably wondering why I called you all in here," he said in a peculiar voice.

"Yes," said Banks. "We are."

He grinned. "Guess not everyone's *au fait* with the cultural references. Never mind. *Garçon!*"

From nowhere, a waiter appeared.

"What," said Poppy, "the fuck?"

"They're trained to be silent," said Lincoln. "And when I say trained, I mean bred."

The waiter looked remarkably like the ticket collector.

"Another one?" said Garland.

"Cheaper by the dozen," Lincoln replied. He picked up a thin leather pad and opened it.

"I'll have the usual," he said, putting it down again.

"They'll have the same."

"Oh, will we?" Poppy said.

"Dude," said Lincoln. "You're eating with me. You're in the favoured position of being at the table with the choicest morsels."

"Is he quoting something?" asked Banks.

"Don't ask me," said Garland, "I just learned to read."

"Oh, that's right," said Lincoln. "Denning did do that."

"You know Denning?" said Poppy, tensing.

"Honey, I know everyone and everything," Lincoln said. "I know, for example, that I just have to press this –"

He produced a small black box from his red parrot shirt.

"– and you'll be jerking like a marionette."

Poppy grabbed at the box. Lincoln put it in his pocket.

"Emits a disruptive charge," he said. "Like an EMP only smaller. Not that you'd appreciate the benefit, seeing as you'd be trying to stop your own hands from clawing off your face."

He smiled at them.

"Let's enjoy our lunch," he said.

• • •

The food came and it was unusually good.

"This is champagne?" said Garland as the waiter filled their glasses.

"Cristal," said Lincoln, and for the first time he looked apologetic. "Rappers used to drink it."

"Used to?" said Poppy.

"Rappers?" said Garland.

"It's very yellow," Banks added.

"You three." Lincoln sat back in his seat and grinned. "You're quite the superhero team-up."

Poppy held up her bear.

"Don't forget Teddy," she said.

• • •

Sometime later, Poppy sat back and belched, deep and loud.

"I wish you'd stop doing that," Garland said.

"You're not my mother," said Poppy.

Lincoln said, "You sure about that?"

Poppy stared at him.

"Joking," Lincoln said.

"Thank God," said Garland.

Lincoln drained his Cristal.

"See," he said, "what I like about you guys is the – what's the word? – the sheer lack of curiosity. Here we are, three courses in, and you haven't asked me one single question. I mean, we're on a train, for God's sake, sixteen coaches long –"

"It's more than sixteen," said Banks.

"I think he's quoting," Garland said.

"– and none of you have asked me, I dunno, why are we on a train? Where are we going? Who am I?"

He leaned in and looked at them, one by one.

"Who are you?"

"That's not true," Garland said. "Everything we've done has been to find out what's happening."

"Not for me," said Banks. "I know as much as I want to know. I just want a quiet life." He helped himself to some more Cristal.

"Strike one," said Lincoln.

"Poppy here wants to know what's going on," Garland said. "She even got off the train."

"Then she got back on again. Strike two," Lincoln said. "Which leaves you."

"Me?" said Garland, looking affronted. "I'm the one who made everyone head up the train. I'm the one who wants to find out. All those questions you asked, that's what I want to know."

"Haven't tried too hard to find out though, have you?" said Lincoln. "I mean, all you've done is walk up the train."

Garland said, "That's not –"

"He's trying to make you angry," Poppy said.

"He's succeeding," said Garland. To Lincoln she said, "All I have done since I woke up on this train is try and find out what is going on."

"And yet you missed so many opportunities," Lincoln said. "There's a whole library here and you didn't open one book."

"What do you mean?" Garland said.

Banks produced the book they'd found from his kitbag.

"Not so literal," said Lincoln, laughing. "That's just a book somebody left behind. Family heirloom kind of thing. I ain't talking about that kind of book or that kind of library at all."

"What are you fucking talking about?" Poppy said.

"I might have to zap you anyway," Lincoln said. He sighed.

"You've all got this place wrong. It's not a train. It's a

book. These aren't carriages – they're chapters. And if you read a book right, if you look for the clues, you'll find what you're looking for."

He looked at Garland.

"But you, lady… you haven't been looking at all. You know why? Because you're scared of what you might find."

• • •

Garland got up and left the table. She walked to the end of the restaurant car and looked out into the night. She could see her reflection in the glass. It looked troubled, and uncertain.

A memory returned to her.

She was standing in a room, on one side of a long black box that had been placed on black trestles. On the other side of the box, Denning was talking.

He said, "You know that if you consent to this, you'll lose almost everything you had?"

She knew he was trying to discern what she really thought, but in the last few years she had become adept at hiding her feelings behind a bland expression.

"Am I consenting to this?" she asked.

Denning nodded. "I admit this is being rather imposed on you from above –"

She raised an eyebrow.

"No," he said, "not from above. But yes, a decision has been made, with which you are not involved, and as such 'consent' isn't perhaps the right word. Nevertheless," and as he said the word, his lips pulled back from his teeth, "you have been offered the option of continuing."

"And what you are asking me to continue is not acceptable to me," she said.

"Shame," said Denning. "It would have made for an easier transition. You are more popular than –"

He nodded at the box.

"Be careful," she said. "He may be gone and I may be going, but you should still choose your words with forethought."

"Oh, I always do," he said. He took a piece of paper from his coat pocket. "As you'll see when you read this."

"A contract?"

"A consent form," he said. "We may be protecting you, but that doesn't mean you can just walk away. You know too much. Sign this, and that problem will be… erased."

She took the paper.

"We both know I'm not going to walk away from this," she said, placing the paper on the black box. Denning produced a pen.

"Then why agree?" he asked.

"What else can I do?" Garland replied, and signed the paper.

• • •

She returned to the table. The ticket collector stood behind Lincoln, as though awaiting instructions.

Banks was finishing the Cristal while Poppy picked her teeth with a fingernail.

"Denning," Garland said. "What did he do to me?"

"Finally, a question," said Lincoln. "Nothing you didn't know he was going to do."

"Did he take my memory?" she asked.

"That was the deal."

"Why?"

"He didn't want people to know who you were. The best way to ensure that was to make sure you didn't know who you were."

"Why can't I read? Was that part of the deal?"

"Not as far as you were concerned. As far as he was concerned, that was a safety measure. Didn't want to prompt any memories."

"How come it's coming back?"

Lincoln shrugged.

"It was a new technology. Untested and faulty."

He stood up.

"I think that's enough questions for now," he said.

Poppy said, "Just like that? I think she's got more questions."

"I can speak for myself," Garland said. "I mean, you're right but…"

"I don't think you understand how things go down round here," said Lincoln. He turned to the ticket collector, who had remained silent through the conversation.

"I need you to stand over there," he said.

"Whatever you say," the collector replied. As he walked over to the far wall, Lincoln took out a gun.

"Is here OK?" asked the collector.

"It's fine," said Lincoln, and shot him in the face. "You see," he explained to Poppy, "from where you sit, this is pretty much my train. Let's move on. There's so much more to see."

Two waiters appeared. They opened the train door and threw out the ticket collector's body.

Poppy lunged at Lincoln and grabbed his throat. Before she could choke him, Lincoln tapped his shirt pocket and she fell to the floor, her legs twisting underneath her. He hit the pocket again and she stopped moving.

"Like I said, my train," said Lincoln, as Banks and Garland helped her stand. "Now come on."

• • •

The next carriage was a conference room. It had a row of TV monitors circled round the walls where the windows should have been, and it was entirely filled by a long, oval wooden table with chairs set around it. The chairs made it hard to manoeuvre around the table, but Lincoln didn't seem particularly bothered by this.

"At least we're moving further towards the front of the train," said Banks.

"Always looking on the bright side," Poppy replied.

• • •

The carriage after the conference room was a bare shell. The floor was covered in zig-zag metal plate, reinforced to carry extra weight. The extra weight was a car. A huge red open-topped car, with white wall tyres and a silver grille.

"I pushed for an enclosed vehicle," said Lincoln, "so we could armour it up a little. But he said it was for personal use, by which he meant sitting in, because he couldn't drive for shit."

"Who?" asked Banks, but Lincoln ignored him.

"There were only three of these built in the world," he

said. "He had the other two compacted, as well as the people who owned them. He wasn't too hot on competition."

"I'm not really interested in cars," Poppy said.

"Shame," said Lincoln. "Because this might be the last one you ever see."

He leaned over the front of the car.

"Look at that," he said. "Beautiful detail."

On top of the grille, at the very front of the car, was a silver ornament, a tiny figure. It was a crucifix, and on it a half-naked figure, arms stretched, head lowered.

"Nice touch, eh?" said Lincoln. "You could never tell with him if he was being serious. I think this was one of the occasions when he wasn't."

He turned and looked at the others.

"You ever think about taste?" he asked.

"Like salt and sweet?" said Banks.

"Like good and bad," said Lincoln. "I mean, to me this thing is beautiful. Imagine how much it cost. The leather on the seats alone is worth more than I am. It's a work of art if you ask me. But Denning – he hated it. He said it was the worst trash imaginable." Lincoln brightened. "Where's he now, eh?"

"He –" began Banks.

"Be quiet," said Garland abruptly.

"It's OK," Lincoln said. "It was a rhetorical question. I have cameras everywhere, I know exactly where Denning is."

"Soup," confirmed Poppy. "Salt, not sweet."

"It was you," Garland said to Lincoln. "You put him in that room. With those things."

"Not me," said Lincoln. "Well, yeah, it was me, in the sense that I gave the order. But I was, y'know, acting in the spirit."

"What spirit?" said Banks.

"The spirit," Lincoln replied, "of the Leader."

. . .

He looked at them again.

"Wow," he said. "They really did a number on you."

. . .

"I know I'm going to hate myself," Poppy said, "but who is the Leader?"

"Was," said Lincoln.

"Is he the reason we're on this train?" asked Garland.

"Honey, he's the reason, full stop. He's the reason the sun comes up in the morning."

"The sun doesn't come up in the morning," said Poppy.

"Good point," said Lincoln. "It will, though. We've been working on that. Just a matter of firing up the ionosphere."

"You're kidding," said Garland.

"You think the explosions in the sky are a big party?" said Lincoln. "Oh wait. You probably think they're the apocalypse."

"I would have said apocalypse," Banks said. "If asked."

"Yeah, well, not asked," snapped Lincoln. "You people. I don't know."

He checked his gun, spinning the chamber.

"Five," he said. "Just making sure."

. . .

They looked at the car some more. Garland reached into

the glove compartment, but Lincoln stopped her.

"No more clues," he said.

He stepped back.

"Hey! Who wants to go into the bedroom?"

Before anyone could reply, he brandished the gun again.

"Rhetorical," he said.

. . .

They squeezed around the car to the next door.

"After you," said Lincoln to Banks.

Banks opened the door and they went in.

. . .

"This is a *bedroom*?" said Poppy.

. . .

The next carriage was opulent. Mirrors hung on every wall, gilt-framed and laden with cherubs. Heavy curtains hung around the windows, and the floor was carpeted in blue and gold.

"What is that symbol?" asked Poppy, pointing at the carpet.

"You don't know?" asked Lincoln. He sounded surprised.

"I've seen it on the carriages," said Banks. "I thought it was the badge of the train company."

"The train company," said Lincoln, shaking his head. "Tyrants have bowed down before that symbol, you know. Nations have trembled at the sight of it. The Leader used to have it branded on the faces of his opponents. It's a sign of fear, and a sign of empire."

Poppy said, "So not the train company then."

. . .

"This room is ridiculous," Garland said. She was looking at the bed. It had a huge gilt column at each corner, carved with more symbols and supporting a thick canopy. The canopy was made of blue and gold satin, as were the bedspread and the pillows.

"Matching collar and cuffs," said Poppy. "Nice."

. . .

There was a dressing table, with a gilt-framed mirror and a selection of hairbrushes. Banks opened a drawer. It was crammed with pill bottles. He took one out and squinted at the label.

"Benzedrine," he read.

"The Leader was often required to stay awake for long periods of time as he planned affairs of state."

Banks picked up another bottle.

"Viagra," he read.

Lincoln shrugged. "Like I said, affairs of state."

"Penicillin," said Banks, reading a third label.

. . .

"He lived here?" said Banks.

"This was the Leader's personal carriage," said Lincoln. "When there was a Leader, and there were places for him to go. This was his personal train."

"So all the things here were his?" asked Garland. "The apartments? The cages?"

"The buffet cars?" said Banks.

"The turtles," Poppy said, wistfully.

"Not all, no," said Lincoln. "Things changed, you see. The world changed. You wouldn't recognise it how it was and how it is now. But it changed, and it changed a lot. So the personal train became the government train, which didn't make a great deal of difference at first, because, you know, the Leader and the government…"

He pressed his hands together.

"… so it was easier. Everyone in the same boat, or at least train. He could get around, he was safe, he could run things and it was a home from home."

Lincoln looked at Garland.

"You remember any of this?"

Garland shook her head.

"I remember Denning," she said. "But that's all."

"It'll come," said Lincoln. "Did everyone drink their Cristal?"

Banks nodded. Poppy froze.

"He poisoned it!" she shouted. "The fucker!"

Before she could move, Lincoln raised the black box over his head.

"I didn't," he said. "Why would I? I've got this, I've got a gun, I've got guards."

Lincoln smiled. "Process of thought," he said. "Synapses firing in the brain, all that. Electrical connections, leading to new ideas and, equally, old memories. There was something in the Cristal, but it wasn't poison."

"Then what was it?" said Garland.

"Call it memory relaxant," Lincoln replied. "Because I think it's time you knew everything again."

He opened another drawer in the dressing table.

"But it's going to take a while," he said, and pulled out a

small paper packet. "So who wants to see some old snaps?"

. . .

There were ten photographs in the packet. The first showed a large, clearly new train festooned with ribbons and rosettes. A small group of people posed in front of the train, one holding a large bottle.

"See anyone you know?" asked Lincoln.

"There's you," said Poppy. "Only less fat."

"While ago," agreed Lincoln. "Anyone else?"

Garland noticed a thin, serious face. "Denning," she said.

"No show without Punch," said Lincoln. "Now, a little test for you all, see if the memories are returning. Can you see our dear Leader?"

They scanned the picture.

"Is it the man holding the bottle?" asked Poppy.

"Nope," said Lincoln. "He's just holding it before the Leader takes it from him. And he's terrified he's gonna drop it."

"Is it one of the men in the big hats?" Banks asked.

"The generals? They wish. They're just there for show."

"He killed them," said Garland. "Denning. He tricked them and he killed them. I was there."

"Right," said Lincoln. "I heard that, but it's nice to have an eyewitness account. But you still haven't identified the Leader."

"I'm bored now," said Poppy.

"And I am tempted to give you a little jolt, young lady." Lincoln sighed. He jabbed the photograph.

"That one," he said.

"No way," said Poppy.

"He looks like he works in a shop," said Banks.

They were looking at a small, chubby man with grey hair and glasses.

Garland said, "Are you sure?" Lincoln walked over to the far wall and pulled away a curtain. Behind it was a small framed portrait of a man. The painter had given him rosy apple cheeks and the smile of a loveable grandpa, but it was still recognisable as the man in the photograph.

"I'm sure," said Lincoln.

• • •

They went back to the other photographs. There was Poppy, in her skiwear, and in formal dress at a banquet.

"You were elite," said Lincoln. "Even if you couldn't ski for shit, you were from one of the Families."

"What families?"

Lincoln ignored her. "It's you," he said, sliding a photograph over to Banks. "My, aren't you pretty. *Weren't*," he corrected himself.

Banks slid the picture back. "I don't need to see that to know who I was," he said.

"I think you look better now," said Poppy.

"I agree," Garland said.

"Gee, get a room," Lincoln said. He sounded disappointed. Then he brightened again.

"What have we here?" he said, handing a picture to Garland.

It was the largest of the photographs, blurry and black-and-white. It showed a small heap of something, white and indistinct. The heap was dead people. In front of it stood someone holding a gun and looking pleased with herself. It was Garland.

"Target practice," said Lincoln. "Don't worry, they were enemies of the state."

. . .

"That's not me," said Garland.

"How do you know?" said Lincoln. "You can't even remember what you were doing last week. Hey! Maybe this is what you were doing!"

Garland took the picture and crumpled it up.

"Three scientists, two of 'em married, and an author," said Lincoln. "Point-blank range. Some people have weird hobbies."

"I don't remember this!" Garland said. She might have been shouting. Poppy put an arm around her.

Banks looked at Lincoln.

"I don't like you," he said, "and I don't like what you're doing. You're an unpleasant man and you're enjoying this, which is disgusting. Stop torturing us and tell us the truth."

Lincoln put the photographs back in the packet.

"Wow," he said. "The worm turns."

He sighed.

"OK then. The truth."

SIX

A long time ago (Lincoln told them) there was a world
and it worked.

. . .

It was degenerate and it was disordered, but it worked.
People walked around in all weathers and told each other
that they liked it. They ate some animals and kept others for
fun, and they did the same with plants too. They didn't eat
each other but they did pretty much everything else.

. . .

They had to work, but less so as time went on. This was
partly because a lot of work was unpleasant and they got
someone or something else to do it, but also because
people didn't really like working. What they liked was
talking to each other and taking photographs of each
other, and taking photos of themselves and each other, and
their animals and plants (both the ones they were eating

and the ones they kept for fun). You can bet they took a lot of photographs.

• • •

They got on, generally. There were wars, but as these were work, little robots started fighting the wars instead. People were relieved, because originally they were going to fight the wars with big rockets, so little robots were a lot better.

• • •

What with the reduction in work, and the robots fighting the wars, and the photographs, everything was very nice. The people had a world and it worked.

• • •

And then one day everybody woke up to find the world didn't work any more.

• • •

"What is this?" Poppy said. "This is a fairy tale."

• • •

"It's not," said Lincoln. "It's what happened. How I see it, anyway."

• • •

"Let him tell it," said Garland.

• • •

And then one day (Lincoln continued) the world didn't work any more. The air wasn't blue, it was black. And the black air killed the animals, and then the plants. The drones started to crash, and so did everything else. The world was broken, and nobody could fix it.

• • •

People couldn't agree on how it had happened. Some said

it was the environment, meaning the world had got too hot or too polluted, which was probably because of all the different ways people had found to avoid working. Some said God was angry with people, which was possible but unlikely, because normally there was an Ark when that happened, and this time there was no way out. And still other people said it was the photographs, because there were a lot of photographs, but nobody was printing them out, or throwing them away, and every day there were more and more photographs.

. . .

"I don't think it was the photographs," said Banks. "That's a joke, surely."

. . .

"Yeah?" said Lincoln. "At one point, people were taking more pictures on their damn cameras in a day than everyone in the entire history of the world had taken in a hundred years. So there were a lot of photographs."

. . .

The world worked, and then it didn't. People kind of went to pieces. This is when the Leader appeared. He was the Leader because he knew how to lead. I mean, really lead. He got the people together, got an army together. He started the world again, and nearly got it working. Made it run, you might say.

. . .

There were people who disagreed with him. They were trouble but not for long. But there were people who were trouble, so there were wars and this time they were wars with big rockets. The skies went from black to white to grey, and some of the cities disappeared. It would have been a lot worse, only nothing worked properly, including the big rockets.

And when the smoke had cleared – not literally, it's still out there – there was nothing left but the trains.

· · ·

"Trains plural?" said Garland.

· · ·

"Let him tell it," Banks said.

· · ·

The trains were the thing now, you see (Lincoln went on). They could hold a lot of people, and they were fast, and hard to stop, and hard to hit. People had mostly given up on the cities, and the country was kind of lawless, so the trains were where a lot of people went. In the end, even us. We were the last government, and we came here.

· · ·

"I have some questions," Poppy said.

· · ·

"No you don't," said Lincoln.

· · ·

He sat back and folded his arms.

· · ·

"And that's the truth?" said Banks.

"All the truth that's fit to print," Lincoln said. "Obviously, I've edited here and there. The whole thing took more than a year or two, as I'm sure you can imagine."

"You've left out everything important," Poppy said.

"Like who Garland is, and how she got here, and why there are *things* on this train."

"I decided to spare your feelings," Lincoln said.

"Don't," said Garland. "I need to know."

"I, on the other hand, don't need to know," said Banks. "I have as much of my truth as I can bear."

"Oh," said Lincoln, "we'll see about that."

"I want the facts," Poppy said.

"I don't," Banks said. "I know who I am and what I did."

Poppy said, "All this is to scare us, isn't it? Smoke and mirrors and vague stories, to make us too scared to ask any questions."

"Ask me a question, then," Lincoln said. "Anything you like."

Poppy thought. "What was his name?" she said. "The Leader."

"That was his name," said Lincoln.

"He was called the Leader?"

"He may have been called something else once," Lincoln said. "But that name wasn't who he was. You know what I'm talking about, don't you?" he said to Garland.

Garland said nothing.

"Knows more than she's letting on," said Lincoln.

Garland faced Poppy. "I don't," she said.

"Stop," Banks said. He sounded angry, and frightened. "Poppy is right, he's trying to scare us, dragging all this up and not being clear, deliberately. He's doing it to keep us in our place, and I don't know about you −"

Banks stopped. He took a deep breath.

"– but it's working. I'm terrified. I thought I knew who I was and where I was from, but I don't know all of it."

"You surely don't," said Lincoln. "You think you were some big cool guy who betrayed this innocent kid. And you were. You did. But you don't know it all."

"Wait," said Poppy. She gave Banks a warm, deep smile. "Banks was cool?"

"Cool for a geek," said Lincoln. "Dressed well for a nerd, all that. And yeah, he was kind of pretty before we got to him."

"They changed my face," Banks said.

"I like it," Poppy said. Garland nodded too.

"Glad someone does," says Lincoln. "I can barely look at it. We didn't do it to uglify him, you understand. We're not monsters. I mean, we make monsters, but we're not actually monsters ourselves."

"'We're not monsters, we just make the monsters'," repeated Garland.

"Lady," said Lincoln, "someone has to make the bad things, to keep the worse things away. Anyway, I was telling you how we made pretty boy here into much-less-pretty boy."

"You don't have to listen to this," Poppy told Banks.

"He does," said Lincoln. "Because he deserves it. We didn't make him like this for fun. We made him like this because it was one of the Leader's dictates. 'People should look like who they are,' he said. 'A good person should look like a good person...'"

"'A bad person should look bad'," Garland finished. She looked shocked that she had spoken.

"It's all coming back to you now, ain't it," Lincoln said cheerfully. "But yeah, a bad person should look bad. And a traitor –"

He stared at Banks's altered face.

"– should look like a traitor."

· · ·

Banks said nothing.

"I deserved it," he said.

"Sure you did," said Lincoln. "You did it to save your own skin, which is kind of funny when you think about it, seeing what we did to your skin. And the rest."

There was a moment's silence before Poppy said, "What do you mean, the rest?"

"Leave it," Banks said.

"Oh no, that's a perfectly fair question," Lincoln said. "Because we didn't just mess with your face. Wasn't all new ridges and contours in your skull to make you less pretty. See, we had a few fellows, medics and such, wanted to try a few things out."

"That's enough," said Garland.

"Go on," said Banks, his face blanched and tight.

"We were getting short of prisoners, and clones don't – well, they don't *fall right* when you work on them. So we opened him up and we let the fellows do what they wanted to."

"Which was what, exactly?" said Banks.

"I don't entirely know. They kind of got in there and played roulette. Took some shit out, moved some shit around. You know the saying, his heart's in the right

267

place? Ain't true in your case."

"He's joking," said Poppy.

"Truth is," Lincoln said, "I have no idea. But hey, they sewed you up again and you're alive. It all worked out fine."

Poppy put her arm around Banks.

Garland took his hand.

"Listen," Poppy said, "whatever you did, you more than paid the price."

"Unlike you," said Lincoln. "Those fancy parts we gave you, you stole them."

"Not much use to anyone else," Poppy replied.

"But they didn't belong to you," Lincoln said. "They were new technology, and expensive too. We were just about to take 'em back when you made a break."

"Good job too, then," said Poppy. "And since you took what I was born with, I feel fair exchange is no robbery."

"Kind of a shame you came here," said Lincoln. He turned to the others. "She thought she was escaping, but she wasn't, was she? She came right back to us."

"I saw Denning," said Poppy. "He was here, too."

"It should have been you in there," Lincoln said. "Once we'd figured out how to get those off you –" he nodded at her arms, "– without damaging them, we were going to put you in a death room, same as Denning, and throw in a couple of vials."

Garland stared at him. "You're not human," he said.

"About the only one here who is," Lincoln replied. "You got your freak face here and your metal girl and – well, maybe you should tell me who you are."

"I'm human," said Garland.

"That remains to be seen," Lincoln said. "No pun intended."

"What pun –" Poppy began.

Lincoln interrupted her.

"I said this train was like a book. Different carriages, different chapters," he said, getting up. "I didn't say which book, though."

He motioned for them to follow him. They did so, uncertain and reluctant.

"Come on, we're nearly there," said Lincoln. "Hey," he added, "you ever hear of a man called Shandy?"

• • •

The next carriage was black. The walls were black flock wallpaper, gloss black decoration on matt black paper, the carpet a thin black pile, while the ceiling was hung with black crepe, and the windows were draped with it.

Music was playing as they entered, a strange high bubbling sound, like a dance but also like a scream.

"What is that noise?" Banks said.

Poppy said, "I like it. It sounds frightening and jolly all at the same time."

"Bagpipes," said Lincoln. "The Leader liked them because they were martial."

He listened for a moment as the tune unfurled.

"'Train Journey North'," he said. "It was the Leader's favourite. I mean, I guess, he was a tone deaf old shit who didn't care about music. Me, I love anything so long as it's a train song."

They made their way with some difficulty through the half-lit carriage. Ornate black brackets held dim candle-shaped bulbs that lit the air a few centimetres around them. In the centre of the otherwise empty carriage was a large box mounted on a pair of trestles.

"I've been here before," said Garland.

"No shit, Sherlock," Lincoln said.

Poppy said, "Who's Sherlock?"

"I was here with Denning," Garland said.

"Denning?" Banks said. "Did you know him too?"

"She never said before," Poppy said.

"I didn't know before," Garland replied. She turned to Lincoln. "How have I been here before?" she asked. "How do I know Denning?"

"Oh, you know Denning well," Lincoln answered. "Matter of fact, you used to rely on him for advice and assistance. He was kind of your factotum. Your gofer."

"I don't know what any of those words mean," said Poppy.

"I do," said Banks, his face severe. "He means that Denning used to work for Garland."

"No," said Garland. "That's not true."

"There's more to her than she lets on, that's for sure," said Lincoln, and he winked at Garland.

"Banks, this is what he does," said Poppy. "He makes us scared so we don't question him."

Banks wasn't listening.

"Is he right?" he asked Garland. "Did Denning work for you? The man who did this to me – did that to her? The man who killed the only person I loved?"

"Strictly speaking," Lincoln reminded him, "you killed the only person you loved. But yeah, I'm here to tell you that our late, recently liquidated friend Mister Denning was employed as an advisor to this lady here."

Garland shook her head. "I know you're right," she said, "but I also know you're wrong."

"Well, that makes no sense," said Lincoln. "Now, I have a question for you all."

He laid his palms on the lid of the black box as if drawing strength from it, then looked up.

"You ever hear of the murder weapon paradox?" he asked.

Poppy shook her head. Banks just looked at Garland, who avoided his stare.

"The murder weapon paradox is this," said Lincoln. "Let's say you commit a murder. Not the kind Banks committed, but a real man's murder, with a knife. The police arrest you, throw you in jail, and they take the knife because the knife is the only proof they have that it was you who committed the crime. Maybe there's fingerprints on it, a couple of hairs. Are you with me so far?"

The three of them said nothing.

"So the trial for some reason is delayed, and in that time someone is cleaning up the evidence room and they drop the knife, and the handle breaks. Maybe it's a cleaner who doesn't want to lose her job, I don't know. But she has an identical knife of her own that she carries in case she gets attacked on the way home. It's a rough town. And she replaces the broken handle on the murder weapon with the handle from her knife."

"This is all very confusing," said Poppy.

"It gets worse," Lincoln replied. "A day or two later the same thing happens again. Only this time it's a painter working in the same room and he needs a blade to open a pot of paint, I don't know. And he breaks the blade. Oh crap. He panics, and runs out into the canteen, and finds another knife with the same kind of blade, pulls out the blade and slots it into the handle of the old knife. Which, you may recall, is not the original handle."

"I wish I had it here now," said Poppy. "I'd kill myself to get away from this story."

Lincoln took out the remote control again. "Don't need a knife," he reminded her. "Anyway, the day of the trial comes, the accused is brought into the dock and the knife is shown to him. 'Is this your knife?' they ask him. And he's about to say yes when something makes him stop. A smile plays on his murderer's lips. 'No,' he says. 'That is not my knife.'

"Well, the place is in uproar. The defence are shouting no fair, the police are saying nobody's touched the knife. When the dust settles, the judge orders an investigation, which of course reveals that the murder weapon is no longer the murder weapon. Because of this, there is no evidence, which means there is no case, which means the prisoner walks free."

"But it was the murder weapon," said Poppy. "It was the knife the murderer used. Wasn't it?"

Lincoln put his hands together. "And that," he said, "is the murder weapon paradox. When something changes, and over time all its component parts are replaced, does its original essence remain, or is it a new thing?"

"Like the Ship of Theseus," said Garland out loud.

Banks said, "Washington's Axe."

"Trigger's Broom," said Poppy.

"Whatever you call it," Lincoln replied, "it was the end of our world."

He thwacked the lid of the box with the flat of his hand.

"Knock once if you can hear me," he said, "twice if you can't."

Silence followed.

"It was the Leader," said Lincoln. "When he came to prominence, when he became the Leader, he was strong. He made decisions and he made our world. People died, because they had to. There was war, and there were all kinds of things, but the Leader had sight, and he followed the sight. Then he got old, and he got worried. What would people think when he was gone? Worse, what would they think when he was old, and ill, and dying? What would they *do*? Would they do it to him? He got soft. I would ask him to make a decision, and he would hesitate. Denning would advise him on a course of action, and he wouldn't take it. You see, he wasn't the same person."

"You mean he changed?" said Banks.

"No," said Lincoln. "I mean *he wasn't the same person*."

He looked at Garland for support, and she saw that Lincoln was not sane.

"People change, that's a common saying. But it doesn't account for the real truth. Every day our cells die, don't they? And they're replaced by new cells. Every cell dies and every cell is replaced. Which means that the person you were as a child, or as an adolescent, is not the same person you are as a grown adult. And that person is not who you become. And so on, until you die."

"That's not how it works —" Banks began. Lincoln wasn't listening.

"A clone," he said. "See, a clone is more than a copy of you. It's a digital copy. It doesn't decay like you. It doesn't change its mind or learn or get swayed by arguments or become more compassionate with age. It stays the same. But people – people change. We all do, unless we have the strength to resist. Some of us can do it. I can. Denning could, until he was taken apart. But the Leader – he was no longer the weapon. And so we had to remove him."

Lincoln looked down at the black box.

"Remove him?" asked Poppy.

"Oh, we explored other avenues first," said Lincoln. "Reason, persuasion, even threats... but he was adamant. He wanted to be *remembered*. We told him he would be. But he said no, he wanted to be remembered favourably. We told him he had saved the world. He just shook his head. So we made plans. We made provision for his removal, for his replacement, and he... stepped aside."

After a while, Poppy said, "And that's him?"

"What?" said Lincoln.

Poppy spoke slowly. "In the box," she said. "That's him in the box?"

"Hell no," said Lincoln. "We burned his body and scattered the pieces. Fuck him and his legacy."

"Is it Shandy?" asked Banks.

Lincoln laughed. "I do not believe so. As a matter of fact," he went on, tugging at the lid of the box, "this ain't a man at all."

He pulled the lid off and it crashed to the floor. Inside the box was a body. It had been preserved with some kind of chemical that made it look fresh but deathly pale, and it was wearing an expensive uniform. In every other respect it was Garland's double.

"A real chip off the old block," said Lincoln. He looked Garland in the eye. "Ain't that right?"

Interlude Three

She was in the room with the black box again. Denning was there and he was talking. Lately, she reflected, Denning was always talking. It was as if he knew the end was near, and the only thing he had left was words. She wished that he would shut up, but she knew he wouldn't.

"Somebody once said that the end of an empire is messy at best," Denning was saying. "They were right. And this one is no exception."

She looked out of the window. The grey sky was getting even greyer. She wondered how that was possible.

"We're trying the cloud bombs again," said Denning, catching her gaze. "Might work, might not. But he promised them blue skies, so we have to try. Of course," he went on, and she realised that he was never going to stop talking because then he would have to start thinking, and when he did, it would all be over for him, "he promised a lot of things at the end, didn't he?"

"He was trying to reform the system," she said.

"He was trying to create his legacy," Denning almost spat. "He was crapping on everything we had created, throwing it all out so he might get a kind word from the history books."

"He wanted to change," she said.

"Everyone does, at the death," said Denning. "They want to be forgiven. They want their mothers. They want to die in a state of grace, so they can be born again."

He looked out into the grey night.

"Mothers," he said.

"I never knew mine," she said.

"Overrated," Denning said. "I had mine arrested. Quite by accident, as it happens, but that's by the by. We can do without them."

He looked at her again.

"All the men we sent to fight," he said. "All of them, at the end, screaming and crying for their mothers. So much simpler to do without, don't you think?"

Denning opened the box. A face exactly like Garland's stared back at him, expressionless.

"It's always the same," he said, looking into the dead eyes. "There's an emperor who isn't really an emperor, just a boy in a crown that's too big for him. His empire isn't even a kingdom, it's four walls and a roof. Or there's a dictator and he's not the great dictator, he's the man who comes after the great dictator. His empire is a bunker and a loaded pistol."

"When are we leaving?" she asked, hoping to stem the tide of words. Denning wasn't listening.

"History is full of these people," he went on. "The small men who follow the big men. Nobody remembers them. Donitz, Constantine Palaeologus, Caesarion… they're the men who run out onto the pitch just as the game ends. The ones who end up poisoned, or in front of a firing squad, or on trial for their grubby lives."

He sighed. "And then we have this young woman. The second and final Leader. She had all the qualifications for a classic last emperor: no qualifications save blood, and an empire that nobody could see. An empire that goes on rails, and has to keep moving, in case its enemies see it. A skulking, tiny empire."

"Did you kill her?" she asked.

"Me? No," said Denning. "There was no need. She – she didn't work. We tried everything but the upgrade was too much."

"Upgrade?" she said, needing to hear the answer but not wanting to. "I thought the process was simple."

"Simple to make a soldier, yes, or a labourer," agreed Denning. "But we weren't transferring basic skills and the rudiments of a personality. We weren't making a worker bee. We were making a *queen*."

He looked down at the corpse, almost fondly.

"We were making a new Leader, who was to have the character and force and mind of the old Leader," he said. "Your father reincarnate."

"She wasn't him," she said.

"For a moment, she was," Denning corrected her. "When we woke her, she *was* him. It was uncanny: apart from her gender, which was necessarily yours, she had his ideas, his voice and even his mannerisms. Unfortunately," and Denning sighed again, "she also had the disease that killed him."

"But his illness took —"

"Years, I know. But the process must have accelerated in her."

He turned to her.

"I was never for using your cells," he said. "I said the moral decay in you was worse than any physical or mental decay. We should have used someone with fibre."

"You, perhaps?"

He was taken aback by the steel in her voice, so different to her usual meekness.

"Why not?" he said. "When you look at the filth who will follow me... why not?"

Denning looked at his watch.

"Oh well," he said. "No use chuntering on about the past. Let's go. We have a train to catch."

• • •

Garland found that she had closed her eyes tight. When she opened them, she saw that the others were standing around her.

"She remembers," said Lincoln. "How was it? Your trip down memory lane?"

"I remember," said Garland. "I'm not sure, but I think I remember everything."

"Who are you?" said Banks.

"Who's she?" asked Poppy, looking at the body in the box. "Is she your sister?"

"Is she your daughter?" Banks asked.

"Of course she's not her fucking daughter, you tosser," said Poppy.

"Then who?" Banks said.

"She's my clone," Garland said, quietly.

"The fuck," said Poppy.

Banks looked confused. "But clones..." he began. "They're not like you."

"They're not," said Garland. "They're not very sophisticated, you mean. They're basic personality templates. But she was meant to be like the Leader. The Leader before he got –"

"– soft," said Lincoln. "We figured that because he was old, and sick, he didn't know what he was doing. Blue skies, for goodness' sake."

"What?" said Poppy.

"Oh, and letting people go free, and make decisions, and all that kind of bull," said Lincoln, contemptuously. "The man was pissing on his own legacy. 'Course, he wasn't well. We knew he was dying, so we had to act in a hurry. Which, unfortunately, we did."

"I don't understand," Banks said.

"Not understanding is your brand, son," Lincoln said.

"What he means," said Garland, "is that the operation was done in a rush. It was botched. The clone had some of my cells and some of his, but his – they were diseased."

"We should have just rinsed your fucking brain," said Lincoln. "Two birds with one stone, know what I mean?"

281

"Why did they use your cells?" said Poppy. "What had you done to him?"

Garland said, "I was his only child, the only one with his DNA."

"Wait a minute," said Banks. "The Leader was your father?"

Poppy looked at him. "Oh, come on," she said.

"I'm sorry," said Banks. "A lot has happened lately, and I'm starting to feel that she's part of it."

"She's done nothing," said Poppy. Less certainly, she said to Garland, "Have you?"

"Well," said Lincoln, filling the silence, "have you... Garland?"

"If that's her name," Banks said.

"Banks!" Poppy shouted. "Of course it's not her name!"

"OK," said Banks. He turned to Garland.

"Tell me," he said. "Tell us."

. . .

Garland told them.

. . .

There was a chess set on the table. At least, she thought it was a chess set. She was eight years old and, as her governess told her when nobody was around, she didn't know everything.

The chess set looked like a normal chess set except for one thing: it was entirely black. Instead of being a pattern of black and white checks, the board was black, and instead of one set of pieces being white and one black, both sets were black.

She found it annoying, because she liked chess, and she

liked things to be right. An all-black chess set clearly was not right.

"Why is it all black?" she asked her governess. Her governess, who didn't like to be wrong but frequently was, said, "You should ask your father," in the hope of ending her interest in the topic.

So she asked her father. He knelt down to her – they were standing on opposite sides of the chess board at the time, as if about to begin an impossible game – and he said, "To remind me of an important lesson." Once, he had been in an art gallery somewhere abroad – somewhere *decadent* – and he had seen another chess set. "Was it black, too?" she asked. "No," he said, "it was white. All the pieces were white and so was the board."

The artist had been there, her father explained, and he had asked her – it was a woman, as is common in decadent cities – why she had made this chess set. Well, he said "asked" (he and his daughter both smiled at this, because he was the Leader and he never *asked* anything, he just said it, and it happened) but really he just told the woman artist that it was a bad chess set because even if you could move the pieces on an all-white board, sooner or later the fact that they were all white meant that both players would become hopelessly confused and nobody could tell which pieces belonged to which side.

And the woman artist had said to him, "Exactly."

• • •

Her father had not liked this, but it wasn't his city and it wasn't his chess set, so when he came home, he had had this set, the all-black set, made.

"In my chess set," he said, not a little proudly, "both sides are black because both sides belong to me. The board is black because the field belongs to me. There is no chance of confusion because I control both sides."

"But you can't play a game. Not with someone else."

He looked at her, and he was smiling.

"Not with someone else, no," he said. "Exactly."

• • •

Where they lived was the palace and it was by far the nicest place in the world. The rest of the world was foggy and lacking the colour that everywhere filled the palace. There were green ferns and white orchids and orange fruit and all kinds of beautiful things. She wanted for nothing, except a pony because there were none to be had, and a mother, because hers had died giving birth to her.

"I am surprised your father did not break it to you more… gently," said the governess.

"I'm surprised you still have a job," she replied, and the governess was silent.

• • •

She loved her father, who was also the father of their country, which meant she had to share him, but she didn't mind, so long as the country only had him during the week and she got him to herself at the weekends. She knew the country loved him because wherever she went with him, people waved and cheered, and held up their own children, as though hoping that her father might take the children home with him. She could understand why they might want him to do that – she could tell from their clothes, crisp and white though they were, that these people did not live in a palace.

• • •

As time went by, she found that even life in a palace wasn't perfect. For a start, she spent too much time in the palace. There were many things to do – she could read, or swim with the turtles – but not enough. By the time she was thirteen, she felt that she had swum with the turtles enough, and the books were very dull (there was one about making films, written, she was sure, by the dullest man in the world: she hoped never to see any of the films he had made).

"I miss my mother," she said to her latest governess, hoping to provoke her into saying something that would get her sacked. But the governess was wise to her tricks now, and simply said, "That is a natural feeling."

• • •

Her father grew older. He was ill, she could see that. He had started to need her, first for simple tasks like finding his glasses and bringing him tea, but then for more difficult things, like helping him with his speeches. He was having trouble finding books and sources for them, he told her, although she also noticed that he was having more trouble finding the right words to put in the speeches.

"We need to – what is the word?" he asked her once. "Not transient, not transfer."

"Transition?" she said. It was a reasonable guess, as lately he had become fond of the word.

"That's it!" he said. "What would I do without you?"

He kissed her. She flinched.

"Your breath," she said apologetically.

"One day," he went on, apparently not having heard her, "all this will be yours."

"The palace?" she said, teasingly. This was one of her favourite conversations, almost a game. But today her father did not seem to be playing.

"I need you to take on my grand plan," he said. "It will take seven years, and I don't have seven years."

"But –"

"You know what my plan is. To – transition – to a limited social democracy. To give the people back their country."

"I thought you were giving it to me," she said, smiling to show it was a joke. She didn't want a country. She just wanted him.

"I am," he said, smiling back. "But only to look after. One day, who knows, you will have a son –"

"Or a daughter," she frowned.

"Perhaps. And he, or she, will preside over the final handing over of power. But it will take many years."

He put down his pen to massage his arm.

"I have many enemies," he said. "I did not want you to know, and I have tried to – what is the word, like confuse?"

"Conceal," she said.

"I have tried to conceal this from you. But they are like weeds. I cut off one head and ten more spring up. Many are here."

"I know," she said. "I trust nobody."

"Good," he said.

He looked away from her, and for a moment she wondered if he was quite present.

"Do you remember when we talked about the chess set?" he said. She nodded yes, and he went on, "I wanted the world to be all the same, all controlled by me. It would be a safer world, I thought, and one without conflict. But you cannot have a world without conflict, without dialectic, without opposing views."

"Shall we get a new chess set then?" she asked.

He laughed. "Maybe not just yet," he said.

• • •

She began to accompany him to official events. Her photograph was printed in the papers. Her face appeared on a coin.

One day, Denning appeared with a doctor. "We need your DNA," he said, without further explanation.

"Why?" she asked.

"Your father is ill," said Denning.

"Open your mouth, please," said the doctor.

"Will this help?" she asked.

"Just going to take a sample," the doctor said.

• • •

Her father was very ill. Every day she helped him dress, helped him to the window so he could see the crowds below who had come to wish him well. He waved at them and they waved back.

• • •

One day he waved at the crowds and suddenly something hit the window and cracked it.

They watched as troops ran into the square below. Smoke filled the air and there were screams.

Denning appeared with two identical men, who gently moved her father away from the window.

"Let's not do that any more," he said to her father as the men laid him on the bed.

. . .

Her father never left the bed again. She saw him give instructions to Denning, but she doubted that they were ever followed.

. . .

One day, a man called Lincoln came to see her. He was sweaty, and looked as though his suit hated him.

"Have you come to make my father well?" she asked.

"No, ma'am," he said.

"Then why are you here?" she said, losing interest.

"There are people who want to kill him," said Lincoln.

"They needn't bother," she replied. "He's dying anyway."

"When he dies," said Lincoln, "they will kill you."

"They can't," she said. "I will be Leader, and I will implement his policies."

"Which is why they will kill you," he said.

"What do you want?"

"I represent a faction," said Lincoln, looking around him as though for spies, "who are opposed to those who oppose you."

She stifled a grin.

"And we want to take you to a place of safety," he went on.

She stood up.

"I am in a place of safety," she said. She tapped her chest with her hand. "So long as I am here, for my father, I am safe."

Lincoln stood too.

"OK," he said, his tone of respect gone. "Just stay away from the windows, that's all."

• • •

Time passed.

• • •

She stood with Denning beside her father's coffin. He was putting a piece of paper in his pocket.

"All right," she said. "Let's go."

Denning nodded, as if relieved. He turned to one of the soldiers guarding the coffin.

"You, Garland," he said, reading the woman's name badge. "Change clothes with her."

• • •

She walked with Denning onto the platform, the green uniform feeling odd.

"This is my father's train," she said.

"It was," Denning said. "We have requisitioned it for the emergency."

She looked the train up and down. It was magnificent, a home from home. But now soldiers were running in and out of it, onto the platforms and back again. Furniture was being loaded out, and food loaded in.

"We've added more buffet cars for the men, so they can eat," said Denning. "And a few – experiments. Work in progress. *Useful* work."

"I don't need to know," she said. "Just show me to my quarters."

"A pleasure," said Denning. He made a strange gesture. Two soldiers appeared from nowhere and one of them pinned her arms behind her back. The other crammed a wet cloth into her mouth and she passed out.

• • •

Denning leaned over her inert form. He jabbed a needle into her wrist and emptied its contents into her veins.

"Fucking bitch," said Denning. "Throw it in the caboose."

SEVEN

"You remembered!" said Lincoln. "You even remembered me. I'm touched."

"I should have gone with you," Garland said.

"He wanted to kill you, I bet," said Poppy.

"Even if he did, I should have gone with him," said Garland. "I'm just as bad as them. Him, and Lincoln."

"You're not," said Poppy.

"She is," Banks said.

They looked at him.

"Banks!" said Poppy. "She wasn't in charge. She didn't do any of this."

"She was there," Banks said. "She could have done something. She could have said something. Stopped all the bad things."

"He's got a point," Lincoln said. "I mean, at least I tried to stop some of the bad things. True, I had my own reasons, but I'm not supposed to be the good guy here. Whereas she was going to be the knight in shining armour."

He looked at Garland. "That was your plan, right? You were going to undo all your daddy's works, good and bad, and make a happy land, where children could play in the street and everyone had pie in the sky for dinner."

"I was going to institute his reforms," Garland said.

"See?" said Poppy. "She was going to institute his reforms. Sounds fine to me."

Banks turned away.

"Banks," said Garland. "This isn't fair."

"You were at the heart of it," Banks said. "The evil... you were right there. For all I know you gave the order to have *him* killed."

"I didn't," Garland said. "Even if I had known, I wasn't allowed to make decisions."

"That's true," said Lincoln. "Which kind of makes all this pointless."

"What do you mean?" Poppy said.

"Ever heard of Kerensky?" said Lincoln. "He was a reformer. Lasted about a week. Ended up in exile, teaching kids who weren't listening to a stupid old man. History remembers him as a well-meaning loser. Cheers, history."

"Banks, I never knew," Garland said. "I never hurt anyone."

"And you never stopped anyone being hurt," said Banks.

"I didn't know anything," she said, near tears.

"You never tried to know anything," Banks said, and walked away.

Garland went to follow him, but Poppy put a firm hand on her shoulder.

"No," she said.

"I couldn't do anything," Garland said. "He needs to know that."

"He needs to be left alone," said Poppy. "And you need to imagine how he feels."

Lincoln clapped his hands.

"All righty," he said. "We had a fine jaw around the old campfire, didn't we? We chewed us some fat and we're all square. Cards on the table, genies out of the bottle, a frank exchange of truths. Is everybody happy? I mean," he said, looking at them all, "in a metaphorical kind of way."

Garland went over to him.

"I want to see the driver," she said.

"I thought *he* was the driver," Poppy said.

"Honey, believe me, I'm not the driver," Lincoln replied.

"He's not the driver," said Garland. She looked at Lincoln again. "The next carriage is the last carriage, isn't it? The locomotive itself."

"That's correct."

"Then take me to him. Take me to the driver."

Lincoln looked at them all again.

"All righty," he said, and beamed.

• • •

The three of them – Poppy on the alert, Garland tense and Banks sullenly silent – followed Lincoln down the carriage.

"Kind of a tricky manoeuvre here," he said as they approached the end. He opened the door. Between the carriage they were in and the next there was a gap. The two carriages were connected by four or five shifting steel panels, like the plates on some armoured creature's back.

"You have to sort of shimmy across," said Lincoln. "Not for the faint of heart."

"The person who designed this train ought to be shot," said Poppy.

"Funny you should say that," Lincoln said. "After you."

Poppy ignored the moving panels below them and jumped across the gap, grabbing the handles on the other carriage and opening the door.

"Now you," she called back to Banks.

"I can't do it," said Banks. "I'll stay here. I don't care about the driver –"

Lincoln shoved him. Garland gasped. Banks staggered across the plates, arms flailing, and stumbled forward. Poppy grabbed him with a free hand and pulled him across.

"Now me," said Lincoln, and stepped into the darkness. He moved across the plates like a man who knows a secret path.

It was Garland's turn. Somehow she got across the panels as they slid away from her, but at the last minute she lost her footing and her legs gave way under her. She thrust out a hand. The nearest person was Banks.

He looked at her hand, as though wondering what it was.

For a moment there was nothing but him and her and the rush of air and sound beneath her.

"Banks!" Poppy shouted.

Without speaking, he reached out and took her hand.

Garland righted herself and Poppy pulled her into the carriage.

"Thanks, Banks," Garland said. Banks didn't reply.

. . .

They were in a short, dark corridor. It was narrow with machinery and hot enough to make them take their jackets off.

"That way," Lincoln said.

Poppy stopped.

"You go first," she said.

"Thanks, but I want you in front of me where I can see you," said Lincoln.

"But that's exactly how I feel about you," said Poppy.

"I'll go first, if it's that important," said Banks.

"You don't have what she has," says Lincoln. "I want her to go first."

He looked at Poppy. Poppy returned his gaze.

"I don't believe this," said Garland. "I want to do one thing and here we are."

Suddenly Poppy reached into her tunic.

"Drop it," said Lincoln, pulling out his gun.

"What, Teddy?" Poppy said, holding the stuffed bear up by its toe. She kissed its head, tucked it into her tunic again and walked up the small corridor.

"Door's locked," she said.

"Security," said Lincoln. "Here."

He threw a key at her. She caught it with one hand.

"Knock first," Lincoln said. "We don't want to startle him."

And he grinned.

• • •

Poppy knocked on the door. There was no reply.

"Open it," said Lincoln.

Poppy unlocked the door and went in. Lincoln motioned with his gun for Banks and Garland to follow.

• • •

The driver's cockpit was roomy, compared to the rest of the carriage. Enormous bowed windows on either side and in front presented a panoramic view of the landscape. Screens filled the walls, some showing maps and track systems, others flicking between closed circuit camera images of different carriages. A rack of weatherproof coats and trousers hung to one side.

Garland put her jacket on a hook, feeling self-conscious and formal. Banks kept his on, as if in defiance, and Poppy dropped her jacket on the floor, first taking care to remove Teddy.

At the dead centre of the cockpit was an enormous chair, white and made of leather or some synthetic equivalent. Poppy spun it round.

"What?" she said.

Garland stepped forward. The chair was empty.

"What is this?" she said. "Where's the driver?"

"There is no driver," said Lincoln. "There never was a driver. Fully automated."

"No driver," said Garland. "Why didn't you tell me?"

"I needed to be sure you wouldn't go against me," Lincoln said. "Helps to use the carrot instead of the stick sometimes, even if the carrot ain't real."

"There has to be a driver," said Garland. "It doesn't make sense otherwise."

"It's a train," Lincoln said. "It doesn't have to make sense."

"No," said Garland, and she could hear the hysteria in her voice. "No, this can't be it. Someone has to be in charge. Someone has to be driving."

"No one driving," Lincoln said. "No need."

Banks bent down. "It's pretty impressive," he said. "Amazing setup, actually."

"Don't touch anything," Lincoln warned.

"Why?" said Poppy. "Will it send us off course?"

Lincoln smiled.

"Off course?" he said.

"What I mean is," said Poppy, "it may be automatic and all that but we are still going somewhere, aren't we?"

"Yes," said Garland. "We're going somewhere. We must be."

Lincoln shook his head.

"What?" said Banks.

"We're not going anywhere," said Lincoln.

• • •

He leaned past Banks and tapped a screen.

"Seen this before?" he asked.

On the screen a simple map appeared. It was shaped like a figure of eight.

"This is our route," he said. "Has been for a mighty long time."

Garland stared at the screen. "My map," she said.

"It was there all the time but you just didn't want to see," said Lincoln. "This train just goes round and round and round on the circuit. Never goes this way, never goes that. Just round and round."

297

"We saw other lines," said Banks. "We saw other trains."

"All the other lines are smashed and useless," Lincoln said. "The other trains, too."

Lincoln gestured with his hands.

"This is it, folks," he said. "This is the only railroad, and the only train."

Garland walked away from Banks and stood at the very front of the train. Oblivious to any human interaction, it nosed on with mindless determination, track stretching endlessly ahead into the night.

For the first time, Garland could see in front of the train. Lights danced in the distance, and the darkness around was as complete as before, but it was unsettling to be able to look forwards and not just from side to side.

"Why?" she said. "Why isn't this train going anywhere?"

"Because there's nowhere to go," said Banks. "That's it, isn't it?"

"Give the freak a coconut," Lincoln said. "This train ain't bound for glory, that's for sure. This train ain't bound for anywhere. It just follows the eight."

Poppy looked at the map.

"It goes past all these orange bits," she said.

"Danger areas," explained Lincoln. "Places that are just too hot to go near. I mean that figuratively and literally, by the way. There are things out there that we can't go near because we don't know if they're physically safe. Installations where the wrong thing melted. Facilities where experiments went a tad awry."

He gazed into the dusty night.

"Sometimes the experiments get out," he said. "I believe you saw a couple of them."

"Teddy certainly did," said Poppy. "Sorry," she added, "that sounded weird even to me."

Lincoln carried on. "And," he said, "there are places where this train can't go because it wouldn't be awfully welcome."

"You mean where there are people?" said Garland.

"I mean places where there are troublemakers," said Lincoln. "Bandits, assholes, nogoodniks. The scum of the earth."

"Rebels," said Poppy. "Dissenters."

"Yeah, well, fat lot of good it did them, whatever you want to call 'em." Lincoln snorted. "The meek inherited the earth, and it's fucked, so they can keep it."

"Your father's plans came to nothing," Banks said. "All that rubbish about reforms and blue skies, whatever that was, was just a waste of time."

"Sure did," agreed Lincoln. "The future's just as shitty as it always was. The world's always been about the people who're on board and the people who aren't."

"What's the point, though?" Poppy asked. "I mean, I get how it's all nice and cosy on this train with all the bad people outside, but it's not much of a fucking life is it? Stuck in here eating out of cans and nothing to do but walk up and down and look out the window at nothing all night long."

"What other choice is there?" said Lincoln.

"When I was a skier," Poppy said, absently stroking Teddy's fur, "I loved to ski. I loved it when people cheered, and I sort of liked the medals, but it was the skiing I loved. And the thing I didn't love, the thing I think I actually hated, was – well, it was everything else. Going to events. Mingling. Talking to people whose only interest in life was owning things. Watches, cars, boats, people... all they cared about was their stuff."

"I see we have a rebel of our own," said Lincoln. He sounded like a man trying to appear bored.

"Whatever," Poppy said. "The thing that got me, though, was how they were always looking round. Like they were scared. Like someone was going to *get in* and take their stuff. Take their watch or their car or their life. And they never did anything. They just stood behind velvet ropes, or on the deck of their boat, and didn't do anything."

"You want to go out there?" asked Lincoln.

"Why not?" said Poppy.

"Because all I have to do is stop this thing."

"You can do that?" Garland said.

"Manual override," Lincoln explained. "A child could drive this train. You can stop it, you can reverse it, you can even change course. I mean, assuming the brave rebel bands haven't pulled the tracks up."

"We could drive this train ourselves?" Garland said.

"We could," agreed Lincoln. "But we're not going to."

He walked over to another console and flicked a switch.

• • •

Outside, speakers set into the sides of the train began to play music.

· · ·

They could hear it in the cockpit.

"Did you just do that?" said Poppy.

"Signal," explained Lincoln. "From my friends who put me on the train."

"Who to?" Banks asked.

"You have friends?" said Poppy.

"How else could I get that ass Denning in a cage?" said Lincoln. "And who do you think sent the security detail? Of course I have friends. And," he went on, "I don't want to spend the rest of my life on this train. I hear there's places you can have some kind of life if you've got what people want."

"And what do you have that people want?" asked Poppy.

Lincoln gestured at Garland.

"Her," he said.

· · ·

"Me?" Garland said. "But I'm nothing. I'm worthless."

"Hey, don't put yourself down," Lincoln said. "You're solid coin to me. Think about it. There are so many uses for someone like you."

"Don't," said Poppy.

"I don't mean anything as sordid as that," said Lincoln. "I mean, here we have a unique specimen. The sole surviving member of – what do we call it? The final dynasty. The last royal family. Who wouldn't pay to have something like that in their collection?"

"She's a human being," Poppy said.

"I'm glad one of you is. Our friend here is the actual, genuine, untouched, unmodified human progeny of the

Leader. The one man who could unite everybody. People like that, you know."

"People hate him," said Banks. "And they'll hate her just as much."

"You ever hear of leadership cults?" Lincoln said. "All around the world, Stalin, Franco, Perón... these guys, with their tunics and their moustaches, they killed thousands, millions of people. They were mass murderers. And what happened when they finally dropped dead?"

"People rejoiced," said Banks.

"Did they fuck," Lincoln said. "People *cried*. People wept in the streets, and they beat their breasts and some of them killed themselves."

"Is that what happened to my father?" asked Garland.

"Not so much," Lincoln admitted. "But that was more to do with a breakdown in communications. World in ruins, social media down, that kind of thing. Which leads me to something much more interesting."

"Finally," said Poppy.

Lincoln didn't reply, just fingered the inside of his pocket.

"Her father dies," he said. "Nobody writes about it, nobody posts about it online, it's on TV but there are no TVs... yet word gets around. Out there, around the bonfires and in the ruins. In the tents and the settlements, people start to get the news. Their Leader is dead. Their father."

He looked at Garland. "How did you feel when your father died?"

"I was devastated," said Garland. "I knew his faults –"

"*Faults?*" said Banks. "He was a sociopath."

"Shut up, freak," Lincoln said. "What else?"

"I knew what he was like," said Garland. "But he loved me, and I loved him. He was my world for a very long time. When he died, there was a hole in my heart, and there always will be."

"Despite what he did?" said Banks.

"He was my father," said Garland.

"And there we have it. As she feels, so the people feel," Lincoln said. "He was their father, and they loved him. When he was there, they felt safe. They had food, and warmth, and he kept their enemies away. Don't you think they want him back?"

"Back?" said Poppy. "Is that what this is about?"

"Relax, he's not coming back," Lincoln said. "He's ashes now. We tried to bring him back, remember, but he was too old and broken. We tried to make a new him, too, but that didn't work. No, there's only her," and he gestured at Garland with the gun.

"Oh my God," said Poppy. "You're not going to sell her to her enemies. You're going to sell her to –"

"To the fan club," said Lincoln. "To the people who want her father back."

"What for?" asked Banks. "She's not him. She says she's not even like him."

"She can be, though," said Lincoln. "Just a tweak here, a cut there. And she can be just like he was. Maybe a little more… malleable. I mean, I was surprised when she got out of the carriage I put her in. I thought she'd just lie there and cry. But people like spirit, don't they? They like to have something to crush."

"No," said Poppy. "You can't do that to her."

"That's wrong," Banks said. "Even I think that."

"Why?" Lincoln said. "Her father did worse than I'm doing. He cut and shot hundreds of people. I'm just keeping the old family firm going."

"She doesn't deserve that," Banks said.

"Stop me, then," said Lincoln. Banks didn't move. "Thought not," said Lincoln. He picked up a weatherproof coat and threw it at Garland.

"Put this on," he said, waving the gun.

"Where are we going?" Garland asked.

Lincoln smiled.

"Out," he said.

• • •

Garland held the coat. It was too big for her and it smelt of diesel.

"You don't have to go with him," said Poppy.

"I don't care," Garland said. "I did what I came to do. I got here, and there was nothing."

"She's right," said Banks. "There never was anything, not for us. We're just leftovers."

"Dregs," Lincoln agreed. "Anyway, you are."

He shot Banks in the chest.

• • •

Banks grunted and fell to the ground. Lincoln watched him twitch, and then be still.

"Like the man said, leftovers," he said, cheerfully.

"You killed him," said Garland.

"He's been dead for years," Lincoln replied. "Who's next?"

Garland suddenly saw that the remote control had reappeared in his free hand. Before she could move, Lincoln pressed it.

Poppy screamed and convulsed.

"Stop it!" Garland shouted. She ran at him and he hit her in the face with the gun. He walked up to Poppy.

"You going to be good?" he asked.

She gave him two fingers.

"We'll take those off first," he said, and jabbed at the remote again. Poppy all but flew across the room, slamming against a bulkhead.

"I'll come back for the parts," he told Garland. "Now get the fuck dressed."

• • •

Shaking, Garland was about to put on the coat Banks had given her when she saw something on the floor.

Poppy's tunic.

"I need to put this on too," she said. "It's cold."

"Just get a move on," Lincoln said.

• • •

She picked up the tunic and put it on. Sliding a hand into the pocket, she felt something soft and almost laughed out loud. Teddy. She tried the other pocket, and this time her fingers found tissue paper. Tissue paper wrapped around something small and hard.

"What are you doing?" Lincoln said.

"I thought there might be some gloves in here," Garland replied. It sounded ridiculous even to her.

"Gloves? What the – *get your hands out of there now*."

Lincoln was pointing the gun right at her.

"Slowly," he said.

• • •

She took her hand out of her pocket and held up the toy bear.

"In the name of fuck," said Lincoln. "Both hands."

Slowly, she removed her other hand, unrolling the tissue as she did so.

In her palm were three vials.

• • •

"Oh," said Lincoln. "So that's your game, is it?"

"Yes," she replied. "Except it's not a game."

"Do you," he said, stepping back a little, "do you even know what's in those things?"

"I know one of them will turn you in a heap of mush," she said.

"You're wrong," said Lincoln. "Won't work on me."

Something in his voice contradicted his words.

"Garland?" said Poppy.

"Yes?" Garland replied.

"Have you had your jab?" Poppy asked.

For a moment, Garland was confused. Then she said, "No."

Poppy looked at her.

"Are you *sure*?"

"Yes," said Garland.

Poppy turned to Lincoln. She was smiling.

"How about you?" she asked. "Have you had your jab?"

The look on his face told her the answer.

"Touché," said Lincoln. "But which vial will you smash?" he went on. "One of them is just water. And one of them is the antidote."

"What?" she said.

"I didn't tell Denning that," said Lincoln. "I was going to, just to spice things up a little, but I never got the chance. So," he continued, gesturing at her hand, "here's your dilemma. You get one chance at this because I'm going to shoot the moment you throw anything. You can't throw one vial, because you don't know which is which. You can't throw all three, because the antidote reacts with the air at the same time as the killer vial does, thereby rendering your actions useless. So you're going to throw two, hoping that the laws of chance are on your side and one vial is fatal and one is water."

Garland put her hands together as if in supplication. She clapped them together.

"Wrong," she said.

Broken glass fell from her hands as she ran at him. Before he could fire the gun, she crammed the bear in his mouth and closed his jaws down on it. With her free hand, she covered his nostrils.

He tried to beat her with the gun, but she ignored the pain.

"You were right," she said. "I've got one chance."

Lincoln used one hand to try and pull her hands from his face, but he still had the gun in his other hand and he couldn't get her off him.

"I knew you wouldn't let go of the gun," she said. "People like you never do. You can't get a shot at me, but you're not going to let go of the gun."

His eyes burned into her.

"And you want to live, but I don't care," she said. "I just want to make it stop. Make it all stop."

"You fuh –" he started to say, but he was weakening.

"So maybe," she said as he struggled, "maybe this is water and maybe this is antidote and maybe it's just a toy bear. Let's see."

She kept her hands over his face. His eyes closed and he dropped the gun. She let go of his body and he slumped to the floor.

. . .

"What do you know, Teddy?" said Garland.

. . .

Poppy woke after a few minutes. She was shaking, but the shaking began to die away.

"How did you…" she asked.

"I smashed all the vials into Teddy," said Garland. "Sorry. Antidote, water, the lot. And I stuck Teddy down his throat until the fucker choked."

"Language," said Poppy.

She reached into Lincoln's throat and pulled the bear out.

"Someone needs a wash," she told it.

. . .

They stood over Banks's body.

"Bullet to the chest," Poppy said. "The bastard."

"Yes," said Garland. "But –"

And Banks coughed.

"What the fuck!" Poppy shouted.

"They moved everything round," said Garland. "Remember? Lincoln taunted him about it. He said they put his organs in new places. So –"

"His heart's not in the right place," said Poppy, and laughed.

• • •

Banks was still in some pain.

"I can't believe I'm not dead," he said.

"You're going to need a lot of rest," said Garland. "And maybe an X-ray."

"The bullet passed through me," Banks said.

"She means we need to find out where everything is inside you," said Poppy. "We need a map."

Garland stood up and looked around the cockpit.

"We need a lot of maps," she said.

• • •

They pushed Lincoln's body out of the side door.

• • •

Banks said, "Can you bring me the kitbag please? There's some cans left."

"No way," said Poppy. "Those things will outlive us."

"Of course they will," said Banks. "That's what cans are for."

He opened one and offered it to Garland. She was about to refuse when Poppy shook her head.

"Peace offering," said Poppy. Garland looked at Banks.

"Blueberry," he said and gave her a spoon.

"My favourite," said Garland.

She took a mouthful of the purple mess.

"Delicious," she said.

"You are such a liar," Poppy said.

• • •

They sat there, eating from the cans as the train ploughed through the night.

"Is it me or have the explosions stopped?" asked Banks.

"You're right," said Poppy. "There are no more lights in the sky."

"Nothing to guide us but ourselves," Garland said.

She stood up.

"Banks," she said. "Can you find me that song? The princess one," she remembered.

"I still don't know how you can speak languages," said Poppy. "You must have had an amazing education."

"I must have had, mustn't I?" said Garland.

Poppy clambered slowly over to the screen Lincoln had used before. She touched a button, scrolled down, and hit a key.

"Music," she said.

> *Meree raajakumaaree chalee gaee hai*
> *Kabhee nahin lautane ke lie*

Poppy studied the consoles for a while.

> *Mainne itanee der intajaar kiya hai*
> *Main har samay intajaar karoonga*

"Doors," Poppy said, and pressed another switch.

All over the train, in compartments and carriages, air rushed in as the doors swung open.

"Rain," said Poppy, and hit a button.

The sprinklers came on and drenched every carriage. Water surged downwards and outwards over the walls and floors and flushed everything out through the open doors.

Garland sat in the driver's seat.

"That one," Poppy said. She was pointing at a switch. "Manual override," she explained.

Garland took the driver's controls.

"Now what?" said Banks.

Garland pressed the override and, as the train screamed and lurched, took hold of the controls.

"There's a world out there," she said. "Let's fix it."

• • •

Poppy swiped screens. New maps appeared, new options.

• • •

"Look," said Banks, pointing out of the window.

Far off, and tiny in the grey sky, was a patch of blue, like a flower in the dust.

Garland smiled.

"Blue skies," she said.

Acknowledgments

Thanks to Cat Camacho, Lydia Gittins, Polly Grice and Julia Lloyd at Titan, and also to Andrew Lownie at the Andrew Lownie Literary Agency. And thanks to Liz Buckley at Ace Records, for sending me *All Aboard: 25 Train Songs* (Ace Records), which is a one-CD jukebox. I listened to a lot of train songs whilst writing this book, by everyone from Chuck Berry and Ozzy Osbourne to the Pet Shop Boys and Cath Carroll, but especially several Indian train songs from the movies, from Mangal Singh's "Rail Gadd" to "Mere Sapno Ki Rana" by Rajesh Khanna and Sharmila Tagore.

David Quantick is an Emmy Award-winning television writer for such shows as *Avenue 5*, *Veep*, *The Thick of It* and *The Day Today*. He is the author of *All My Colors*, *Sparks*, *The Mule*, and two writing manuals: *How To Write Everything* and *How To Be A Writer*. Find him at www.davidquantick.com or @quantick on Twitter.

For more fantastic fiction, author events,
exclusive excerpts, competitions, limited editions and more

VISIT OUR WEBSITE
titanbooks.com

LIKE US ON FACEBOOK
facebook.com/titanbooks

FOLLOW US ON TWITTER AND INSTAGRAM
@TitanBooks

EMAIL US
readerfeedback@titanemail.com

was proving pointless, the websites and books were inaccurate. North Norfolk in May should have lower-than-average rainfall. It should be neck and neck with Cornwall in terms of daily sunshine hours and be the driest county in England. But look at it out there – streaming and soaking and that huge sky dense with more to come. She'd overheard Sam calling it Norfuck yesterday.

Alice – we have a book to write.

But there was neither sight nor sound of Alice. Frankie trickled a little wine onto the page, folded it in half and vigorously rubbed her hand over it. She opened it out and stared hard. It looked nothing like the butterflies or strange beings that the children had created with poster paints at nursery school all those years ago. Even Freud – or whoever it was who'd used the exercise in therapy – would have had a hard time reading anything into it. It was simply an amoebic splodge and a waste of wine.

Alice and the Ditch Monster Do Absolutely Nothing.